ROSIE COLORED GLASSES

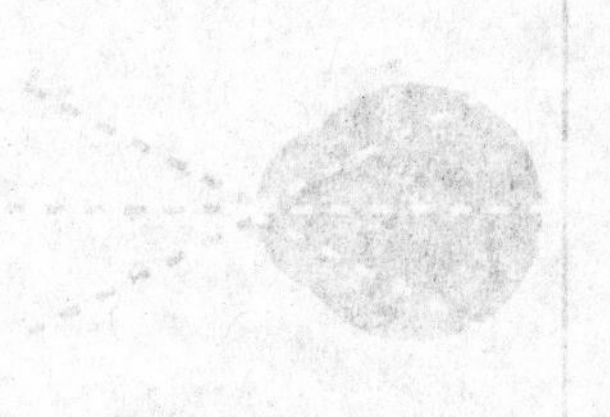

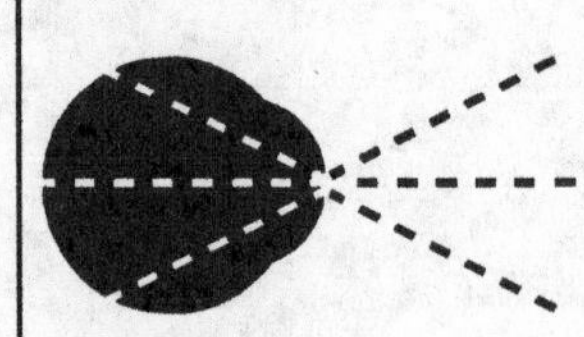

This Large Print Book carries the Seal of Approval of N.A.V.H.

Rosie Colored Glasses

Brianna Wolfson

THORNDIKE PRESS
A part of Gale, a Cengage Company

Farmington Hills, Mich • San Francisco • New York • Waterville, Maine
Meriden, Conn • Mason, Ohio • Chicago

Thorndike Press, a part of Gale, a Cengage Company.

Thorndike Press® Large Print Core.
The text of this Large Print edition is unabridged.
Other aspects of the book may vary from the original edition.
Set in 16 pt. Plantin.

LIBRARY OF CONGRESS CIP DATA ON FILE.
CATALOGUING IN PUBLICATION FOR THIS BOOK
IS AVAILABLE FROM THE LIBRARY OF CONGRESS

ISBN-13: 978-1-4328-5098-2 (hardcover)

Published in 2018 by arrangement with Harlequin Books, S.A.

Printed in Mexico
1 2 3 4 5 6 7 22 21 20 19 18

To my mad and moonly mama,
whom I still think about each day.

Prologue

Willow Thorpe knew friction. The heat it created when one thing rubbed against another. When one world rubbed against another.

Willow felt it every time she got into the back seat of her mother's car, buckled her seat belt, grabbed her brother's hand and prepared to return to her father's house. Every time she stared out the window of her mother's car, and traced the familiar turns of the street on her way to her father's. Every time her father opened the big heavy front door and grumbled, "Late again, Rosie." Every time her mother casually responded with a smirk and a "Catch you later, Rex."

Every time she looked up at her father and became self-conscious of the way her knees knocked together. Every time she went from art-covered walls to plain white ones. Every time she went from Mango Tango crayons to yellow #2 pencils.

Willow had a sense that the children of other divorced parents fantasized about what it might be like for their mother and father to be in love again. For their mother to tighten their father's tie in the morning before work. For their father to zip up their mother's dress in the evening before dinner. For their mother and father to share a casual kiss on the lips when they thought their children weren't looking. For every picture frame around the house to display an image of a whole family: mother, father, and brother and sister tangled around one another.

But Willow didn't think about any of that.

She thought about her tough and serious father in one world, and her warm and glimmering mother in the other. And the three times a week when one world grated up against the other.

But that grating of worlds, all that friction and heat, was worth it for Willow whenever she could return to her mother's world.

Because in that world, her mother's love was magical and it was fierce. Willow felt this kind of love could crystallize inside of her and fortify her. That it could fulfill her in the truest, realest sense. That it could keep her safe and happy forever.

But Willow was wrong.

In her life there would soon be confusion and sadness and pain and loss. And her mother's manic love for her daughter could not protect Willow from any of these things. In fact, it might have even caused them.

1

Twelve Years Ago

At twenty-four, Rosie Collins believed that love was both specific and all-consuming. She believed that true love accessed the back of the earlobe as much as it accessed the heart. She believed that there was one, special, nuanced way one human being could love another human being. And she thought of those nuanced, invisible, loving forces whenever she saw lovers together in the park or the subway or on a bench. She imagined the names they called each other before bed. His favorite place to put his hand. Her favorite shirt of his to wear to bed. The silly thing she said that made him laugh and laugh. The ugly painting he bought for their apartment that she loved seeing on the living room wall.

Rosie took the job at Blooms Flower Shop on 22nd Street and 8th Avenue as soon as she moved to Manhattan in part for the money, in part because she liked the idea of someone named Rosie working in a flower shop. But mostly she took the job so she could gain access to those loving forces. Like all of her other petty jobs, she would have to perform certain mundane tasks — this time, arranging flowers, manning the register and transcribing messages onto cards. But Rosie thought she might be able to keep this job for longer than the usual six weeks because at Blooms Flower Shop, she saw the greater meaning in her work.

She saw herself facilitating love. She fantasized about the thousands of love stories of which she would witness the tiniest glimpse, as patron after patron would call her up and share a little piece of themselves. They would tell her about their girlfriend's favorite flower. Their fiancée's favorite poem. How they wanted the perfect bouquet to show up at their wife's desk for her birthday. How they wanted the perfect arrangement to say Happy Anniversary. Or to send something just because.

She was so excited that she spent the entire Sunday before her first day of work practicing her calligraphy. Rosie wanted to ensure that each letter was original and ornate enough to reflect the beauty and originality of the love behind the note. She barely slept that first night with the anticipation of her access to the authentic, naked, unabashed voice of love. It was a voice she loved so much, even though it wasn't a part of her own life yet.

But Rosie's heart broke the first week at Blooms when, day after day, men called in requesting a dozen red roses be sent to their girlfriend or wife or lover with a card that simply read "Love, Jim" or "From Tom," or just "Harry."

Didn't some women prefer hydrangeas or chrysanthemums or lilies? Wouldn't some of these flowers go to women who preferred pink or white or a mix of colors? Didn't men in love know these sorts of things about their lovers? Hadn't they wanted to fill that tiny card accompanying the arrangement with the kindest, truest, most perfect words?

When you sent flowers to your wife, didn't you want it to mean "This is the way I still feel when I look into your eyes"? When you loved someone, didn't you want to tell them in the most perfect, specific, unconcealed way? How did all of these men love women in the same twelve-red-roses-and-a–"Love, John" or "From Rob," or just plain "Colin" way?

It broke Rosie's heart to think that love could ever, ever, ever be that banal.

But Rosie was also not the type to sit around with a broken heart for long. Especially when it threatened her worldview. If the men of Manhattan could not express love properly, she would help them along. She would infuse their gestures with nuance and specificity whether it was authentic or not.

So Rosie took it upon herself to ensure that no card left Blooms Flower Shop with a generically and heartbreakingly boring signature. She replaced all requests for dull notes with ones she deemed more appropriate for a gesture of love. "You looked beautiful last night. Love, Alex." "I was just thinking about how charming you looked when you had that piece of food stuck in your teeth. Love, Ryan." "I'm better with you around. Love, Charlie." "I hope we hang out so many more times. Love, Ian." And she would smile wholly as she tied each card around a stem and sent it out the door.

These were the love stories Rosie wanted to be a part of. Even if they weren't real, Rosie still believed them in some way to be true.

For weeks and weeks no one ever mentioned her love nudges. No one until Rex Thorpe called and requested that a dozen red roses be sent to his girlfriend at 934

Columbus Avenue.

"And what would you like the card to say?" Rosie asked dully.

Rosie had talked on the phone to this type with the Upper West Side girlfriend before. Brash. Probably had a high-paying job. Probably handsome but also deeply jerky. Probably had a pretty girlfriend to whom he seldom said, "I love you."

"The card? What card?" Rex responded curtly.

"The card that will accompany the dozen red roses."

A momentary pause.

"Sir?" she added as she rolled her eyes and pressed her condescension through the phone.

"I don't fucking know."

Silence. And then the repulsive chomping sound of gum-chewing came through the phone.

"To Anabel. Love, Rex. I guess."

Click.

Rosie found Rex and the whole interaction to be entirely and maddeningly insulting to her and to the verb *love.* Again.

And so Rosie filled out the card in the manner that she felt appropriate, with her favorite e. e. cummings poem:

love is more thicker than forget
more thinner than recall
more seldom than a wave is wet
more frequent than to fail

it is most mad and moonly
and less it shall unbe
than all the sea which only
is deeper than the sea

love is less always than to win
less never than alive
less bigger than the least begin
less littler than forgive

it is most sane and sunly
and more it cannot die
than all the sky which only
is higher than the sky

And then she signed it on his behalf: "I love you, Rex."

This was the first time Rosie had ever used anyone's words besides her own on these notes. She had never invoked any of her favorite poets. But this time, with Rex Thorpe's supreme jerkiness to counterbalance, it felt just right.

Even to Rosie, it was unclear whether she was trying to rescue Rex's girlfriend in some small way, or whether she was tacitly trying to tell Rex something about how love ought to be. Either way, now her effort was written in ink and it would be showing up on Anabel's doorstep in thirty-six hours.

And Rosie was happy.

When Rex arrived at his girlfriend's doorstep to receive credit for the flowers he had sent, Anabel immediately and energetically threw her arms around him. Unbeknownst to Rosie, Anabel was a literature student and a great fan of e. e. cummings.

"Your note is perfect," Anabel told her boyfriend.

"I will treasure it always. I love you too," she said.

Rex knew Anabel felt sure they would get married and Rex hadn't yet thought of any reasons why she wouldn't be correct. Rex received his undeserved hug without a word in response.

But when he saw the card on that bouquet, he was furious. Because he was not interested in flowery language and he was definitely not interested in anybody doing anything without his explicit permission.

At thirty-one years old, Rex Thorpe was both serious and particular about the things in his life. About his Brooks Brothers pants and steamed, button-down shirts. About the Eames furniture in his apartment. About the Upper West Side restaurants he frequented and the academic degrees of the people he interacted with. About the whiskey he drank and the shape of the glass it came in. About the brand of black ink in his ballpoint pen. About his vision of himself as a respected and successful man. About being a man of authenticity.

Rex focused his attention so meticulously and intensely on all of these things that he never felt it logical or worthwhile to spare any energy on Anabel DeGette. He never cared enough about her to go out of his way even though she was both pleasant and beautiful enough. Rex, himself, was acutely aware that if a pleasant and beautiful woman were not part of his idea of what a "successful" life looked like, he probably would not concern himself with women at all. But since it was, Rex knew he needed occasionally to express some sentiment of affection while simultaneously ignoring his girlfriend and spending all of his time at work. And a bouquet of a dozen roses with a note that said "Love, Rex" was what he had decided on.

"What the fuck did you do?" Rex shouted rhetorically at Rosie that next day even before he had both feet in the door of Blooms. "I gave you very clear instructions for my note. And nowhere did those instructions include a poem from fucking e. e. cummings. Who the fuck are you to interfere and manipulate my words?"

He was prepared to continue his rant, but stopped abruptly at the sight of Rosie in her knee-length paisley dress. Her messy brown hair slipping out of a loosely tied braid. Her bangs that nearly hid the curvature of her thick eyebrows. The flower-stained gloves that were comically too large for her undoubtedly tiny hands at the end of her tiny wrists. Her petite bones. The slight scoop of her nose. Her freckles. The way the corners of her eyes turned down. The way she jaggedly swayed her hips and hummed the tune of Stevie Nicks and Don Henley's "Leather and Lace." The way she radiated.

And most importantly, the way she casually ignored his fury.

Rex was struck breathless by it all.

He stood in his place, mouth agape, disappointed that Rosie had yet to look up at him. He thought he could catch her eye. Just for a moment. He wanted to catch her eye. He wanted to gaze right into it and see something new.

■ ■ ■ ■

Without even looking up from her daily thorn trimming, Rosie knew it was Rex stomping through the door. She peeked out quickly from underneath her bangs. Handsome and jerky, indeed.

She tried keeping her eyes cast downward at the roses in her hands as Rex spoke at her but lost the battle when his words stopped. She met Rex Thorpe's eyes for just an instant and there everything was. His unruly eyebrows. His strong shoulders. His smooth skin. The creases in his cheeks. His black hair.

His presence.

Rosie couldn't bear being in the shop with that overwhelming toughness. That simultaneous repulsion and attraction. So she shook her hands until the canvas gloves fell to the counter. And then Rosie picked up her tote bag full of scribbled-in notebooks and sweet-tooth fixings and scurried past Rex without saying a word. She put such focus on getting out the door and such little attention on what was happening in that shop, that she didn't even stop to acknowledge the blue crayon and couple of pennies dribbling out of her bag as she dragged it behind her. As Rosie walked toward the door, she felt another twinge.

Although she did not share Rex's principle, she quite admired his authenticity. Not all people, all men, spoke their mind like this. Not all were willing to let others know what hurt them. Vexed them. Pleased them. Excited them. There was a sexiness in Rex's assuredness. His masculinity. His convictions. But even with all of those thoughts about the man standing so firmly in the middle of Blooms, Rosie waltzed right out and decided to take the afternoon off.

She hopped on her bike and, without a care in the world, headed straight for her favorite branch on the willow tree in Central Park. Just the tune of "Leather and Lace" playing in her mind. And Rex's sylvan scent lingering in her nose.

2

As it were, Willow Thorpe hated Wednesdays. Per the rules of the divorce, Wednesdays were always Dad's days. And Dad's days were full of homework and piano practice and chore charts and manners.

But it wasn't long before her mother found a way to make Wednesday nights Willow's favorite night of the week. Another adventure, another opportunity for so much love.

Willow tugged her favorite Keith Haring T-shirt over her thick hair until it fell onto her shoulders. She smiled when she looked in the mirror to brush her teeth and saw herself wearing it. She loved that oversize T-shirt with the thick squiggly lines and bright colors. She loved how it exuded excitement all around. How the figures were so simple and so happy dancing around together.

She washed the toothpaste from the edges

of her mouth, then wiggled herself under her sheets. And then she waited. She squeezed her eyes shut like she was sleeping. But she wasn't even close. And then she waited some more. And when Willow's midnight alarm went off, it simultaneously felt like all the time in the universe — and no time at all — had passed.

With a tingle just under the surface of her skin, Willow tucked her feet into her slippers, picked up her flashlight from her bedside table, slid her pillow under her sheets in case Dad might check on her and walked delicately on her tippy toes all the way down the back stairs. She gripped the railing for balance, but made her way down the steps so naturally. It was a shame that Willow was her most graceful on that dark staircase in the middle of the night when no one would ever see her.

Willow pressed her toes slowly, purposefully into the lush carpeting that covered each step. She crossed the kitchen, slipped out the back door and made her way to the far end of the backyard. This moment, standing on the edge of the manicured grass with nothing but towering trees in front of her, made Willow's heart tremble. It was just Willow alone in the dark. Nothing but the syncopated buzz of cicadas and faint crackling of the woods. Nothing but the crisp acidity of October nighttime air filling her lungs.

Willow could feel the excitement pulsing through her nerves. She was on the edge of her father's world and on the precipice of her mother's. Here was the entryway to happiness.

Willow launched off the thick lawn into the depths of the trees. *Only thirty-seven and a half steps,* she told herself as she hurried over fallen leaves and flimsy sticks to the tree house. She and her mother had counted the number once. Rosie had even made sure to account for the length of Willow's stride instead of her own.

And when Willow reached the base of the ladder that led up, she made the signal — three clicks of her flashlight. Then she waited, her eyes big and her heart rumbling. And without another moment of quiet, Rosie returned the signal and popped her head out the base of the tree house floor.

Willow always wanted to zip up that ladder so badly at the sight of her mother, but she knew her loose knees were no match for the rickety wooden rungs. She was barely able to keep herself upright on the smooth ground of the fifth-grade hallway, let alone an old ladder. So she took her time wrapping her fingers around each wooden rung and then gripping her tightest grip as she carefully let her feet climb up slowly, one step at a time.

And when Willow finally got to the top, her mother would lift her by her arms and kiss her so hard, so decidedly, on the cheek. And together Willow and her mother would sing and dance and talk and draw by flashlight. They would paint and have thumb wars and play Twister and spin quarters. They would take turns performing tongue twisters. They would love each other so much.

And when the tree house walls were coated with new drawings, and when their mouths were coated with Pixy Stix sugar crystals and their bellies were filled with cream soda, and when the tree house air was saturated with the sounds of Elton John through her mother's tiny speakers, Willow would lay her small head in Rosie's lap and exhale.

Willow's soft and raspy voice moved through the stillness. "Mom, why did you and Dad get a divorce?"

"Well, do you like waking up to the sun or an alarm?" Rosie replied.

"The sun," Willow answered. And she was quick to it.

"Me too, baby," Rosie said calmly as she kissed Willow on the middle of her smooth forehead. And then Willow exhaled again in her mother's lap.

When Rosie's watch beeped at 1:00 a.m., Willow and Rosie packed up their wrappers and toys, clicked off the flashlight and shimmied back down the ladder. Rosie with ease and Willow with full concentration.

And when Willow got to the back door of her father's house, she waited and watched as her mother walked down the driveway away from her. She watched Rosie's hair bounce weightlessly as her thin arms scrambled to maintain the pile of soda and candy and colored pencils stacked precariously against her chest. Willow watched her mother in all of her coolness, all of her effervescence, until she was gradually absorbed by the darkness.

Inevitably, before she disappeared, Rosie would drop a pencil or crayon or marker from her grip and let it roll along the ground without the slightest motion to pick it up. Her mother didn't even pause to make sense of the faint clicking sound of the thing as it slipped from her arms and hit the blacktop. Rosie just got into the front seat of the car, where the dim car lights revealed her silhouette once again. And then she rolled her windows down, pressed both hands into her lips and extended her arms out toward Willow. She was sending a kiss all the way through the velvet darkness into Willow's soul.

Then her mother drove away.

Willow returned to the driveway with her flashlight on dim to retrieve the lost crayon and bring it upstairs with her. She rolled the dark pinkish waxy cylinder in her hands and scanned the crayon label — Jazzberry Jam — then tucked it into her pajama pocket.

On Wednesday nights, as Willow drifted into sleep for the second time, she would replay the image of her mother's red lips turning into a smile and the feeling of her mother's long manicured fingers playing with her curls. And just like that, she could fall asleep happy.

It never mattered how tired Willow's time in the tree house made her feel for school on Thursdays. Wednesday nights with her mom were definitely Willow's favorite night of all the nights of the week.

Willow woke up the next morning in her room at her father's house to the sound of her alarm. She slowly opened her eyes to the blue walls and the white wicker dresser.

To the lacy throw pillows on the floor. To the taste of quiet. And then back to the beeping alarm.

Rex had told Willow that the trick to not snoozing through your alarm was to place the clock across the room. "Then, the only way you can stop the buzzing is to get up!" he told Willow one morning when she overslept. He told her this as he moved her alarm clock from her bedside table to the edge of the dresser by the far wall.

Willow slapped down on the clock and started the tasks of the morning checklist her dad had made for her. She also made sure that her little brother was on top of his morning checklist too. But as usual, he wasn't.

At six years old, Asher Thorpe was always forgetting things. Spilling things. Breaking things. Knocking into things. But he was almost always forgiven for all of it. Because of his full cheeks and round chin, his clear blue eyes and his silky blond bowl cut. And, most importantly, his missing front two teeth and his trouble with the letter *R*.

It surprised everyone that two brunettes like Rosie and Rex could produce a blond-haired, blue-eyed little boy. But it made sense to Rex, Rosie and even Willow that Asher would have the kindest, most gentle, most nonthreatening features. There was a lightness to Asher that none of the other Thorpes possessed. A lightness that Willow was reminded of every time she reached Asher's room across the house and found him pleasantly asleep beneath a pile of stuffed animals. Every time she nudged her brother awake and he smiled at the sight of his big sister.

"Morning checklist, Ash," Willow said, and kissed her brother on the forehead.

"Alwight, alwight!" Asher said through a sleepy smile and sloppy cheeks.

Willow left her brother's room and completed her checklist.

Brush Teeth — 30 seconds top, 30 seconds bottom
Wash Face — Face soap only
Make Bed
Brush Hair
Fold Pajamas
Get Dressed — Clean clothes!
Pack for School — Do you have all your homework with you?
Take Vitamins
Family Breakfast

Willow had her morning checklist memorized, but Dad insisted that it remained taped to her door next to her afternoon checklist, which was taped next to the nighttime checklist. And Willow was very diligent about completing all but two items on this list up to her father's standards.

The first thing Willow had trouble with was "Brush hair." Because Willow's hair was too curly and wild, and brushing it only made it worse. Mom told Willow that this was the kind of thing that boys didn't understand and to just ignore that item on the list. But Willow didn't like disobeying so instead of skipping the step, she guided the smooth back of the brush over the top of her tight curls every morning.

And then there was "Get dressed." And while Willow didn't have a problem doing so, her father never liked the clothes she chose to get dressed in. And the things she got dressed in were the same every day — shiny purple leggings, a black T-shirt with a silver horseshoe on it and black high-top Converse sneakers. The same thing every day for the last five years. She had several pairs of purple leggings and several of the same T-shirt. And today, a few weeks into fifth grade, she was still wearing that same outfit.

Her father never said a word about the outfit to Willow. At least not with his mouth.

But he didn't have to because Willow could always tell how he hated seeing her in that outfit. Every morning when Willow said good-morning to her father, she could tell she had disappointed him all over again. He said it with his eyes and a subtle drop of his chin and a faint shake of his head. Maybe it was her outfit or maybe it was her collapsing knees. Maybe it was something else entirely. But no matter what, her father never looked at his daughter in the same way her mother did.

Rex was posed in the big wooden chair at the head of the breakfast table exactly as he always was. Right leg crossed over left. Reading glasses perched at the tip of his nose. A steaming cup of coffee in his right hand. A pile of furiously scribbled notes scattered across the table. Dressed in a suit that looked like it was brand-new.

Looking serious. Looking powerful. Looking the same way he always looked.

Rex Thorpe was tall and broad and his shoulders pressed forward. If you were up close enough, you could see that his black eyes were always *tick, tick, ticking* back and forth. He was always scanning the room and the people in it. And his lips were always pursed like he was ready to say something. But the way his eyebrows pressed in toward one another and the way he held his jaw tense, you knew you didn't want to hear what he had to say. But whether he was talking or quiet, looking at you or ignoring you entirely, Rex Thorpe commanded your attention when you shared space with him.

Willow sat down at the table and poured a bowl of Lucky Charms cereal for her brother and then one for herself as Rex tilted his right arm up and down like a steel machine taking sporadic sips of coffee. Willow and Asher used their heavy silver spoons to scoop the nonmarshmallow bits into their mouths first. They liked seeing the color that the specific mix of horseshoe, pot-of-gold and heart-shaped marshmallows might tint the milk. It was a game they played at their mother's house too. After the Lucky Charms milk settled into a certain color, they would each scramble through the box of crayons at the center of the table and search furiously for the one that best matched the color in their bowl. Whoever announced the closest color first earned a big red kiss from Rosie.

When they played this game at their father's house, Willow and Asher just stirred and observed the milk quietly. But at least they were both having fun.

Asher broke the silence when he loudly

asked, "Can we go bowling this weekend?"

"Maybe once all your chores are finished," Rex said without lifting his eyes from the notepad next to the coaster he put his coffee on.

Willow already knew her dad would say something like this. Because the set of things that Dad said yes to was specific and almost always conditional. You could watch TV for fifteen minutes, if your laundry was already folded. You could have ice cream, two toppings maximum, if you finished every last pea on your plate. You could go outside, jackets zipped all the way up, only after you practiced piano for thirty minutes. You could open a new cereal box when the old one was finished, and then you could fold up the old box so it was efficiently flattened and put it in the recycling bin. It didn't matter to her father if none of your favorite horseshoe-shaped marshmallows were left in the old box.

Asher returned to his cereal bowl with an "Oh, man!" and then dipped under the kitchen table to play with his action figures. Which meant that everything went back to quiet at the breakfast table. Back to a quiet that disappointed Willow. She liked noise and chatter and music and games.

She liked her mother's house.

Willow looked up from her bowl and considered whether to ask her father what color he thought the milk looked like. But his temples flared with each chomp on the wad of pink Bubblicious gum in his mouth. He looked so serious sitting there like that. So intense. So engrossed in his notes.

So Willow took her creased word search book out of her backpack and scanned the page for the next word on the list — *ZIPPER*. Willow searched the grid for a letter *Z*. She tapped the Jazzberry Jam–colored crayon on the paper as she stared at the page. Willow smirked at her secret. The secret of how she came upon that crayon. And even though no one even noticed that Willow was smirking or holding a crayon, she was still proud of that dark pinkish cylinder of color in her hand. Proud that she had a mom who loved her so much she met her in the tree house in the middle of the night. Proud that she had a mom who played with her hair every Wednesday night. Proud that she had a mom who always let her win in thumb war.

Right before the "bus alert" that Rex had set up sounded, Willow found her word. There it was, lettered straight across the middle. *Z-I-P-P-E-R.* She circled all the letters, closed her word search book and tucked it into her backpack. She needed it to keep her company on the bus. And at her lunch table. And under the slide at recess. And in her mind's eye.

Willow brought her and Asher's empty bowls to the kitchen sink, zipped up her jacket, then her brother's, then said, "Bye, Dad," loudly enough for him to hear as they left for school.

"Bye, guys!" Rex shouted back from his seat at the kitchen table.

If Willow created a morning checklist for her father and taped it to his wall, it wouldn't say check your notes or tighten your tie. It would only say one thing:

Kiss Willow and Asher goodbye.

3

Twelve Years Ago

When Rosie got to her favorite willow tree by the Jacqueline Kennedy Onassis Reservoir for the fourteenth time in fourteen days, she took off her helmet and leaned her bike against the rugged bark of the trunk. Then she started climbing. The fourth branch up on the left side was Rosie's favorite to sit in. She could hear the ripples of the water and the murmurs of conversation below, but no one ever saw her up there. She sat up in the tree and made drawings, scribbled doodles and wrote notes to friends in faraway cities.

Two weeks ago, she walked out of Blooms Flower Shop after Rex came in yelling, and she decided she wasn't going back. And if she had ever bothered to check her messages, she probably would have learned that she had been fired anyway.

Rosie pulled a few straggling Pixy Stix out

of her tote bag and tore them open. She poured some of the sugar into her mouth and the remainder onto her notebook. The purple crystals scattered so beautifully on the page. She added some orange and then some red and swirled them around with her fingertips.

Art, she thought. *Ha.* She stuck her tongue in the pile for a taste, and then blew the rest of the sugar off the notebook. Rosie watched the colorful crystals scatter into the air and trickle down toward the ground.

"What the fuck?" boomed a familiar voice from below. She couldn't forget that voice. The incisive way with which Rex Thorpe said "fuck."

Normally, Rosie might have apologized, but there was no way she would say she was sorry to that handsome jerk of a man. Not after the way he treated her. Not after the way he treated love.

She shimmied down the tree prepared to walk away from him for the second time in two weeks. And as she did, her dress flipped up above her head revealing her polka-dot underwear. As soon as the paisley fabric fell back into position, Rosie and Rex locked eyes.

There was a pause.

"Hey, I know you. You work in the flower

shop. You wrote that card to my girlfriend. The one with the crazy e. e. cummings love poem."

Another pause.

"That was fucked-up."

Rosie adjusted her dress, squinted her eyes and decided to do battle. But only for a second.

"Your note was fucked-up."

"Yeah? What about it?" Rex came back quickly, ready to spar.

Rosie almost walked away with her grimace, but then something just slipped out.

"Even Maleficent had something original to say to Sleeping Beauty."

Instead of firing back, Rex just stood there staring at her. And then he laughed. He found Rosie's retort bizarre, immature and adorable.

Rosie tried to make her escape from Rex for the second time, tote bag in hand. Rosie's body jerked just as awkwardly and charmingly as it had two weeks ago at Blooms Flower Shop. But this time there were strange comebacks and endearing polka-dot underwear.

Rex thought about Anabel. She never moved like this. Or dressed like this. Or talked like this. She always had a tall spine and a straight neck and a freshly dry-cleaned shirt.

Rex was surprised to find that everything about Rosie right here under this willow tree was warming his heart. Especially the awkward manner in which she tried to wiggle out of their encounter. Rosie marched determinedly in one direction. Then abruptly she turned around and marched equally determinedly in the opposite way.

But Rex had positioned his body right in front of Rosie's and stared down at her.

And Rosie slowly lifted her head and stared right back into his eyes.

Rex saw right through her big brown eyes and into her soul. Her bones that had finally stilled. And into her heart. Her heart that was racing.

Rex felt his heart do the same, and right then and there started to believe in the nuanced, invisible, loving force of the world.

And it made Rex want Rosie. So wholly. So viscerally. And when Rex Thorpe wanted something, he made it happen.

So right there next to the Jacqueline Kennedy Onassis Reservoir, Rex Thorpe pressed Rosie Collins up against the bark of a willow tree, and then pressed his lips against hers so gently.

It was the best kiss Rex ever had.

Even though there were Pixy Stix in her mouth and in his hair.

Rosie still had her eyes closed when she asked Rex slowly and calmly, "Think I'll ever see you again?"

Then Rex stared into Rosie's still-closed lids and said simply and honestly, "Sure do."

Rex Thorpe went home, made a reservation at the most impressive restaurant he could think of and told Anabel simply and honestly that he was sorry, but he didn't love her.

Because Rex Thorpe finally knew what love was. And she tasted like Pixy Stix and wore polka-dot underwear.

4

Willow dragged her feet getting onto Bus #50. How was it one of the most difficult parts about going to Robert Kansas Elementary School. Because #50 was cruel to a fifth grader with tightly coiled hair that sprung out in all directions. It was cruel to a fifth grader who preferred a CD player to hopscotch with friends. And to a fifth grader who sat in her seat engrossed in word searches. It was cruel to a fifth grader who wore the same outfit every day or had once, just once, even peed in her pants at recess in front of everyone.

Bus #50 was a nightmare for Willow Thorpe.

Willow couldn't go back on that bus. Not one more time. So she told her father about Bus #50. She told her strong, sturdy father. About the hair-pulling while having the word *boing* yelled in her ear. About the pointing at her favorite black T-shirt with the horseshoe while everyone laughed and laughed and said "she's wearing it *again.*" About the tearing of her word search pages right when she was going to circle *S-L-I-T-H-E-R* on a backward diagonal. Willow's voice crept over the lump in her throat as she told him.

But Willow was devastated when her father's only suggestion was to fix it herself.

"Stop sitting near those kids, Willow," he said nonchalantly. "Sit in the seat right behind the bus driver. He can help."

Willow did her best to clear the lump in her throat once more to protest, but as usual her father was insistent and unwavering. Rex walked Willow all the way up into the bus, pointed at that green vinyl seat with the duct tape covering up a hole in the back and said, "Sit here, Willow."

He said it in front of everybody. He was already making things worse.

"Sit, Willow," the fifth graders, and even some fourth graders, mocked as they patted on their legs like they were talking to a dog.

Willow might have been even more upset if she didn't think those fifth, and even some fourth, graders had it right in some ways. Her father *did* talk to her like she was a dog. A dog being trained. And not just this one time on the bus. All the time.

"Eat your broccoli."
"Take your plate to the sink."
"Finish your homework."
"Make your bed."
"Tie your shoes."
"Help your brother."

Her father said those things without a smile or a *please* or a morsel of warmth. Her father was firm and direct, and Willow didn't like it. Not now on Bus #50. And not any day at his house.

In an effort to avoid eye contact with everybody else on that whole entire school bus, Willow turned her attention to the duct tape on the seat. She wished Asher didn't have to take the designated kindergarten bus. She wished he was sitting right next to her. And as she wished, Willow picked at the sticky edges compulsively until she revealed the entire hole in the back of the seat. But when she looked into the hole, she saw something unusual in there. Willow reached her hand into that hole to see what it was.

Tucked inside the hole she discovered two grape-flavored Pixy Stix with a string tied around them and a typed note that said, "For Willow."

For the first time all year, Willow smiled on Bus #50. She smiled to herself and sneakily stuck her secret candies into her backpack.

But then she took one right back out, ripped it open and poured the sugar into her mouth. She couldn't hold out for even a second. She loved Pixy Stix. She loved the loving force that put them there. And Willow thought she knew exactly what, who, that loving force was. There was only one person in this town, on this earth, in this universe who loved Willow enough to surprise her with her favorite flavor Pixy Stix.

As Willow walked down the hallway with her remaining Pixy Stix in her bag, she almost forgot that the kids at Robert Kansas Elementary School were going to be so mean. She almost forgot they might put diapers in her cubby. She had almost forgotten about the first time she saw diapers in her first-grade cubby after she peed in her pants a few days after her parents told her about the divorce. The day of that big thunderstorm. That big, booming, terrifying thunderstorm. She had almost forgotten that she would have no one to sit with at lunch, and that everyone would avoid being her partner in gym class. That her teachers wouldn't call on her even though she knew all the answers. That at some point during the day, she was inevitably going to trip and fall in front of everyone.

Gravity worked differently on Willow than it did on everybody else. It yanked her down randomly. It pulled her toward the earth whenever it wanted to. It gave a quick but firm tug on her knee, her elbow, her hip — and her body would buckle, leaving Willow in a contorted pile of bent skinny limbs on the ground. And while this often caused minor scrapes or bruises, Willow actually didn't mind falling down like this. She thought that it made her special. She thought it made her distinct. The very idea that somewhere, sometimes, the world around her had singled her out. It singled her out and pulled her close to itself. Willow liked the idea that gravity was thinking of her from time to time. And she liked the idea that it would always let her know, with a tug on the knee, exactly when that time was.

When the lunch bell rang, Willow took her time retrieving her bagged lunch from her cubby and then took her time walking down the hallway to the cafeteria. It helped minimize the time in which she was sitting alone at her lunch table in the back. She put one foot slowly in front of the other and traced her finger along the green elementary school walls.

But before she even rounded the corner for the lunchroom, Willow could hear Amanda Rooney and Patricia Bleeker giggling even though she couldn't see them. This was a trick Willow recognized from last year. Amanda and Patricia had waited for Willow to turn the corner, then they stuck out their clean white platform shoes, causing Willow to fall over right in the middle of the floor. They laughed, and then walked away with their arms linked at the elbows.

Today, Willow knew better than to fall into their trap a second time. So, she made a very wide turn and exposed Amanda and Patricia huddled together on the other side. They were both wearing big blue bows in their blond hair and had on pink-striped T-shirts. Willow could barely tell which one was which, given the way they were tangled up in each other's matching outfits like that. Willow looked right at them, smiled only slightly and let her eyes tell them, *You're not going to trip me twice!*

But just when Willow thought she had escaped the taunts, gravity yanked down on her so hard she fell all the way to the ground. First her right knee, then her right hip, then her right shoulder.

Amanda and Patricia squealed equally

high-pitched squeals. And with the sound of their laughter ricocheting in her skull, Willow just stayed on the floor and closed her eyes tightly and hoped that she would hear Patricia's and Amanda's shrieks soften.

But their sounds only got louder.

And when Willow opened her eyes, the two blond-haired, blue-eyed girls were standing over her and dumping handfuls of pencil shavings all over her body, making sure to get them into her curly hair.

Willow just lay there watching as the apple from her lunch bag broke loose and rolled halfway down the hallway.

And then finally Patricia's and Amanda's voices trailed away as they left Willow to her bruised elbow and her bruised apple. To her messed-up lunch and her messed-up hair.

Willow got up and shook her head back and forth, expecting flakes of soft yellow wood to flutter out of her hair, but nothing did. The shavings hooked themselves so assiduously into her jagged curls that not a single one fell to the ground. Willow walked into the bathroom to find a mirror, thinking perhaps there would be enough time to pick out the pieces before lunch was over. But on the wall next to the mirror, in thick black Sharpie, it said, "Willow, Willow, hair like Brillo." She wondered if someone had just added it here or whether it was left over from last year.

Either way, after the quick glance she got of herself in the mirror before turning around, Willow thought the yellow flecks looked sort of cool in there. They had that same jagged in-motion effect as the design on her Keith Haring T-shirt. Mom would like that. Plus, tonight was pizza night so she could show her then.

5

Twelve Years Ago

Although Rex was not Rosie's usual type, her soul had already succumbed to Rex in so many ways. Rosie was equal parts nervous and excited for their first date.

She mixed and matched printed dresses with vintage jewelry until she was pleased. She twirled around in the mirror and blew herself a kiss after applying her favorite red lipstick and scanning her final choice of outfit.

Rosie shouldn't have been surprised when their first date included a highly coveted reservation at a fancy Manhattan restaurant with high ceilings and a bathroom attendant, but she was. She was surprised and uncomfortable in her twenty-dollar dress on a six-hundred-dollar gold-adorned chair. And she was annoyed and uncomfortable as Rex ordered an appetizer of oysters for the two of them to share without consulting her.

Rosie hated oysters. And Rex didn't even pause for one moment to consider that he wasn't going to impress Rosie with them. He was going to scare her with them. He was going to gross her out with them. Because Rosie thought they looked like boogers. And tasted like them too.

Rosie considered putting one of them up her nostril when the oysters arrived to ease the tension between them, but Rex was too enraptured by the wine menu to have noticed.

When their second course was set down by a waiter with a napkin folded over his forearm and the one-hundred-and-fifty-dollar wine was poured by a sommelier, Rex finally looked up at Rosie.

"Cheers," he said innocently.

But Rosie was indignant and it bubbled out of her immediately.

She positioned her tiny arms to push her stupid, gold-adorned chair back and leave Rex alone at his expensive fucking table with its boring white tablecloth and its overly formal waiters who bent from the hips with straight legs and backs when you walked by.

"I hate oysters," she stated a little too firmly and a little too loudly. "And this wine is, like, stupid expensive."

A pause.

"And so is this stupid tablecloth and this stupid napkin, I bet!"

"Ugh, I think you're right," Rex said, finally dropping his shoulders. "Let's finish this stupid bottle of stupid expensive wine and get out of here. I know a good pizza spot around the corner."

And just like that, Rosie nuzzled her knees back under the table, finished her wine and found herself ready to be smitten all over again.

As they munched on cheap pizza while expensive wine coursed through their blood, conversation flowed easily between them. Neither Rex nor Rosie had any idea what the other was saying because Rosie was focused on Rex's deep, dark eyes. And Rex had his eyes locked on Rosie's expressive, red lips. And just as Rex was about to take the last bite of his crust, Rosie grabbed his hand and whisked him out the door.

"Music time," she whispered in his ear as she pulled him in toward her on the sidewalk, and then twirled her body around.

They walked a few brisk blocks, and then ducked under the red awning of Ray's, Rosie's favorite piano bar. Rosie loved everything about Ray's. The dark corners and the red lamps at the tables. The smoky scent of cigars and the bottle-lined bar. The sexiness of it all.

She loved that she could never guess who from the audience might stand up and play a tune for the rest of the room. She loved that one minute, a man with quiet eyes and deep wrinkles would be slowly sipping a whiskey neat, and the next minute he was slamming his fingers against the keyboard and filling a room with music. She liked the idea that anyone, everyone, in a given space might have a gift to share.

Rex and Rosie sat in the back with another bottle of wine as, one by one, different members from the audience took a seat onstage and used their entire body to make sexy, full, stunning music. Rex and Rosie searched around the room and tried to guess which patron they thought would perform next. They tried to guess what song might be played. Billy Joel for the man about their age in the rugged baseball hat. Frank Sinatra for the gray-headed man with strong and wrinkled hands tapping his foot in the back. And while they were never right, not even once, Rex and Rosie both opened themselves fully to the game and to each other.

When Rex slid away from the table, Rosie assumed it was to order another round of drinks. But then he was onstage under the foggy red lights. In a thousand-dollar jacket on a five-dollar piano bench. And he looked great.

The crowd sang along to Rex playing "Bennie and the Jets" as he pressed his fingers deliberately but naturally into the keys. And right there, Rosie saw the most important thing she could see in a man. Rex Thorpe had soul — and she could work with that.

So Rosie joined the rest of the room and sang along as her soon-to-be boyfriend moved the crowd and Rosie's heart into motion.

Rex left the stage after a standing ovation and a familiar handshake from the bar owner. And then Rosie kissed Rex deeply and proudly linked her arm in his as they walked out of the red-lit piano bar.

She didn't mean to stumble into Rex's arms when he walked her back to her apartment, but she was drunk with wine and whiskey and new love.

6

Willow fixated on the second hand of the clock in Mrs. McAllister's classroom as she waited for school to be over. As she waited for pizza night. Waited for her mother to come around the bend of the parent pickup circle in her rattling blue car with its googly eyes stenciled on the front of it. Waited to spend the night swaddled in fun.

When the three-thirty bell rang, Willow shoved her spelling list into the bottom of her backpack, confirmed that her laces were tied on both shoes and fast-walked all the way to Asher's classroom. She grabbed her brother's hand and pulled him toward the parent pickup circle. Then Willow exhaled for the first time all day and locked her eyes on the entranceway.

Rosie was typically late to pick up Willow and Asher from school. She never wore a watch and often found herself in a daze somewhere, completely oblivious to the time. But Willow didn't want to miss one second with her mother, so she rushed to the pickup circle anyway every Tuesday and Thursday after school. Willow noticed that all of the other moms wore jeans, a T-shirt and dark sunglasses. They drove black or white cars that sparkled permanently. They kept their hair in neat ponytails and never got out of the car to say "hi" to their children.

But that wasn't her mother. Her mother's car was bright blue and made loud clanking noises. Rosie had named her car Lili Von after her favorite character in *Blazing Saddles*. The googly eyes that were stenciled just above the headlights always caused side-eye glances from the other mothers too. But that didn't faze Willow or Asher. They loved that car and they loved those googly eyes.

After only three games of tic-tac-toe, Lili Von appeared around the bend with Prince blasting out the window. Willow saw her mother's left knee poking out the driver's seat window. Her wavy brown hair was blowing around excitedly. Her big brown eyes and arched eyebrows were sticking out above her neon pink, thick-framed sunglasses that were resting on the tip of her nose. Lili Von screeched as her mother pulled up to the curb in front of where Willow and Asher were standing. And almost before the car had fully stopped, Rosie jumped out of the front seat to give each of her children separate, tight hugs.

Rosie looked as cool as she always looked in her cutoff jean shorts and long fur coat even though it was a perfectly temperate fall afternoon. She looked as cool as she always looked with her shoes with the holes in them and her polished red nails. She looked as cool as she always looked with her bright red lips.

"I missed you little noodles!" she said with a full-teeth and full-heart smile as she got back behind the wheel. "Hop in, already. It's pizza night!"

But just before Rosie got back behind the wheel, she snapped her head around and looked back at her daughter. She tilted her head to the side, pulled her sunglasses down farther on her nose and said, "Cool hair, baby." She said it quickly and honestly, and then drove off, leaving Willow smiling so big in the back seat.

They hadn't even reached the edge of the school parking lot when Rosie reached for the volume knob and said to her children the thing she always said on the way to pizza night at Lanza Pizza.

"Let's rock 'n' roll."

And when Rosie said that, she meant it in the literal sense. She turned the volume knob so many revolutions to the right that the speakers started throbbing and the floor started vibrating.

Cymbal. Cymbal. Bass. Bass.

Willow recognized the song right away. It was Prince's "Let's Go Crazy," and it was one of Mom and Willow's favorites.

Rosie, Willow and Asher all sang the lyrics in tandem and whipped their hair around as the music played.

Cymbal. Cymbal. Bass. Bass.

They sang as loudly as they could until they reached their parking spot at Lanza Pizza. Even Willow and Asher could see how Rosie filled with even more life when they arrived there. It was Rosie's favorite pizza place in town, tucked on a side street with a neon sign that was rare for the suburbs of Virginia. It had orange and yellow plastic booths, an old pinball machine and a deep bucket of half-used crayons.

The moment Willow, Rosie and Asher walked through the door of Lanza Pizza, they simultaneously tilted their noses toward the ceiling and pressed their chests forward as they inhaled the smells of bubbling cheese and hot tomatoes. As Willow and

Asher grabbed handfuls of crayons, Rosie bounced straight to the counter and asked for three large cups for fountain soda. And just like every Thursday, John had them waiting already right next to the register. As Willow sat down to put her crayons to use, she saw her mother wink familiarly at John in his sauce-stained apron. And then she saw John wink familiarly back at Rosie as he swirled a freshly floured heap of pizza dough around his thick sausage fingers. Willow couldn't help but smile at the warmth between near strangers. The ease between opposites. The electricity created when her mother entered a room.

Asher and Willow snatched their large paper cups from Rosie's hand and dashed to the soda fountain, where they filled their cups with a fizzing mixture of orange, root beer, Sprite and Hawaiian Punch. Rosie met them at the fountain, but filled her cup with nothing but cream soda. It was her favorite drink. And every time she got her big, icy cream soda from the fountain — not the bottle — she poked her straw through the plastic top, took her first gulp and said, "Nothing like a cold fountain cream soda." She did it so often that it had become tradition for Willow and Asher to say the words right alongside Rosie and then for all to take a big slurp of soda.

While the pizza warmed in the oven, Rosie took a roll of quarters out of her tote bag and handed it to Willow. And then Willow and Asher took turns on the pinball machine, clicking the flippers and encouraging each other on. They cheered when they hit a bonus and booed when their final ball slid between the flippers.

And when they got back to the table, a big slice of hot pizza was waiting on each of their plates. Willow bit into her slice, and then looked back up at Rosie, who had a big gooey piece of cheese hanging from her nostril.

"Mom!" Willow said half laughing, half embarrassed, but not at all surprised. Asher looked up too. He clutched his tummy and laughed so hard at his mother with that cheese in her nose.

"What?" Rosie said in thinly veiled awareness, now barely able to hide her smirk. Asher pointed right at her nose, unable to get a word out between giggles.

"Is my nose running? I did feel a cold coming on," Rosie said, restoring her poker face.

Now Willow was laughing too.

"It's a cheese booger! A huge one!" Asher screeched between breathy giggles as he pointed at his mother's nose.

Asher peeled a piece of cheese from his pizza, still vibrating with laughter, and stuck it in the gap where his front teeth should have been. He shook his head back and forth, the cheese swaying too. "Look! It's cheese teeth!"

Now Rosie was giggling uncontrollably too.

Rosie looked at Willow with urging eyes. And then Willow peeled a piece of cheese from the gooey pizza and draped it over her right ear. "Cheese earrings!"

Right there, in the middle of Lanza Pizza, Rosie, Asher and Willow were just one big pile of cheese and giggles and love.

For Willow, every time she was with Mom was like having all the pizza and soda and candy and ice cream in the world and never getting a tummy ache.

7

Twelve Years Ago

Rex and Rosie planned to walk around Central Park for their next date. Rosie thought about it every night as she fell asleep in her downtown apartment with the creaky stairs and tattered comforter. She wondered if she and Rex were going to hold hands. Or kiss. Or continue falling in love.

When 2:00 p.m. on Saturday afternoon finally arrived, Rosie was scanning the crowd for Rex on the front steps of the Metropolitan Museum of Art. She spotted him right away when she looked up as he leaned against the base of one of the Corinthian columns next to the entrance with his left leg crossed over his right and his hands in his pockets. He was so tall and handsome with his broad shoulders and thick black hair. And Rosie was giddy at the sight of her strong, sturdy man leaning on that strong, sturdy column. She skipped up the steps, two at a time, and surprised both herself and Rex when she did a little hop right in front of him and gave him a quick kiss on the cheek. She didn't plan to kiss him right away like that so early in their relationship, even if it was on the cheek, but it felt so natural.

Rex raised one eyebrow at Rosie, and then hooked his arm around her shoulder and said, "Hey, you." Then they walked down the steps slowly in lockstep toward the park so that they could soak in every moment of each other as they listened to each other with full attention. They each told stories about living in Manhattan and the sets of events that got them there. They talked about art and philosophy. Music and stories of past travels. They paused every few moments to digest each other's words. They nodded in agreement and sometimes blissful disagreement. And, in no time at all, on that fall afternoon, Rex was drunk with Rosie and Rosie had Rex sloshing around in her tummy. The air was crisp and clear in the height of a Manhattan autumn, but neither of them noticed the weather. There was only each other. In the whole park, the whole city. Among all the buildings and people and planets and stars.

When they reached the boathouse lake, Rex sat down on the grass and Rosie joined him. Rosie was pleased and surprised that he hadn't brought a blanket. Pleased that he wasn't worried about getting little pieces of crunchy leaves stuck to the back of his pants. And Rex and Rosie simultaneously opened the bags they had each been carrying. Rex's had turkey sandwiches, two bags of chips and two apples. Rosie's had old scraps of scribbled-on paper, a dozen flat stones and a few grape Pixy Stix.

Rex unwrapped the sandwiches and offered one up to Rosie, who was already standing up with a fist full of stones. She inadvertently ignored Rex's extended arm and pranced a few feet away to the edge of the lake and counted out loud as her stone skipped across the surface of the water. "1-2-3-4-5-6!" she shouted and made three little hops. And then held her stone-filled hand out and offered a stone to Rex. "No thanks," he said, his mouth half-full of turkey sandwich.

Rosie rolled her eyes dramatically, ensuring that Rex could see. "What do you mean, *no thanks*? Come on."

"I mean, *no thanks,*" Rex said now a bit

more firmly.

Rosie pranced back toward him. "Oh, come on. Take a stone. Skip it on the water. Live a little!" Rosie was now yanking Rex by his arm from his position on the grass. But Rosie's slim five-foot-one-inch body could barely shake Rex's single muscular arm.

"I don't like skipping stones," Rex said with his body stiff on the grass and the agitation in his tone escalating.

"Everyone likes skipping stones."

Rosie was still tugging.

"Not me. I don't like skipping stones. And I'm not good at it so can you just give it a rest, please?"

And, just like that, Rex accidentally revealed his vulnerability to Rosie. It was the first time it had been done. And it just slipped right out.

And Rosie wasn't gentle about it. She responded like Rosie. "Oh, I see! You don't like it because you're not good at it. Well that, babe, we can fix."

It may have been the way she called him *babe,* and it may have been that he was weary of her little body tugging on his arm, and it may have been the cuteness of her candor, and it may have been that he actually believed her, but no matter what the reason was, Rex stood up and allowed Rosie to be his teacher just this once. In skipping stones and in letting go.

Rosie reached around Rex and guided his arm in proper stone-skipping motion. She demonstrated how and when to flick your wrist. How to position the stone in your hand. She showed him how to choose the flat side of the stone so that it would slide most efficiently across the top of the water. And she was warm and enthusiastic through all of it.

She stood full of excitement as Rex tossed stone after stone, waiting for each to skip just once. And even when each stone sank into the water with a plop and a few fat ripples, Rosie pushed Rex to try again. Never once did she crumble under the weight of his frustration.

And when Rex finally got one little stone to skip twice, they both jumped and cheered and smiled. And then Rex picked Rosie up and spun her round and round. She was as delicate and airy as Rex thought she would be as he whipped her around in her loose floral-printed dress and draped scarf.

Rex liked holding Rosie. And Rosie liked being held by Rex. He liked feeling her lightness. And she liked feeling his strength.

Rex put Rosie back down onto the grass

and they packed up the remaining traces of their lunch and shared a grape Pixy Stix. And then Rex picked Rosie up again, this time for a piggyback ride all the way back to the steps of the Metropolitan Museum of Art. They stopped for a brief kiss and then parted ways.

As soon as Rosie got back to her apartment, Rex called and asked to see her again. And Rosie immediately invited him over to her six-story walk-up on the Lower East Side.

8

Willow and Asher got in the car to go to school the next morning with a little bit of the previous night's ice cream still dried on their cheeks. And Willow's bones relaxed with relief. Sitting in the front seat next to her mother, she observed her in all of her coolness. Her long fingers with the red painted nails curved around the gear stick. Her left foot casually perched up on the seat. Her head bopping from side to side as she drove. Her wavy brown hair swaying back and forth as the wind moved through it.

Willow was in awe of the way Rosie's hair moved so pleasantly. The mellow manner in which her locks draped over her shoulders. The way it looked like her hair belonged piled on top of her head. She wondered if her own tight curls would ever fall into smooth waves like that.

Willow was distracted from her thoughts

by the jolt of Lili Von coming to a red light. And Willow watched Rosie as she pulled down the sun visor and fumbled around in her purse. She watched her mother pucker her lips in the mirror, and then locate a tube of red lipstick in the depths of her tote bag. Then she watched her mother twist her lipstick stick and spread the bright red color slowly and deliberately around her lips.

Rosie smacked her lips together and winked at herself in the mirror. Then she caught her daughter's eyes fixated on her lips as if she were aching for something. And Rosie was happy to give her that thing.

So when Rosie reached the elementary school drop-off area, she asked Willow to stay in the car for a moment while she said goodbye to Asher. Willow felt a tickle in her tummy waiting for her mother to return as she watched Asher express his typical embarrassment over the dramatic hug that Rosie gave him when they were dropped off. And like all the other mornings, Asher rolled his big blue eyes as his mother pressed her whole body into him.

Willow watched with a smile until her mother got back into the car. And then, with minimal digging in her bag, Rosie pulled out that same stick of red lipstick and presented it with a flick of her wrist to her daughter.

"You want some?"

Willow didn't have to say anything for her mother to know that, yes, she wanted to put some lipstick on. She wanted some of her mother's lipstick on more than anything in the world. She wanted pieces of her mother with her all the time.

Rosie leaned over to Willow and delicately painted her daughter's lips red with full attention and precision. Then Rosie snapped up, looked at her daughter and smiled warmly.

Willow could see how much her mother loved her. How funky Rosie found Willow's purple leggings. How cool she found her wild hair.

"Check it out, noodle," Rosie said as she unfolded the mirror from the sun visor in front of Willow.

Willow looked at herself in that tiny mirror. She knew she looked so much like her mother with those bright red lips. Willow smiled a big, big smile as she hopped out of the car with only the tiniest stumble and walked toward the building door.

"Wait!" Rosie hollered after Willow as she marched away. "You forgot something."

Rosie tossed the stick of lipstick through the passenger side window and right into her daughter's hands.

"It's all yours."

And just like that, red lipstick was added to Willow's permanent outfit.

"Oh! Willow. One more thing!"

Willow stumbled again when she turned back around toward her mother. You would have never guessed that Willow was feeling more confident than ever in her new red lips, the way she turned around with her knees and ankles wobbling.

Rosie held up her pointer finger and curled it back toward herself three times as she raised her left eyebrow. Willow smiled, ran up to the car and stuck her little head and big hair through the window.

"Yeah?" Willow asked.

And then Rosie leaned over and pressed a big kiss into Willow's cheek. And she shook her head all around as she did it. It left a big blob of red on Willow's cheek that Willow didn't even consider wiping away.

There was a moment of quiet love as Willow and Rosie looked straight at each other. But then Willow snatched it up.

"Hey, Mom. Can I ask you something?" She was looking right into Rosie's brown eyes. Right down into her full heart.

"Did you leave those Pixy Stix for me on the school bus from Dad's?"

Rosie tilted her head to the side and scrunched her eyebrows.

"Hmm. I'm not sure about that, noodle. What do you mean?"

Willow smirked. It was so like her mom to pretend like it wasn't her.

Willow turned around and walked into the building feeling a second wave of her mother's love. But ignoring the sincerity of her mother's confusion about those Pixy Stix.

Willow Thorpe had gotten a lot of things privately wrong about her mother. Her father too. As parents and as people. And Willow got a lot of things wrong about the ways in which her parents showed their love. But of all the things that Willow got wrong about her parents and about love, Willow's assumption that those two Pixy Stix were another one of her mother's displays of the right kind of love would turn out to be the most detrimental.

That next night at her mother's house, Willow and Asher helped Rosie prepare for Spaghetti Sunday. Asher shoved his hands into a bowl and squeezed and smashed plump red tomatoes until he couldn't squeeze or smash anymore. And then he thrust the bowl at Rosie and said, "Hewe's youw tomato guts!" through his toothless smile. As Willow stirred the bubbling pot of tomato sauce, the house filled with the aroma of garlic. And as soon as Mom got her hands on the record player, the house filled with sounds of Elton John too.

Rosie danced around as she set the table, and then served big piles of pasta and tomato sauce on her children's plates. Rosie hadn't yet finished chewing her first bite of dinner when Asher announced to the table that he had something to say. Rosie put her fork and knife down and urged Willow to do the same so that they could listen properly to Asher.

Asher stood up, pushed his chair in and swallowed.

"I don't weally like the colow of my woom," he said nervously, wobbling over each mispronounced word.

"What?" Rosie yelled quickly as she slammed her fists down onto the dinner table. She slammed them so hard that their glasses shook and the soda in them fizzled. Willow thought for a moment that her mother might be mad. She had never seen her mad before.

"That is a terrible thing!" Rosie continued, fists still clenched in tight balls next to her bowl of pasta. Rosie paused for a moment as if she was contemplating the best and quickest way to indulge her son.

"We have to fix this right away."

Another pause.

"Willow, Asher. Shoes on. We're going to the store."

And both Willow and Asher quickly, and excitedly, obeyed. Willow twisted her feet into her high-top Converse sneakers and then helped Asher tie his light-up shoes, bunny-ear style. And then Rosie whisked her children into the car and drove, windows down, Prince blasting, straight to the paint store.

She guided Asher quickly down the aisles by his hand as Willow jogged and stumbled behind them. And then Rosie stopped in front of a giant wall of every color paint in every size bucket.

"All right, sweetie. Up to you. What color do you like?" Rosie said to her son so earnestly.

Asher's eyes stretched all the way up to his hairline and his jaw fell all the way down to his belly button. And then his lips tightened as his nose crinkled.

"I have an idea," he said firmly.

It was rare that Asher found a sentence without an *R* to fumble over. It gave his words a certain un-Asher-like seriousness.

"What if we get a lot of diffewent kinds of colows and put ouw hands in thum, and then put that on the walls?"

And just like that, Asher was back to Asher. And Rosie was ecstatic at the idea.

"Yes!" she cheered. "Let's do it! Pick out all of your favorite colors. This is going to look fabulous!"

It was only natural that Rosie said yes so passionately. So openly. Because the list of things that Rosie said yes to was infinite. It was infinite on top of infinite. And whenever Willow or Asher wanted to have something or wanted to do something, their mother said yes and piled another thing right on top of it. Yes, you can play. And I want to play too. Yes, you can have candy. Have you ever put a Rolo inside of a marshmallow? Yes, you can have ice cream. Do you think it would taste as good with Swedish Fish *and* cookie dough on top? And, tonight, yes, you can paint your room. And you can do it all different crazy colors.

She kissed Asher on the cheek. Hard. Hard enough to make his lips look like a fish. And then Asher ran up to the paint chips and started pointing.

After only a few minutes of Asher running and pointing and comparing colors, Rosie,

Willow and Asher were walking out of the store with five new buckets of paint.

When they got back to the house, Rosie tossed Willow and Asher some old T-shirts she had in her closet so they wouldn't ruin their clothes. The T-shirts smelled like Dad. And everyone noticed, but no one said a thing about it. They just walked over to Asher's room and pushed his solar-system themed rug into the closet and spread newspapers across the floor. And then, the paint cans were opened and Prince's "1999" came on full blast.

All three of them stood on opposite sides of the room, shirts rolled up to their elbows, and prepared for their fun.

Rosie dived in first, but it wasn't even a full second before Willow and Asher had their arms elbows deep in paint too. At first, Willow and Asher were deliberate with each stroke of the paintbrush. Each handprint on the wall. Each little detail by the doorway. But they changed their style as soon as they noticed the way their mother had slipped right into creativity. The way she twirled around the room. The way she fanned her brushes causing the spray of paint to add a gentle dusting to the wall. The way she threw handfuls of paint at the wall, creating bursts of color. She did it so effortlessly.

And the walls looked so good. And soon Willow and Asher were following Rosie's lead in ignoring boundaries. In accessing an internal kind of freedom. In living fully and blindly immersed in the things you love. In doing the crazy things that made you happy even if they were temporary. And in this moment, dancing and singing with paint on their hands and faces, it could not have been more apparent just how wonderful all of those feelings were.

And once the walls were covered, everyone signed their name in their favorite color paint and lay down in the middle of the paint-colored floor. It was the kind of tired that only happened after an hour of laughing and dancing. It was the kind of tired that hit your bones all at once. It was the kind of tired that allowed you to keep smiling even though your eyelids were getting heavy.

As the three of them lay there quietly on their backs, the track changed to "Purple Rain."

Willow wasn't used to hearing slow songs from Prince. She was used to the kind of Prince song that begged you to dance all around or sing at the top of your lungs in the car with the windows down. But she welcomed the restrained drumming and intermittent cymbal chime. She imagined what purple rain might actually look like. The sky dripping with little beads of her favorite color. Nothing in the world scared Willow more than a thunderstorm with its whipping wind and relentless rain and sharp cracks of lightning, but a purple one might be okay.

And then, just when Willow and Asher thought the night was winding down, Rosie broke the silence with an offer of ice cream and a wink on the way downstairs to get some.

In no time at all, Willow, Asher and their mother were huddled together in Rosie's bed, scooping Ben & Jerry's Phish Food with every topping in the pantry straight from the container. And then Rosie put on *The Twilight Zone* episode she had recorded and her children sank into her.

9

Twelve Years Ago

Rex impressed Rosie that fall in Manhattan. He did it with his firmness. Because in every interaction, big or small, meaningful or trite, Rex was firm. And Rosie admired his commitment to it.

Rex was stubborn and he grumbled and stomped his feet even when he just meant to walk. And he was easily agitated. By a taxi driver taking a questionably efficient route or someone blocking the entrance of the subway. By the checkout lady at the grocery store taking more than one try to slide a quarter out of the register. By long lines and oversalted soup. And whenever Rex was agitated, he made it known. He would huff and tap his foot and tense his shoulders. He would chomp down on his Bubblicious gum so hard his temples flared. He would jut his lower jaw out to expose his crooked bottom teeth. And although all of these things were unpleasant, Rosie loved how people responded to Rex. She loved that baristas made his coffee with exactly the right amount of milk. That barbers never left a piece of hair out of line. That waiters never made him wait too long for his dinner. That Rex got everything he wanted from his world by the force of his will. Rosie admired his high expectations for his world and those around him. She liked how he pressed firmly through the day. She liked that if you were on Rex's side, mountains would be moved for you.

Rex emitted strength and Rosie liked nuzzling up next to it. She was flattered at the idea that someone like Rex might want to take care of someone like her. But most of all, she liked being taken care of.

She felt a change within herself. She had never found stability interesting before. She used to pick up books and put them down. Eat a few bites of a sandwich, and then forget about it. Talk briefly and intimately with a stranger she knew she would never see again. She took up odd jobs, and then quit them without warning.

But with Rex, she craved his steady presence. She felt a visceral urge to pull him in so close and never let go. She loved the feeling of safety when Rex was around. She loved his strong back and arms. His tough eyes that turned so loving when they got into bed. Not all women, not all people, could put up with Rex, but Rosie liked that she was strong enough, perhaps even aloof enough, to handle this caliber of man.

By Rosie's definition of love, she loved Rex very much. And while she desperately hoped she could stay still enough to find a great, enduring love with this man, she knew in her bones that it could never be. She knew in her bones that one day she would want to twirl her way into a whole new orbit. That this love was most likely the transient kind.

She wondered, but doubted, if Rex would be willing to come on her life's adventures with her. She wondered what she might say or do to try to convince him.

For now, however, Rosie would sink into her love with a man who was the opposite of everything she was.

Rosie entranced Rex that fall in Manhattan. She did it with her funkiness. Because in every interaction, big or small, meaningful or trite, Rosie was funky. And Rex admired the magic in that.

Rosie never matched her socks or cleaned the windows in her apartment. She ate pizza for breakfast and fell asleep in the middle of movies. She would casually put on a white T-shirt but cut off the sleeves or bedazzle the cuff before leaving the apartment. She refused to set an alarm, or the microwave timer, or the volume on the television to an even number. She was distracted by graffiti and never exited a subway car without saying goodbye to the person standing next to her. She waved and smiled as she did so even if they hadn't exchanged a single word or glance.

Rosie had a simple laugh and she was quick to it. She never wanted to make anyone work too hard for it. She always had a dozen things in her bag she would have trouble keeping track of. And she would dig through her tote for her wallet to no avail to find her sunglasses already on her head, a pen already in her mouth, or the book tucked precariously under her arm.

And although all of these things might seem bizarre to Rex, he loved how everything dazzled when Rosie was around. He loved the way that sullen man in the subway car would smile as the doors closed on Rosie's waving hand. How she'd share a park bench with a homeless man without hesitation. How an old piece of chocolate dug up from the bottom of her purse still tasted delicious.

Rex enjoyed getting into the crannies of the world with Rosie. He liked the sensation that the air was clearer and the sun was warmer when Rosie was near him. He felt a change within himself. He spent so much time glossing things up — his shoes, his résumé, his apartment — that he didn't know until he met Rosie that things could be so beautiful, so raw. He felt overwhelmed with desire to see things through Rosie's eyes. To explore all the tiny, forgotten corners of the universe with her next to him. Guiding him.

He loved the feeling of ease when Rosie was close by. The feeling that the next adventure, the next thing of beauty, was right around the corner.

Not all men, not all people, could put up with Rosie, but Rex liked that he was curious enough, perhaps even aloof enough, to handle this peculiar type of woman.

By Rex's definition of love, he loved Rosie very much. And while he desperately hoped he could remain engaged enough to find an all-encompassing, enduring love with this woman, he knew in his heart that it could never be. He knew in his heart that, one day, he would want to be still again. That this love was mortal.

He wondered, but doubted, if Rosie would ever sit calmly next to him in bed on a Sunday morning. He wondered what he might have to say or do to stay true to himself.

For now, however, Rex would sink into this love with a woman who was the opposite of everything he was.

10

Willow found it peculiar when she came home from school and found her father in jeans and a T-shirt waiting on the front steps. He was usually locked away in his office with all of his buttons still buttoned and his tie still tied at his neck.

There were two brand-new bikes leaning next to Rex on the front steps. Asher hopped on the silver-and-blue bike immediately and zoomed away on his new toy, training wheels included. Willow assumed that the purple one was intended for her, but was unnerved to see that it didn't have any training wheels.

"Hop on, Willow," Rex said. "Want me to teach you how to ride this thing?"

Dad always asked questions that had an answer he wanted and an answer he didn't want. Are your teeth brushed? Are the dishes clean? Did you finish your homework? But Willow found herself delighted that Dad wanted her to say yes to this. She was happy to spend some time together. She was happy her father wanted to spend some time together too. She was happy that she would be a girl who learned how to ride a bike from her father. She was happy that she would be a girl with a father who taught her how to ride a bike.

She was happy at the vision of her future self, zipping down the street on that purple bike.

She wondered how long it would take to bike to Mom's.

"Sure," Willow responded shakily to her dad.

Rex held up a helmet and some knee pads and wrist guards. And Willow put them on and pulled the Velcro extra tight on each piece of protective gear. She saved the helmet for last, but her hands were too encumbered by the plastic protrusions of the wrist guards to properly pull the chin strap. She tried a few times, wrist guard clicking against the base of the helmet until Rex noticed what was happening and gave a hearty chuckle.

A chuckle.

Willow smiled sweetly at the sound of that rare noise escaping her father's mouth. And then she felt her heart speed up and her cheeks tingle as her father bent down in front of her and pulled on her chin strap until her helmet was just the right amount of tight. It was the closest her father's face had ever been to hers as Willow could remember it.

Willow loved how her father looked when she was up close. His skin was tan and smooth and his eyebrows were unruly and excited. Willow had noticed the creases between his eyebrows before, but the creases in his cheeks were new to her. Because while the eyebrow creases were undoubtedly a sign of how hard he was always thinking, the cheek creases must have been a sign that he used to smile. Perhaps even a lot. When Willow gazed down, she loved seeing how her father's big hands tugged at her helmet strap, ensuring her safety. Caring about her.

Then, right before Rex pulled away, Willow and her father made eye contact. It lasted for only half a second, but it happened. And it made her heart speed up and her cheeks tingle even more.

Willow floated on top of her bicycle seat and felt ready to learn. And ready to be taught.

Her dad told her how to swing her left leg over just as the bike started moving. And then Rex did what dads are supposed to do.

He told her to pedal, pedal, pedal. He told her to try again. And again. And again. He told her not to give up. Not to worry about falling. He told her he wouldn't let go of the handlebars until she said she was ready. He was energized and encouraging. Willow's heart was in her throat over the thought of crashing down onto the concrete, but she was having a version of fun. Because right there on the road outside of Dad's house, something was happening. Something unlikely. Something unusual. Something meaningful. Something important. Something between Rex and Willow. Between father and daughter.

"Go over there and try pushing off the curb," Rex suggested to Willow when she was so close to balancing herself.

And so she did. Willow gripped her handlebars, pushed off the curb and was suddenly in full motion. She felt the wind passing through her helmet. She felt the uneven surface of the street beneath her wheels. She felt fast and competent. And although she looked neither fast nor competent as she wobbled around on her seat with her arms rigid with fear, Willow also felt graceful and in control. And graceful and in control were brand-new feelings for Willow Thorpe. And she felt happy, so grateful that her father had drawn these feelings out of her.

"Dad! Dad! I'm doing it!" she shouted as loudly as she could with the air whipping by her. Willow picked her head up, looking forward to seeing her dad as excited as she was. Looking forward to him jumping up and down on the grass. She imagined him running over to give her a high five. Picking her up and swinging her around in circles. Kissing her on the face and telling her how proud he was.

But when her eyes found her father, he was staring down distractedly at his notepad and chomping down on a new piece of Bubblicious gum. Rex looked up to give his daughter a brief closed-mouth smile and a silent thumbs-up, and then he scribbled something on his notepad as he stormed back inside.

Willow rode her bike all around until she was alone in the dark and the trees were starting to creak in the wind. Then, when she was ready to go inside, she made sure to remove her wrist guards before attempting to take off her helmet by herself.

11

Eleven Years Ago

Rex was accustomed to elevators and doormen, and so he tensed up the first few times the stairs creaked as he climbed the flights to Rosie's apartment. But it wasn't long before he found the smell of musk by Rosie's doorway profoundly alluring. The palpable dampness. The dusty crannies. The hum of the flickering light. The sticky crackle of the floor. Rex enjoyed his ability to access this kind of rawness when he was with Rosie. He was saving clean modern lines and well-dusted corners for another life.

After a year of dating, Rex already knew that the heart of all things beat more deeply when Rosie was around. Even her apartment vibrated. The walls were covered with annotated Polaroids and handwritten notes from friends. The refrigerator door was collaged with old ads featuring Cheryl Tiegs and Faye Dunaway. The walls were covered with posters of Elton John and Prince and Blondie. The corners of the couches had stuffing coming out the seams ineffectively covered by discolored pillows. There were markers and paintbrushes sprawled across the table. It was so clear to Rex that this was a place where art was made and drinks were spilled. It was a place where friends put their feet on the table, and no one bothered to replace old light bulbs. It was a place where people breathed and moved and talked and created. It was a place where people lived. And were happy. And he could see it in Rosie's face that this was where *she* lived and was happy.

Rex took off his scarf, kissed Rosie gently, and then the two of them sank into her worn-in couch. They oriented themselves on the cushions as if they had been doing it just this way for years; Rex seated upright, shoes on, while Rosie placed her head in his lap and stretched her ankles over the arm of the sofa to let her clogs fall to the ground. This had already become Rex's favorite part of the day, inhaling all of the scents of Rosie's life — the flowery scent of the beautiful world around her lingering on the surface of her skin. It was no surprise to Rex that beautiful things clung onto Rosie and didn't let go. It felt good being close to her. So good and so warm and so comfortable.

Rex wondered how he would eventually let go of all of the beautiful sweet things Rosie Collins was, but the thought quickly burrowed itself in the back of his mind when Rosie reached back and, without looking, wrapped her fingers one by one around Rex's bicep and squeezed it enticingly.

Rex swept Rosie's bangs away and traced his pointer around her temple, across her forehead and along the bridge of her nose. Rosie tried to follow his finger and giggled when she found herself cross-eyed as a result. Rex was a serious man and always assumed his girlfriend would be equally so, but Rosie's quirky style of intimacy fulfilled him in a way he'd never thought possible.

And just as Rex was about to bend over and kiss Rosie, Rosie's roommate Chloe burst out of her room, spewing on and on about the attractive man she'd locked eyes with at the café down the block, and ignoring Rex's presence entirely. Rex did everything he could to keep from staring at Chloe's nipples plainly visible through her sheer white shirt as she spoke. Rosie just half chuckled and shook her head as Chloe's small breasts bounced up and down while she gesticulated her way through another mundane story.

And when Chloe finally exhaled, she lifted Rosie's legs, wedged herself under her knees and pulled out a marijuana joint. Rex's belly tensed at the sight of it.

Rex was uncomfortable with drugs, even the mere sight of them. He wanted to get up, rip the joint away from Chloe and throw it out the window. But Rosie lifted her eyes to meet Rex's eyes and stroked his thigh gently. It was an indication that, yes, this was something she found to be acceptable in her home. And although Rex had never heard Rosie mention drugs before, the effortlessness with which she handled the joint between her fingers indicated that this was an activity she partook in regularly. Rex's muscles tensed and his jaw clenched as he watched Rosie exhale a cloud of smoke, but in the newness of the scene, he didn't protest.

And then Rosie brought the joint to her lips a second time.

Rex watched suspiciously as Rosie inhaled and the tip of the joint flared orange. He watched as Rosie gave in to the feeling of smoke in her lungs right away.

Rosie let her arm hang off the side of the

sofa and slowly allowed her eyelids to close. As her breath deepened and her high began, Chloe's voice, the clamor of the city streets, her lingering uncertainty about Rex and anything else grating about the world, drifted quietly away.

Rex could see the release in her face as he watched the smoke roll around in Rosie's mouth, and then overtake her red lips, like fog rolling over a hill. She looked so calm, so beautiful. He felt Rosie's body loosen, allowing herself to fully sink into his lap. This stillness, this quiet, was something Rex had never seen in Rosie before. He was used to her intense energy. Rex knew that Rosie was someone in tune with all of the tiny ripples of the world. All of the individual, human-to-human forces in it. And that those forces moved in waves through her. And that Rosie absorbed those waves deep within her body. It was the thing that made Rosie, Rosie. The thing that made her so special. But it also seemed to be the thing that exhausted her. Caused her to crave the calm of that high. And Rex could see that happening right there on Rosie's old couch.

Rex was surprised to find an overwhelming sensuality in the feeling of Rosie melting into him. Rosie opened her eyes and looked deeply into Rex's. She slowly reached her hand back and squeezed his inner thigh and walked her thin fingers delicately toward his crotch. Rex looked back at Rosie and kissed her forehead as his heart and his groin pulsed.

Then Rex, leaving Chloe to the rest of the joint in the living room, took Rosie's nearly drooping body to her bedroom where, at her beckoning, he entered her slowly and entirely. As he moved inside her, Rex could feel Rosie's body surge with pleasure, and then dissolve again back into her high. Rex found Rosie sexier than ever beneath him.

It was a version of Rosie he would enjoy only this one time, he told himself, in her bedroom with the old chipping paint. And then never permit this again. He didn't want drugs to be a force in their relationship. He didn't want drugs to be a force inside of Rosie. No matter how beautifully calm they enabled her to be.

Rex returned home from Rosie's apartment late the next morning, heart and mind still spinning. He couldn't keep all of these feelings, these ripples ricocheting around his brain. So he picked up the phone and called Roy Andrews, his oldest and closest, most dependable and most trustworthy friend.

"Roy," Rex said solemnly. "This girl is going to be trouble."

Rex knew he would need someone he could call on if Rosie was going to stick around in his life. And he had a feeling Rosie was going to become a part of him. For the first time, Rex was facing the difficulty of trying to hold on to something that vibrated. First, the sensation tickled a bit. Pleasingly. But then the energy started to move through him. Shaking his hand and then his arm and then his whole body. And even though those ripples in his body were briefly pleasant, they quickly started to become uncomfortable. Because his body was not meant to ripple like that. Vibrate like that. He wanted to release his grip, but his body couldn't catch up with his brain. Finally he managed to let go, knowing he should keep his distance in the future. But still, he wanted to feel that first little tickle again. Even for just a moment. So he came back to Rosie again and again.

12

After dinner at their father's, Willow and Asher met in the den to play their favorite game: Lava Floor. It was the only game in Willow and Asher's repertoire that was more fun at Dad's. Because the den at Dad's was full of so many surfaces to jump onto once the floor turned to lava. It was full of big leather couches and thick wooden tables and velvety ottomans. All were perfectly sized for far leaps and smooth landings. Willow moved the ivory-and-ebony chessboard that her father left out on the coffee table as a not-so-subtle attempt to get his children to play something more worthwhile than Lava Floor. And then she hopped up on the couch and poised herself for a leap. And even though Willow's unreliable legs made her pretty bad at Lava Floor, Willow liked watching her brother jump from surface to surface while his silky blond hair flopped all around.

And also, it couldn't be discounted that she thoroughly enjoyed hopping all around the same couch she was asked to sit on earlier that day with folded hands as her father introduced another one of his girlfriends who ended up staying for dinner. This one had boring blond hair and ate teeny tiny bites at a time. Her shirt was too stiff and her hair was too straight and her pocketbook looked too perfect on her shoulder. Willow liked the idea of jumping wildly up and down on the same surface that lady sat on with a straight back and forced smile.

Willow looked over at Asher, who was squatted down on the end table across the room with his knees bent, elbows tucked by his side and eyes full of determination.

Willow laughed at the intensity of this stance. "Ash, do you have to poop or something?"

And Asher laughed right back. Quickly and loudly. Until they were both interrupted by Rex's booming voice.

"Hey! You two! Is that Lava Floor?"

Willow knew that her father could always tell when fun was about to be had because his jaw would tighten and his shoulders would press upward. And even if he was three rooms away in his office, undoubtedly reading from his stack of notes and tapping his ballpoint pen, Willow could feel the pulsing tension radiate.

"No shoes on the couch!"

Willow and Asher met eyes, shrugged sneakily and threw off their shoes as if they had never been on and giggled quietly.

And then Asher made his first leap toward the couch a couple feet away. His feet flew into the air, and then sank down into the leather cushion.

"Yeah!" Willow shouted instinctively, and threw her arms in the air to celebrate the first triumph of the game.

Then their father's voice boomed again.

"Can we keep the noise down, please?"

Willow turned to Asher to shrug again, but he was back in his squatted position, prepared for his second leap to the ottoman next to the fireplace mantel. It was a far leap that Willow had only seen Asher complete once before. And he had tied his blankie around his neck like a cape in order to do it.

Asher pulled his arms back and jumped up again. His straight, blond bowl cut flapped around as he moved through the air. His feet reached the ottoman, but his upper body was off balance. He swung his arms around like windmills before grabbing onto the mantel of the fireplace for support. His hands slid across the top of the dark wood, knocking her father's favorite vase off balance. It teetered one way, and then the other, and then rolled along the mantel and dripped over the edge. Willow braced herself for a shattered vase but instead, it dropped delicately into the cushioned embrace of the ottoman.

Asher's eyes widened as far as they could go, and he put both of his little hands over his O-shaped mouth.

And suddenly, Rex was standing right next to Asher, arms folded across his chest and his crooked bottom teeth thrust out.

"What did I say?"

Rex picked up the vase from the ottoman, gripped onto it tightly in anger and slammed it down on the mantel. Rex slammed the vase down so hard that it shattered. It shattered into little flecks of pink and blue and green and clear. And all of those little flecks scattered all across the dark wood floor. They spread under the couch and table and the ottoman.

It got so quiet as the clicking of glass hitting floor trailed off into stillness. Eye of the storm stillness.

And then Rex's storm came.

"You've got to be fucking kidding me! Go

to your rooms!" Rex shouted as he thrust his pointer finger in the direction of the staircase. "Now!"

A deep red drop of blood fell from his finger as Willow and Asher stood stunned.

"I said, *now*!"

And then Willow and Asher scurried upstairs without returning the chessboard to its place on the coffee table or refluffing the pillows or picking up their shoes. They were on the cusp of the giggles. They wanted to laugh so hard at the irony of the event. Of Dad's favorite vase in pieces by his own doing.

But Willow also felt the sadness of having a father who loathed the sight of shoes on the couch so deeply, so thoroughly, that blood was spilled. Even if it was just a drop. Willow entered her room and sat down on her bed with the weight of her father's anger pressing heavily on her shoulders and her heart.

The next words Willow and Asher heard from their father were, "My office for 'The Box,' please." Willow dropped her shoulders and shuffled into the office alongside her brother.

"The Box" was the culmination of Rex's week collecting misplaced items from around the house — toys, sweatshirts, books, sneakers — and placing them in a blue milk crate. And when the week was over on Sunday night, Rex would dangle each individual object above his head and announce the name of its shameful owner.

"Sock with holes in it. Asher."

"Purple crayon. Willow."

"Silly Putty with comic imprint?"

Asher reached his hand out excitedly, not really understanding the purpose of the ritual.

"Look. This is the one whewe Calvin and Hobbes make a snowman," he explained excitedly. And then he gloated when Rex returned it into his possession.

Rex ignored the non sequitur and got back to business.

"Batman mask. Asher."

"Hulk action figure. Asher."

And this continued until the crate was clear. And once it was, Willow and Asher could finally escape Rex's office and move on to the nighttime checklist.

Toys Away
Homework Finished — Are you forgetting anything?
Laundry in the Basket
Shower — Armpits included

Floss Teeth — Top AND bottom! Molars too!
15 Minutes of Reading — More is OK!
Tuck In

And when it was complete, Rex would slide his hand through the door frame, flipping the light switch into the off position, and then saying, "Night."

As Willow drifted into sleep, she thought about what it would look like if she created a nighttime checklist for her father. It wouldn't say tell Willow and Asher about the things they left around the house or to count backward from sixty as they brush their teeth to make sure they aren't missing any spots. It would only have one thing on it:

Kiss Willow and Asher good-night.

Willow barely realized that she had fallen asleep when a loud, booming thunder and the knocking of rain woke her up. And when her eyes burst open, her heart was beating furiously and her bladder was pulsing. Her thoughts carouseled around in her mind.

Don't go. Don't go. Please don't go. No accidents. Don't go. Please don't go.

Willow closed her eyelids as tightly as she could and put her pointer fingers deep into her ears. But her pointer fingers were no match for rain that sounded like thousands of pebbles had been dumped onto the roof of her room. When a crack of lightning and second explosion of thunder shook her entire body to its core, Willow instinctively leaped out of bed and ran to her father's room. He would be able to protect her. Calm her.

Willow walked quickly down the long hallway to her dad's room with panic fluttering inside her and her fingers still in her ears. She gently pushed the door open, trying not to wake her father as harshly as the thunder had woken her up.

"Dad," Willow whispered, walking toward his bed.

"Dad."

"Dad."

"Willow?" Rex said with a raspy voice and his eyes still closed. "What's going on?"

"The storm," Willow confessed.

No response.

"I'm scared."

"Willow, it's the middle of the night. We're inside. Go back to sleep."

But the wind was still howling and the rain was still slapping against the windows. And her heart was still racing and her bladder was still pulsing and she was too scared to go to the bathroom alone. Being inside didn't make any of it better.

Willow stood in her father's dark bedroom, Keith Haring T-shirt down to her knees, shivering with fear. Willow couldn't bring herself to leave just yet. She watched her father's shadow rolling over in bed, turning his back to her. She stared at the empty space next to him in bed, wishing she could jump in there. Wishing she could jump in there for a hug and then a back tickle. She stared at that space so hard. She wanted to be in that space so badly.

And then that space moved.

And a second shadow appeared.

The shadow of a woman. A stiff, thin woman with long straight hair strewn across the pillow. Willow was sure it was the same woman she had seen before.

Willow's right knee buckled as she turned around and walked back to her room. A single tear formed in her chest, and then made its way slowly into her eye and down her cheek.

When Willow woke up, her entire bed was wet and everything smelled like urine.

13

Eleven Years Ago

After a year of dating, Rosie decided she loved Rex despite, and sometimes because of, his supreme jerkiness. Because his moments of jerkiness often illuminated his strength, his confidence, his masculinity. But sometimes, those moments just made him a jerk. And usually, the combination of his handsomeness and her love for Rex outweighed all the jerkiness. But not today. Not today when Rosie and Rex made plans to eat crabs by the water downtown.

Rosie could tell that Rex was stressed as soon as she saw him. His shoulders were so tense they nearly brushed up against his earlobes and he was chewing a big wad of pink Bubblicious gum. His temples were flaring intensely and his responses were curt.

It was one of those days in which Rex had a big gray cloud around him. All of Rex's prior girlfriends hated this cloud. And they would either run scared of the impending storm or would shine extra bright hoping it would go away. But these approaches worked neither for Rex nor his prior girlfriends. Because no matter what, when Rex showed up with a big gray cloud around him, everyone always ended up enduring a storm. Everyone always ended up soaking wet. Everyone except for Rosie.

Rosie wasn't scared of rain and she wasn't scared of Rex. And she never changed her approach to her day on anyone's account. So despite Rex's stiff shoulders and bulging temples, she continued walking down Allen Street in her long black dress, cozy knit hat and tiny white shoes. And Rex stood alone under his dark cloud.

"That gum is grossing me out!" Rosie finally told Rex as she peered into the window of the antiques shop on the way to the restaurant.

"Well, I'm hungry," Rex said, refusing to accept a truth without a retort.

"Oh, you're hungry?" Rosie said sarcastically. "Well, don't fill up on gum, all right?" She winked smoothly at Rex before skipping into the musty store filled with old armoires and dusty lamps.

Rex almost smiled, but swallowed it. He didn't like any outward concessions. Especially while he was under his cloud.

Rex tapped his right foot outside and stared down at his watch. He huffed audibly as he watched every *tick, tick, tick* of the second hand. Rosie observed him doing this from inside the shop, but it didn't make her move one bit faster. She returned to her shopping and slowly traced her hand along the intricate carvings of a wooden desk from the 1920s. She inspected every millimeter of a rusted metal windup toy from the 1950s. She leafed through a pile of old postcards. It was Rosie doing what Rosie always did. Absorbing her world. Soaking it in. With great attention. And great warmth. Letting everything ripple through her and fill up all of her senses. And she did it all with Rex Thorpe standing outside, tapping his foot and staring at his watch.

But Rex couldn't stand to be outside for one more instant, and he burst inside the musty shop furiously. The same way he had burst into Blooms Flower Shop.

"I just *told you* I was hungry. Can the postcards wait so I don't have to?"

Rosie looked up from the crooked pile of postcards with only her eyes, leaving her chin and the rest of her body leaning in toward the box.

"Of course, my darling," Rosie said gently

and with a smile. It was almost genuine.

"I was just finishing up. But first look at this photo! It's amazing!" Rosie thrust one of the postcards right into Rex's face, and Rex was charmed all over again. He pretended to reluctantly scan the postcard but his mind was fixated with how strange and lovely Rosie was there in that old shop in her long black dress with those little shoes.

Rosie lifted up her dress an inch as she started to walk, revealing her tiny delicate ankle. She pranced away and waved at the short and wrinkled shop owner. "See ya, Jonny," Rosie said like they were old friends.

And then Rosie and Rex made their way back to the street and continued walking toward the restaurant where their crabs were waiting. A fabric shop caught Rosie's eye and she waltzed in prepared to examine all of the prints, take in the scents of the lace, feel the silks against her cheek. But as soon as Rosie's foot stepped through the doorway, Rex burst with rage.

"You've got to be fucking kidding me, Rosie."

He grabbed her wrist.

"I just said I was hungry."

Clenched jaw. Silence.

"Twice."

Bottom crooked teeth out.

Silence.

Eye of the storm silence.

And suddenly, it wasn't about Rex's hunger or Rosie's delight in silk. Or Rex's flaring temples or Rosie's casual strut. Or Rex's handsomeness or Rosie's red lips. It was about friction. There was too much of it. And no amount of Rosie's funkiness or Rex's firmness could mitigate that.

So quickly, and without putting much thought into it, Rosie decided to forgo the crabs and the evening with Rex. She wiggled her wrist from Rex's fingers and walked down Allen Street back toward her apartment.

When Rosie got home, Chloe was sitting on the couch stoned. Her arm was flopped lifelessly over a cushion and her eyes were closed lightly.

"Hey, babe," Chloe mumbled, barely even moving her lips. And then she sat up, rubbing one eye but not bothering to move her hair away from the front of her face. "I thought you were out with Rex."

Rosie huffed.

"Ugh, I *was.*"

Rosie reached for the joint sitting on the coffee table.

"He's such an ass sometimes though." Rosie threw herself onto the couch, splaying her arms out in defeat. She swung her tote bag over the back of the sofa. A few pens dropped out without Rosie even noticing as she sat up slowly and pulled her fingers to her lips for a drag of the half-smoked joint.

But Chloe placed her hand over Rosie's before it met her mouth and guided it back down to the coffee table.

"Try this instead, doll," Chloe said, handing her a white round pill. "*This* will take the edge off."

And Chloe couldn't have been more correct. Within thirty minutes, that single white pill of Vicodin soothed Rosie, warmed Rosie, hugged Rosie, consumed Rosie. It left Rosie with her arm flopped lifelessly over a pillow too.

The high from that white pill was so thoroughly calming. So thoroughly relaxing and soothing in a way she had never felt before. In a way she felt she needed.

Because Rosie expected so much from life and the people in it and she loved to feel and experience every last ounce of everything, but it exhausted her. And those little white pills allowed that all to melt away. It allowed her to relax. To find stillness. To find quiet.

Rosie let her afternoon with Rex and all the other vibrating things evaporate into nothing as she drifted into a half sleep. Drifted into her high.

And it was a high Rosie would have again and again. Even when it stopped making things better, and started making things worse.

14

The next night at their mother's was the night of the monthly viewing of *The Rocky Horror Picture Show,* and Willow, Asher and Rosie dressed for the occasion. They each wore different permutations of fishnet stockings, big pearl necklaces, thick eye shadow, bright red lipstick and fitted tank tops. And as the three of them stood in front of the mirror to examine their outfits, Rosie held up the framed photo of Tim Curry as Dr. Frank-N-Furter that usually hung in the hallway. She winked with one eye and then the other at each of her children.

"Stunning," she said in all earnestness.

Asher had no idea what he was saying or doing when he slipped into his mother's high heels, struck a pose and smiled, mimicking a line from the film. But Rosie couldn't help hugging him so tightly. And then she joined Asher in his dance and guided him through the rest of the lyrics as they held hands and kicked their feet up.

When the "Time Warp" came on, Rosie, Asher and Willow took their places right in front of the TV and jumped to the left, stepped to the right and thrust their pelvises alongside the characters. They got up on the couches in their makeup while they did it. They laughed and sang until they were out of breath. And when the music was over, Rosie, Willow and Asher retreated to their separate rooms to put on their matching squiggly patterned pajamas with plans to reconvene in Rosie's room.

But when Willow and Asher got back to their mother's door, it was uncharacteristically closed. It was so strange to see their mother's door like that. It was strange to see any barrier at all in their mother's house. Their mother's house was always so open. Open to air and life. It allowed music and laughter to move around freely. Before her heart could start beating any faster, and more nervously, Willow turned the doorknob. But it didn't move with her hand. It stayed there locked in place, silver and cold.

"One second, noodles," Rosie said but without enough breath from the other side of the door.

So Willow and Asher waited at their mother's door with matching pajamas and bouncing legs. Ready to curl up next to their mother for bedtime.

And after only a moment, Rosie pulled the door open and smiled warmly at her children with a word search in hand.

"Should we play?" Rosie asked, extending a word search book out in front of her children's already-vibrant eyes.

Willow and Asher nodded vigorously and in sync. They hopped into their mother's unmade but cozy bed and prepared to tangle themselves up in Rosie. And as soon as Rosie wiggled herself between her two children and then underneath the covers, Willow pressed her ear into her mother's shoulder and hooked her right thigh over her mother's leg and locked her eyes on the grid of letters. And Asher nuzzled under his mother's arm, tucked his knees into his belly and locked his eyes on the same grid of letters.

"Robot," Rosie announced slowly, mumbling a bit. "Can you find me the word?"

Willow and Asher scanned the grid of letters on the page with intense focus. And then Asher yelled out and pointed down at the paper.

"Thewe!"

Asher and Willow waited for their mother to trace the outline of the word and announce the next word to be found, but Rosie was silent. Willow looked up at her mother to urge her to move the pen, but her eyes were nearly closed and her head had fallen unnaturally to the side.

"Mom," Willow said firmly as she nudged her hip into her mother's thigh.

But Rosie just lay there with her mouth a bit agape and her shoulders sunken.

"Shhhhh," Rosie said, with lazy lips and cheeks. Her eyes were still closed as she sank even deeper into her pillow. And then Rosie's wrist went weak. And the word search book fell slowly from her hands and onto her lap.

Willow had never seen her mother's lips producing a *shh.* It was so strange for Willow to see her mother's body draped so lifelessly across her pillow. She was used to her mother lighting up with vitality. Pulsing with energy. But even with Rosie so physically loose, there was something so heartbreakingly rigid about her in this state. The thought occurred to Willow that her mother had perhaps hardened against her world. That she had detached in some way. Even if it was just the littlest bit.

But Willow pushed the thought away as quickly as she could. And she hooked her knee right back over her mother's thigh and wrapped her arm around her mother's waist. And Asher followed his sister's lead and curled right back up in the tiny space between Rosie's arm and ribs.

Rosie, Asher and Willow all drifted into sleep with the lamp on and the book of word searches on Rosie's lap right there in her bed. Without back tickles or head scratches.

The next morning, Rosie, Asher and Willow were all surprised to wake up simultaneously to Rex's shouting.

"Rosie!"

"Rosie!"

Rex's voice echoed aggressively throughout the house. It was so strange to hear Dad's voice knocking around Mom's walls.

"Rosie! You've got to be kidding me! It's ten thirty. The school called again to ask where the kids are."

Rosie exhaled fully. And then she rolled her eyes and rolled out of bed. But not before full-lipped kisses for each of her children.

"Stay here, noodles," she whispered, and raised one eyebrow as she slipped out the door of her bedroom.

Willow and Asher made their way onto the staircase, where they watched and listened to their parents yell coldly at one another.

"Rex, relax," Rosie said while rubbing her right eye with the heel of her hand. "The kids were up late. I wanted to let them sleep. It's not a big deal."

"It *is* a big deal. It's a school day, Rosie. They need structure. They need discipline. This isn't good for them."

Rosie poured Froot Loops and milk into a bowl and scooped a spoonful into her mouth. A bit of white liquid dribbled down her chin.

"You can't be so freakin' cavalier with everything anymore! Wake up, Rosie! You are a goddamned mother!"

A few drops of spit flew from his mouth as Rex cut into Rosie and as he turned toward the staircase.

Willow and Asher scurried back into their mother's room and took their place under her comforter and lay still.

"What were they *up late* doing, anyway?" Rex added as he stomped harshly up the stairs.

But Rosie didn't have to answer his question.

Because he saw the answer as soon as he swung open the door. The sight of Willow and Asher in faded lipstick and smudged eye shadow told the whole story of the prior evening. She saw her father's face as she made eye contact with him and could see all the disappointment in it.

Disappointment at how she looked there with her makeup on. Disappointment at how she had enjoyed her time in her boa. Her father's eyebrows pressed together and his jaw tensed. And then his breathing became audible and his fingers gnarled as all the disappointment twisted into disgust. Disgust at how she was so happy at her mother's. Disgust with the scene of last night's makeup. Disgust with everything.

"Wash your faces. Get dressed. We're going to school," Rex directed. His voice was steady but his body was shaking.

Willow ushered Asher into the bathroom where they could clean their faces. She wiped Asher's face and then her own until they were clear of any trace of their time with Mom. Willow sent Asher to his room to get dressed, then stared at her own face in the mirror. It looked so bare. So empty. She reapplied some red lipstick and felt replenished.

Willow returned to her room and tugged her purple leggings on, one leg at a time. She pulled her black T-shirt with the horseshoe over her head and thought about how her outfit and lipstick would only disappoint her father all over again this morning. But then she remembered that day in kindergarten when she walked downstairs for school and overheard the forcibly quiet fight that ensued when her mother walked through the door with bags upon bags filled with the purple leggings and black horseshoe T-shirts in all different sizes.

"It's just a phase," her father shouted through clenched teeth, ripping one of the shopping bags out of Rosie's hand.

"No. It's not," Rosie said casually, and continued to walk by her husband.

"Even if it's not a phase, this is not the kind of behavior I will encourage from my daughter," Rex said sharply.

"This is *exactly* the kind of behavior I will encourage from my daughter," Rosie retorted. This time with a rare fire in her eyes and grumble in her voice.

Willow just smiled from the top of the stairs. Hearing Mom say this made Willow want to wear that outfit every day forever. And right there at the top of the stairs, a few weeks into kindergarten, she decided to do just that and never changed her mind since.

Rex had opened his mouth, undoubtedly with a retaliation, but Rosie got to the moment of pause first.

"I won't let you take this from her. I won't let you strip Willow of any and all of the weird, beautiful things that make Willow, Willow. You hear me?"

And that was the end of the conversation.

Willow smiled at the memory playing in her mind's eye as she returned to Asher's room. She took him by the hand and walked him downstairs to say goodbye to her mother. Rosie was already waiting by the front door with her eyes crossed and tongue out. Before Willow and Asher were too far out the door, Rosie tossed brown-paper-bagged lunches at her children and winked as she watched her ex-husband continue to pull them down the driveway.

Rosie blew kiss after kiss to her children as Rex's car pulled away.

15

Eleven Years Ago

The idea of a single apartment suiting both Rosie and Rex was nearly unthinkable. But the idea of Rex and Rosie continuing to alternate back and forth between beds was even more unthinkable.

The apartment that Rex picked out with the strangely shaped rooms and old light fixtures was his first concession for Rosie. He would have preferred a modern condo with sharp lines and stainless steel appliances, but Rosie could never survive in such a place. She needed colors and patterns and nooks and crannies. She needed quirk. And Rex would do that for this woman he loved. Just this once.

When Rex lifted his hands from Rosie's eyes to reveal their new apartment on the Upper East Side, they both immediately became aware that Rosie's dress matched the toile wallpaper in the entranceway exactly. And, accordingly, that Rex had picked out the perfect place for his girlfriend. Rosie grabbed the back of Rex's head and pushed her lips and cheek into his. It could barely be considered a kiss the way Rosie smashed her face into his, but it was all the more intimate for it. It was Rex's second-favorite kiss he ever had.

And even though the look and feel of the apartment was not to his taste, he loved the look and feel of Rosie in it. And just this once, that was enough.

Rosie ran over to the wall and stretched her arms and legs into the shape of an X.

"Can you see me? Am I camouflaged yet?" she said as she posed.

And Rex and Rosie just laughed and laughed. They laughed and laughed straight from their bellies as they stared into each other's eyes from opposite ends of the entranceway.

And then Rex activated the record player that he had already cued up. The introductory chords of "Leather and Lace" filled the room.

Rex met Rosie at the wall and uncupped his hand to reveal a tarnished gold chain and locket, an antique he knew she would appreciate. Then he turned the locket over to show her the engraving he'd had etched into the back of it.

299 East 82nd Street, New York, New York. Apartment 5.

He swung the necklace over Rosie's head and watched it dangle around on her chest.

Rosie clutched the locket, then held her small hands over her beating heart. Her beating heart filled with Rex's big love.

Rex lifted her gently off the ground. It got so quiet as they swayed back and forth in tandem to the melody of their song.

It was happiness. It would be brief in the grand scheme of things. But right there in their apartment entranceway at 299 East 82nd Street, it was so real.

And suddenly, without warning or words exchanged, Rosie was crying. But there was an atypical passivity to it. An atypical tremble accompanying it.

Rex waited patiently for Rosie to explain her tears.

And then Rosie whispered, "I'm pregnant."

To Rex and also to the rest of the empty room and also to herself. It was the first time she had been able to say it out loud. She stared vacantly over Rex's back as she said it. Tears still dancing in her eyes.

Rosie pressed her forehead into Rex's shoulder. His strong, steady shoulder. And for a moment she felt okay. It, too, was brief in the grand scheme of things. But right there in the apartment entranceway at 299 East 82nd Street, it also was so real.

And then, without saying a word, Rex pressed his lips firmly and deeply into the top of Rosie's head.

"Do you think we can do this?" Rosie finally asked timidly.

"I think we have a special kind of love, Rosie Collins," Rex said kindly and matter-of-factly.

Rosie knew it wasn't an answer, but it was perfect enough.

"We do, Rex Thorpe. And it's 'most mad and moonly.' " Rosie pressed her head even farther into Rex's shoulder.

"That crazy e. e. cummings love poem!" Rex said through a smirk. And then Rex kissed Rosie again. This time with a renewed levity in his lips.

It was Rosie's second-favorite kiss she ever had.

Even though both of their hearts were beating nervously and out of sync.

When "Leather and Lace" faded out, Rosie wiggled herself from Rex's embrace and looked at him lovingly. He had already done so much for her. The apartment. The locket. The strength in his body. The love in his heart. She wanted to think about it every day. She wanted everyone to see it. She knew a single piece of jewelry never stayed on her body for long. So she took the locket off her neck and hung it from a nail head on the wallpapered wall. As a manifesto to love at 299 East 82nd Street. As a manifesto to unlikely, meaningful, profound love.

And then she wiggled right back into Rex's embrace.

16

Willow sat down in the school cafeteria with her lunch bag, her body still tense. She was uncharacteristically shaken up by her morning with her dad storming through her mom's house. She no longer liked seeing her two parents in the same room.

Willow focused on her lunch and uncurled the tinfoil on her peanut butter and jelly sandwich. A handwritten note rested right on top of the white bread.

> See you by the far fence at recess time! I love you oodles and oodles of noodle poodles.
>
> — Mom

Willow ate her sandwich in a few excited bites, then ran out to the fence as fast as she could, stumbling only twice. At the fence her mother skipped hellos and leaped straight to the purpose of the meeting.

"I realized this morning that I've never taught you how to climb a tree."

Willow felt a buzz in her blood.

"I also haven't rescued you from school yet this year! And what kind of daughter of mine can't climb a tree? Come on, hop this fence. I know a perfect spot."

And without another thought, Willow wrapped her fingers and toes around the cold chain links and started to climb. Her left leg slipped once, but her mother's supporting hands and spirit were right there with her as she urged her over the fence and then into the front seat of her car.

Rosie and Willow drove with the windows down to the park around the corner as Willow filled with happiness.

"There it is," Rosie said, pointing at an enormous willow tree with its waterfall of tiny leaves pouring toward the ground while all of the other trees were bare. Its strong dark trunk radiated into dozens of thin branches that supported thousands of dripping leaves. The afternoon light crawled through its rich green leaves in smooth golden rays that cut through the chill of late autumn. Rosie stood there, so still, admiring the tree. Inhaling deeply. Exhaling deeply. Willow could see a faint cloud of breath form and then dissolve at the tip of her mother's red lips. Her eyes were so wide and Willow thought she saw a tear forming in one of them.

A force of something moved Rosie from both the outside in and the inside out as she took her daughter's hand with an unwavering grip and walked toward the tree. Rosie hoisted her daughter onto the lowest branches and helped her with every move to climb deeper into the willow. Right hand, this branch. Left foot, that branch. Willow wrapped her fingers around each branch and pulled her body up, up, up. She pressed her black Converse into the willow tree's sturdy trunk. Its coarse bark kept her foot in place as she climbed up, up, up some more. It felt so strange for something so rough to feel so safe, but Willow welcomed the tree's jagged embrace. And oddly the higher Willow climbed, the more comfortable she was feeling. The more those draping leaves shielded her and enveloped her. Created another secret space with her mom. Just like the tree house. But this one was in the daylight.

And finally her mom was just below her. When they had reached the thinnest branches they could sit on, Willow and Rosie stopped climbing. They sat on top of the branches and let their feet dangle weightlessly.

And then Rosie looked at her daughter with a rare expression of seriousness. A rare lift in her earlobes and stillness in her cheeks.

"Did I ever tell you why your father and I named you Willow?"

Willow shook her head side to side.

"Your father and I had our first kiss under a willow tree while we were both living in New York. I think we already loved each other right then. Even though neither of us knew that much about the other one."

Willow was already surprised at what her mother was telling her. It was hard to imagine them happy together. Her mother so full of energy, loving her father so full of intensity. Her father so full of rules, loving her mother so full of fun.

"And one day, I taught him to skip stones not too far from that willow tree. Imagine that, baby. Your father skipping stones. And me teaching him how to do it!"

Rosie straightened her spine as she shared the anecdote.

Willow nodded as her mother's words floated out of her mouth, through her ears and out into the abyss beyond the leaves. She kept her eyes locked on her mother's lips the whole time. With her head gently nodding. With her heart forward. Not moving an inch of her little body. Even as the tip of her nose got cold.

"We lived in an apartment together near there too. Not too far from Central Park in Manhattan. Your father picked it out. It had wallpaper on every wall, and a different knob on every door. I remember when he surprised me. We danced in the entranceway and slept on the floor because we didn't have any furniture yet. Yes! And he got me a locket. An old golden tarnished locket. I couldn't believe he picked it out all rusty like that. He even got the address engraved right on the back. I loved that locket so much I hung it right up on the wall," Rosie said slowly as she continued tracing the memory down the long dark tunnel in her mind.

"And that's when I told him we were having a baby. That's the first time he knew about you, noodle."

A pause. Another little cloud of hot breath meeting cold air.

And then Rosie drifted off somewhere.

"Yeah. The very first time."

It was no longer clear if Rosie, vacant brown eyes looking out past the dangling leaves, was talking to Willow or herself. To the tree or the air around them. To something else entirely. Because there was a sadness deep inside her mother. A sadness Willow had never seen before.

Rosie blinked and focused her bold eyes back on her daughter. And then she came back to the branches.

"There's a poem I like by e. e. cummings. He says love 'is most mad and moonly,' and I think he's right. Your father calls it a crazy love poem. But I think he likes it too. Because love is crazy and magical. It's right and it's wrong and it's simple and it's complicated. But no matter what, you feel it all over, you let it in, and it twists through your insides. I loved your father back then in New York. It was definitely 'most mad and moonly.' And I love you and Asher. And that love is the 'most mad and moonly' kind too."

Rosie stared off blankly over Willow's back and into the leaves, drifting again.

And Willow thought about what it meant to be loved in a "most mad and moonly" way. What it meant to love in a "most mad and moonly" way. In her mother's fierce and magical way.

Willow looked back at Rosie but didn't have any words as her mother drifted. Drifted and said things Willow did not understand. As Rosie said things she wasn't sure anyone could understand. Not even Rosie. But still, Willow sat on that branch and continued nodding slowly. She was still so present, so alive, trying to take Rosie's words in. But when she looked at her mother, Rosie was barely there. She was off somewhere else in the invisible distance with that rigidity in her body again.

When Willow looked in her mother's eyes, she knew she had to say something to bring her mother back. She knew her mother needed her to say something to help her back into the cocoon of the leaves of that willow tree. Something to keep her from floating away permanently to that invisible place.

So Willow came up with the truest thing she knew to say.

"I love being up here with you, Mom."

"Me too, baby. Me too."

Rosie pulled Willow's entire body into hers, tucked her chin over Rosie's shoulder and closed her eyes. Willow had probably been hugged by Rosie one million times, but never like this.

Willow watched her mother soak in all of her attention and all of her love. She could tell how much Rosie loved the way she was listening to her mother up in those willow branches. She could tell how much Rosie loved how wholly Willow breathed in her mother. Here, in these branches, and all the time. With every song, every story, every dance move, every crayon, every kiss. She could tell by the buzzing calm of her mother's beating heart. The warmth radiating from her as they hugged.

"You and me, Willow. We'll go back to that apartment in New York City together."

Rosie stayed like that for a few seconds, breathing deeply, and then pulled her arms even tighter around Willow. There was a heaviness to Rosie's embrace that Willow hadn't felt before. It wasn't the light and breezy intimacy she was used to. It was intense and sharp. But, even still, Willow took it all in. The magic and the love. Just like her mother said to.

"Yeah, baby. Maybe we'll even stay there in that apartment."

Rosie's voice had slowed and moved to a whisper as she kept her arms and heart wrapped around Willow. And then she pulled away and looked straight at her daughter.

"I know you don't like it at your dad's. I wouldn't either. All those rules. All that toughness. You need a relief. I did too."

A short cold breeze came and rattled the

leaves and branches.

"I even still do sometimes. I wish I didn't. But I do. From your father and from everything." Rosie hugged her daughter tightly again. And this time, Willow got the sense that her mother was pressing a secret into her. Trying to move it from her body into her daughter's. But Willow could not decipher what it was.

Rosie looked at the swinging leaves, blinked hard and then continued.

"And one day, when it's right, we'll go to that apartment and live happily ever after together. I promise."

Rosie gripped her daughter so tightly. And Willow hugged her mother tightly back, but she had her eyes open the whole time.

"We can eat candy all day, noodle," Rosie whispered softly. Her lips were already right at her daughter's ears.

And Willow made a silent vow that wherever her mom went, she would follow. And eat candy and feel loved. And feel happy.

As Willow hugged her mother half as tightly as her mother was hugging her, she was so close to seeing what was going on behind her mother's words. So close to seeing the pain and the worry pressing up against the two of them.

■ ■ ■ ■

But unfortunately, when Willow made her silent vow, she had gotten it wrong again. Because even though her mother had candy, it didn't mean Willow would be happy.

17

Ten Years Ago

As soon as Rosie told Rex about his baby, their baby, he wanted to prepare everything. He wanted to make sure it was all going to go just right. Because that's the kind of man Rex Thorpe was. He was a good man with strong morals and a plan. He was a man of preparedness and information. He was a forward-thinking man with firm ideas about his future. And while a baby at thirty-three with a woman like Rosie was not part of his early vision, it was his reality now. And unlike Rosie, who was energized by adventure, unlike Rosie, who could casually dip her tiny toes into the unknown without flinching, Rex was terrified.

Could he do this? Could he do this with Rosie? Did he have the patience? A heart that was big enough? A mind that was open enough?

Rex wanted so badly for the answers to

these questions to be *yes.* He willed them to be *yes.* Because the woman he loved was carrying his child in her belly. And that child would carry pieces of him in him or her. And they would be a family. So the answers to those questions had to be *yes.*

In his head, Rex started crafting a list of rules for his future home. He started building out the structure, the spine of his future life. Because when Rex got scared, or felt out of control, following the rules worked best for him. And Rex was so scared. Not as much for himself, but for his future child. Rex shared his ideas about sleeping schedules and healthy foods and the differences between pacifier brands with Rosie, who smiled and rolled her eyes.

But then Rex got serious and focused. About the challenges of raising a child in Manhattan. Where there were distractions and small spaces. Polluted air and gum-stained sidewalks. Honking cabs and rushing pedestrians.

And so Rex decided that they should move to Virginia, where he grew up, and he would tell his clients he would be available remotely. But first he would visit his favorite things in New York. His favorite painting at the Met. His favorite scone at the coffee shop down the street. He would say goodbye to his friend Roy over their favorite burgers and a long, tight hug. And then, they would go. To suburban Virginia, where he was comfortable and it was quiet. Where they could have a big backyard and kind weather. Where Rex could work from a home office and Rosie could have a room for her art. And Willow could have a big quiet room to herself. And a home full of toys. Where Rex would buy the safest crib and most comfortable stroller and the most advanced baby monitor. And there would be a library of children's books that they would read to their daughter. And there would be schedules and bedtimes. And music lessons. And puzzles. It would be the best, safest, environment for his daughter.

It would be the best, safest, environment for Rex as a father.

Up until this moment it almost appeared as if Rosie had shaken Rex to his core. May have un-Rexed him. But as Rosie's belly grew, so did all the Rex inside of Rex. And all things Rex bubbled right back up to the surface. And before Rosie could twirl around and ask questions or kiss the Rex away, a new home was purchased and the moving van was packed.

Rosie waved goodbye to the printed wallpaper and mismatched doorknobs and walked through a big heavy door into a spacious home in Virginia with box-shaped rooms, smooth hardwood floors and naked walls.

It had the clean lines Rex envisioned all along. And even though Rosie didn't like it, she felt that this was a concession she could make for the baby growing inside her. A concession she could make for Rex. Just this once.

But the moment Rosie stepped through her new, thick, heavy front door, she knew it felt so wrong. The bare walls, the stillness in the air, the distance from their neighbors. The silence. The manicured lawn. The trees planted in precise rows. She needed crannies. She needed quirk. And noise and buzzing and energy. And there was none of that in this home. She tried pushing those thoughts aside, for Rex and for Willow.

She tried and tried but no matter how much Rosie didn't want to want those things, she did. She wanted them so badly. She needed them. Because they were the things that kept Rosie, Rosie. The things that kept her breathing. The things that kept her alive.

When Rex looked at Rosie in his new home

with her swollen belly, he loved his girlfriend and his daughter so much. He had a feeling that there was a little girl inside of Rosie. He had that feeling because Rosie willed there to be a little girl in there. And the world around Rosie usually bent to her. Like plants toward the sun. And even though Rex would have preferred baseball gloves and science experiments with a son, he didn't mind the idea of a little girl. He already loved her so much.

And when Rex slipped a diamond ring onto Rosie's finger on their first Sunday morning in bed in their new house, it was for his daughter. Yes, he was in love with Rosie. But no, this was not the woman he envisioned himself marrying. A man like Rex found comfort in stability.

He didn't want the walls of his bedroom to be a new color every other week. He didn't want every topping in the shop on his ice cream. He didn't want a ticket to the movies to turn into a triple feature. He didn't want to have a thirty-minute chat with the homeless man on the corner about his favorite pizza place. He didn't want to be force-fed poetry. He didn't want Pixy Stix for breakfast. He didn't want to cover his face in makeup on Halloween. He didn't want to feel boring for liking plain white walls. He didn't want to go to a museum and look at a single painting the entire time. He didn't want to waste all of Sunday skipping stones.

Rex thought about that e. e. cummings poem Rosie loved. All the crazy things it said love was. He thought about all the crazy, loving feelings he felt now for Rosie and that little girl in her belly. All the "most mad and moonly" love he felt for Rosie and their baby.

He felt it especially when Rosie turned over, finger sparkling, smiled her biggest brightest smile and said, "Okay, yeah, let's do it!"

Even though both Rex and Rosie were willing to give so many things up, it still made the day Rex asked Rosie to marry him in their big new house in suburban Virginia the beginning of the end of their relationship.

And somewhere inside, Rex knew this. Because the day they arrived in Virginia, he decided he would not put the apartment on the market. And then he tucked his and Rosie's keys to 299 East 82nd Street into the back of his desk drawer.

18

The next time Willow boarded Bus #50, she was surprised when Robbie Hawkins lobbed a Brillo pad at her. She had made it all the way through the beginning of November, and she hadn't had one of these thrown at her once yet this year. It was Robbie who started the "Willow, Willow, hair like Brillo" chant last year. The chant that caught on like a hot burning fire on Bus #50. All those hot and burning words as it spread from fifth grader to fifth grader, row to row, until the whole bus was yelling it. Willow hadn't thought about that day in a while, and didn't want to now. So she pushed the Brillo pad off her lap, put on her big purple headphones, hit Play on her CD player and ignored the taunts. She bobbed her head to the sound of Fleetwood Mac's "Rhiannon" and started digging around her backpack for her book of word searches. And then that piece of silver duct tape stretched across the seat caught her eye again.

She slowly peeled it back purposefully and willfully. A zing of excitement went up her fingertips and into her cheeks when she reached into the seat and pulled out two more Pixy Stix. Both grape. Same typed-out note that simply said, "For Willow."

A typical fifth grader might think she had a secret admirer in the back of the bus. A secret admirer waiting and watching and leaving her treats. But not Willow. She didn't think she had the kind of secret admirer who would watch her from the back of the bus or the other side of the classroom. Or the kind who would send his friends to ask her if she liked anyone. Or the kind who might invite her to play hide-and-seek at recess. Or pass her notes in the lunchroom. Willow had a different kind of secret admirer. The kind of secret admirer she thought was simply her mother. Her mother who loved her in a better, more fun, more special way than any fifth grader could possibly love another fifth grader. Willow tucked her Pixy Stix away and saved them for later. For later when she would inevitably need something good to distract her from another day at Robert Kansas Elementary School.

When the recess bell rang, Willow wiggled herself into her usual hiding spot underneath the slide of the jungle gym. She nestled herself in the sand, rested her back against the plastic of the bottom of the slide, hit Play on her Fleetwood Mac CD and opened her word search book.

The next word to locate was *GYPSY*. Willow smirked at the coincidence and then scanned the grid of letters. She liked coming across words with *Y* and this word had two of them. It was an uncommon letter, making the word easier to spot. And there it was. Right smack in the middle of the grid. *G-Y-P-S-Y.* But just as Willow went to uncap her purple gel pen and circle the word, Roger Wallace ripped her word search book out of her hands.

"Whatcha doin'?" Roger said as he dangled Willow's book high in the air.

"Give it back, Roger."

Willow was scowling, but she refused to reach for the book and try to grab it. She didn't want to end up with her face in the sand.

"Word searches, huh?" Roger leafed through the pages. "I like word searches."

Willow stayed seated under the slide with her arms crossed, nose crinkled and eyebrows scrunched together.

"I think there are a couple of words you missed though," Roger said, and took a pen from his back pocket. Willow was confused. She never missed a word.

Roger pressed Willow's word search book against the plastic yellow slide and took his pen to the page. When Roger was done scribbling, he threw the book down onto Willow's lap and walked away.

Despite the bit of sand that Roger kicked onto Willow's lap when he walked toward the slide, it was a relatively painless interaction. Willow had already completed most of the word searches in the book so it wouldn't have been too bad if Roger just scribbled some silly mess across the page. But when Willow opened her book back to her unfinished puzzle, she saw that Roger had added to her list of words to be found.

Diaper

Ugly

Pants Pisser

Chicken Legs

Stupid

Didn't Roger know how word searches worked? None of these words could be found in the grid. And you couldn't do two words at once. This was not how word searches worked at all. Roger was the one who was stupid.

Willow threw her book down into the sand and went on listening to her Fleetwood Mac CD. She had a new word search book waiting at Mom's house anyway. But she'd have to wait until tomorrow to get it. Tonight was another night at her father's.

19

Ten Years Ago

It was as if the whole house in Virginia warmed as Rosie's belly grew. It was almost as if the corners rounded and the lights softened. Perhaps it was because more of Rosie's forces were filling the world as little Willow grew and grew. As soon as Willow came out of Rosie's belly, Rex could tell that she was just like her mother. Willow had the same big brown curious eyes as Rosie had. The same eyes that turned so kind when you looked into them. And Willow was the only baby in the nursery with a full head of brown curly hair. Willow's was thin and soft, but Rex knew that it would grow into the same thick twirling locks as her mother's.

It couldn't have been said for certain just yet, but Rex knew in his heart that Willow would adopt so many of Rosie's qualities. Her bouncy gait. Her loose knees. Her knobby elbows. Her smooth skin. Her tiny frame. Her snort when she giggled. Her awkward rhythm. Her sweet tooth. Her careful attention to the tiny things in between the big things. Her love and appreciation for those things.

And when Rex watched his wife hold his daughter for the first time in the hospital, his entire body filled up with so many things. It filled up with love at the sight of another, smaller version of a person he had already loved so much. It filled up with pride that he could make a thing that looked so perfect. It filled up with excitement about how many more times he would get to see these two people he cared about tangled up in happiness. It filled up at the sight of a tiny Willow needing tiny Rosie. A little Willow who already looked just like little Rosie. A young Willow reaching for young Rosie's breast.

But then Rex filled up with fear. Fear that he would never, and could never, have the bond a mother has with her daughter. He filled up with anxiety that this small and helpless thing would need things from her father. So, so many things. But of all the things that Rex filled up with, he mostly filled up with a new truth. That all of this, good and bad, Willow and Rosie, was his new world. And nothing was more important than loving these two girls. And he would love them in the best way he could.

The next morning, the nurse ushered Rosie down the hallway. Rosie had Willow tucked into her arms as Rex pulled the car up to take his wife and daughter home. And as Rex drove off, he filled up with all those things all over again when he looked in his rearview mirror and watched his wife absorbed in his sleeping newborn in the back seat.

When Rex and Rosie set their tiny daughter in her crib for the very first time and looked down at her, they each, separately and together, shared the feeling that maybe this would work. They just stood there in the dark watching Willow sleep, and neither Rosie nor Rex knew exactly how long it was, but they were holding hands the entire time.

And just before the new parents retired to their bed, Rex put the familiar tune of "Leather and Lace" on the record player to the quietest audible volume. And the two of them slow-danced in the hallway with their heads on each other's shoulder, their hands on each other's hip and their hearts on each other's heart.

20

This day in early winter was the best day Willow Thorpe would ever have at Robert Kansas Elementary School. It was the only day she ever liked. It was the only day she was truly happy within its brick walls. The days when her hair was pulled or her cubby was covered in diapers were unpleasant. And the days when she walked through the hallway and ate her lunch without a single interaction were bearable. But this afternoon was wholly and entirely likable. Because not only did Willow laugh on this day at school, but her classmates were also happy she was around.

It happened during show-and-tell when Alexandra Phillips got up in front of the class to show off her favorite necklace. Each letter of her name dangled elegantly from the gold chain as she stretched it out between her thumbs and showed it to the class.

Alexandra told everyone that it was a family heirloom. And then she defined the word *heirloom* for the class at Mrs. McAllister's urging. As the sun caught the corners, every fifth grader in the class could see the intricate details and careful work behind each letter: *A, L, E, X, A, N, D, R, A.* Each was etched into its own golden bead. She held the necklace up above her head and tilted it around with pride for everyone to admire.

But then the chain broke.

And each of the golden letters scattered across the tiles of the classroom floor. They skidded off in every direction across the tiles and under desks and into cubbies. Alexandra immediately dropped to the floor. She crawled around frantically, her eyes tracing some beads, her fingers tracing others. Alexandra was in a twisted mess of panic and scattered beads on the floor of Mrs. McAllister's classroom.

Everyone remained glued in their seats as they watched Alexandra and the letters of her name and her hands and her knees scramble all around the tiles. Everyone but Willow. Because Willow was good at a few things and one of them was identifying letters. And another one was being on the floor unexpectedly. So Willow joined Alexandra on her hands and knees on the floor of the classroom. And Willow effortlessly navigated the tiles and easily located each letter one at a time. Little *A, L, E, X, A, N, D, R, A* beads each quickly moved to the safety of Willow's cupped hands.

After Willow handed a fistful of golden letters to her classmate, she walked away not thinking that anyone would have much to say about it. Not because she didn't do something special. But because she was Willow Thorpe. The girl with the weird music and weird outfit. The girl who peed in her pants and had frizzy hair. So Willow followed the interaction the same way she followed all her interactions with her classmates. Head down. Eyes down. Quiet.

But as Willow turned to sit down, Alexandra came up behind her and gave her a big tight squeeze. "Thank you, Willow! Thank you!" she said, meaning every word. And then everyone else in the class started cheering. Cheering and clapping. It was the best thing that happened to Willow in Mrs. McAllister's fifth-grade classroom and Willow was beaming.

She was still beaming when she got on the bus to head home from school. And on the walk from the big yellow bus doors to the big heavy doors of her father's house, she told Asher, whose bus was right behind hers, all about it and he listened with big eyes and a big smile. And as soon as Willow stepped inside her father's house, she wanted to tell her father all about it too. Asher zipped up to his room to play and Willow headed straight for her father's office, where he usually was.

But Rex wasn't there.

"Daaaad!" Willow yelled as she walked through the living room with the stiff couches.

"Daaaad!" she repeated as she walked through the dining room with the glass table with its Do Not Touch sign. But still no response. She made her way up the spiral staircase and burst right into her father's empty bedroom with the inertia of the day's excitement in her wobbly legs. "Daaaaad!" She walked toward the octagon-shaped entranceway to the bathroom with its mirrors on every wall, and a rare fuzzy memory of her mother in there came to her.

Willow was sitting in her mother's lap making silly faces. They were sticking their tongues out and pulling their cheeks in opposite directions. They laughed and laughed at the repeating image of each silly face extending infinitely behind them in the mirror. She pushed the memory out.

Separate worlds. Separate lives.

Willow yelled again, feeling that her father was close by now.

"Daaaaaad. Are you in here, Da—?"

But before she could finish her sentence, Rex jumped aggressively out of the adjacent room with a big scary gray cloud around him. His shoulders were tense and his big hands were pressed into his hips. His bottom teeth jutted out between aggressive chomps of his Bubblicious gum.

"You don't just walk in here, Willow," he said firmly. His teeth now clenched to prevent yelling.

Willow froze.

"This is Dad's space and you don't just walk in here yelling without knocking. Do you hear me?"

A few flecks of spit hit Willow's face, and she accepted them without blinking.

Rex stared down at his daughter angrily, leaning his broad chest forward. Seeing her father like that made Willow think about just how much smaller she was than he was. How his bigness would always overpower her littleness. How his bigness could crush her littleness. How for all of time, her father would be big and broad and tall, and she would be small and thin and unsteady. How, for all of time, his bigness would not hesitate to crush her littleness.

There was a long static pause as Rex continued chomping loudly on his gum. His temples flaring and then relaxing. His eyebrows twitching.

Willow was momentarily distracted by a noise she thought she heard in Dad's closet. Like there was someone moving around in there. Willow instinctively tried to peer around her father's broad torso to make sense of the sound. Find the undoubtedly slender body behind the noise. Willow felt sure that the same woman she had seen the other day was in there. Hiding.

"I said, did you hear me!"

Willow immediately turned her attention back to her father's crooked bottom teeth and tense bottom lip.

Willow's head tilted slowly up and then slowly back down. Still without blinking. Of course Willow heard him. He had shouted it all right at her. Right into her.

And as quickly as Alexandra's hug brought happiness to Willow's day, Rex's flaring temples and crooked teeth yanked it right out of her.

Rex thrust his pointer finger in the direction of the door, and Willow's right knee buckled.

She walked out of Dad's room exactly the way she originally walked away from Alexandra earlier. Shoulders slumped. Eyes on the floor. Afraid to be noticed any longer.

But this time, no one came up behind her and hugged her.

Willow retreated to her own room and curled up in her beanbag chair with her word search book. She stared at the page looking for the word *FAUCET.*

She scanned the grid of letters for all of the *F*s. And then she traced her eyes a box around each one, looking for an *A.* And then continued along that line of letters looking for a *U.* It was repetitive but not boring. Just entrancing enough to make the rest of the world melt away. Just engaging enough to make her forget about what just happened with her father. Just simple enough to make the game approachable. Word searches always made sense to Willow. They allowed her to have many, many small victories in a day. And each of those victories was marked in different colored pencils or crayons surrounding all sorts of words with all sorts of letter combinations and all sorts of meanings. It was fun to flip back through the pages and see the rainbow of her little successes. How many times she made sense of the mess on the page and illuminated a word. A meaning.

There it was. *F-A-U-C-E-T.* Going backward on the last row of letters. She pulled out her purple crayon to circle the word.

When she looked up from the page, her father was standing in her bedroom doorway.

He was posed with his left elbow resting against the door frame. Willow quickly ran through the afternoon checklist in her mind. Was her homework done? Did she miss any chores? Had she left anything downstairs? Did she leave the door open?

But when she ran out of reasons for her father to be standing at her door like that, she simply and kindly said, "Hi, Dad."

Willow considered that her father may have come to apologize, but instead of saying sorry, or bending down for a hug, Rex pulled a soccer ball out from behind his back.

"I was thinking we could go play some soccer in the basement?"

And while this wasn't the apology she was expecting, perhaps even aching for, Willow was pleasantly surprised at the gesture. But then she was a little bit nervous. She wasn't any good at sports. She wasn't even any good at standing. "Should Asher come?" Willow asked earnestly. She usually sat on the side while Rex and Asher played sports together.

Rex said, "How about just us this time?"

"Okay," Willow said a little bit shyly.

Rex was pleasantly surprised at his daughter's willingness.

And there it was, father and daughter, Rex and Willow, surprising each other. You could feel it in the air. In the space between their rigid bodies. In the too-long pauses between questions and answers.

"Yeah. Okay. Let's go."

Willow nervously followed Rex down to the basement in her purple leggings and black Converse shoes. As Willow fumbled down the stairs, she wondered if she would be able to do this with her father. For her father. She really hoped she could.

Willow stood there with straight spine and stiff hands, waiting for her father to kick the ball to her. And when he did, the black-and-white orb rolled its way across the floor toward her. It rolled to the left of her legs, which were staked rigidly into the ground. When the ball rolled behind her and then stopped when it hit the wall, Willow looked up at her dad.

Now what? she asked Rex with her eyes.

"Just put your leg out if the ball is going to go by you. You can stop it with your foot or your shins," he said in thinly veiled impatience.

Willow nodded, then continued to look up at her dad. Legs still staked into the floor.

"Okay, go and get the ball now," Rex instructed.

Willow could see that he was struggling to stay calm.

Willow walked toward the ball, already worried what it was going to look like when she had to kick it back. She imagined herself doing it. She imagined herself doing it gracefully. She imagined herself kicking the ball a few yards ahead and racing her father toward it. She imagined him picking her up and tickling her and playing keep-away until he eventually let her take the ball from him. He would playfully knock her over onto the floor, and then she would pick the ball up and toss it away from both of them. And when she did, Willow and her father would be on the floor, out of breath and happy. She could see it so clearly. She wanted it to happen as it did in her mind's eye and right there on the floor. She wanted it to happen so badly.

But the reality was that Willow could barely get control of her gangly legs enough to walk competently. Kicking the ball forcefully and accurately enough to cause it to make a full revolution was a physical impossibility. She tried her hardest anyway. But when she lifted her right leg to kick the ball back toward her dad, her left leg collapsed immediately. It left the soccer ball right where it started and Willow toppled over next to it.

Couldn't they just dance and sing to a movie? Or play word searches? Do something that didn't involve so much body? So much coordination?

"It's okay. Try again, Willow," Rex forced out through clenched teeth.

And Willow did try again. And this time she even made contact with the ball. But it just wobbled a little bit, and then came back to stillness in the same spot it started out in.

Rex huffed over toward Willow and demonstrated a proper kick. He waved his leg back and forth like it was so easy. Like everyone could do it.

But everyone couldn't do it. Willow couldn't do it. His daughter couldn't do it. And maybe she was the only person in the whole universe who couldn't do it. But Willow was Rex's only daughter in the whole universe. Didn't that earn her a few moments of extra instruction? A little warmth? A little patience? A little love?

After no more than two minutes of Rex swaying his legs and Willow looking confused, Rex had his hands over his eyes in frustration and Willow had her hands on her thighs in disappointment.

So Willow and Rex silently agreed to go upstairs.

It wasn't working. This father-daughter soccer pass in the basement.

This father-daughter anything anywhere.

21

Eight Years Ago

That ache that had crept up within Rex in the hospital never left Rex's bones throughout the first years of Willow's life. And he saw it happening every time Rosie held their daughter. Willow plainly and simply loved her mother more. He saw it every time Rosie swayed Willow back and forth in her arms. Every time Rosie effortlessly ran her fingers through Willow's tight curls. The same curls that snagged Rex's fingers every time.

Still, Rex relentlessly made time with his daughter. Adamantly made time for loving his daughter in all the ways Rex Thorpe knew how. With puzzles and books and instructions for tying shoes. With obstacle courses and scavenger hunts and guided science experiments. With reading exercise after reading exercise. He showed her little words on the thick pages of early-reader books. He slowly enunciated every letter or every word as he guided his finger along the page. He picked up objects from around the house and asked his daughter what letter they started with. He sang the alphabet with her and asked her to repeat it. And sometimes she would.

But other times she would just stare up at her father with big, blank, brown eyes. And when Rex would draw a big letter *A* on a mini blackboard and ask his daughter what letter it was, sometimes Willow would tell him correctly. And sometimes she would tell him incorrectly. And sometimes she would divert her attention to the chalk in his hand and scribble all over his big letter *A* without saying a word. And sometimes Rex would write a big *W* and *X* and *Y*, and she would tell him correctly. And sometimes she would tell him incorrectly. And sometimes she would divert her attention. And sometimes she wiped her tiny hand across all of the letters, and then rubbed her freshly chalked hands on her father's shirt.

And although Rex would smile at Willow's clear eyes and smooth chin, his heart would also break at her disinterest. Her inconsistent attention. Because Rex wanted to be a father that taught his daughter things. And he wanted to have a daughter who learned things from her father. He wanted to have a daughter as engaged in knowing as he was. He wanted to impart that to her. He wanted it to fortify her bones. But Willow and Rex were already speaking different languages. Because for Willow and Rex alike, it often, and inadvertently, went in one ear and out the other.

And one afternoon, at the end of another failed alphabet lesson, when Willow's hands and Rex's shirt were completely covered in chalk, Rosie walked into Willow's room with a book of word searches. Rosie had picked it up earlier that day in the bookstore while Rex had been perusing the parenting section. As soon as her mother walked in, Willow teetered her way toward her and stumbled into her lap. Rosie and Willow both looked so comfortable, so whole, sitting there intertwined. As comfortable and whole as they always did together.

"I'm looking for the word *heart,*" Rosie said to her daughter softly, enunciating each letter.

"It starts with an *H.* Can you help me find an *H* on this page?"

And without hesitation, Willow pointed to the letter *H* among the whole big grid of letters on the page. And Rosie wasn't excited or surprised by Willow's response.

She was just present. Content. And totally in sync with her tiny beautiful daughter who looked more and more like her every day. Rosie kissed her daughter on the cheek. It was a kiss filled with warmth and love and mutual understanding.

Rex wanted to cry. At the beauty of mother and daughter in perfect coexistence.

And at the tragedy of his incipient exclusion from it.

22

Rosie roared around the corner of Robert Kansas Elementary School with her left jean leg peeking out the window and her red lips bright as ever. Willow could hear the familiar sounds of Elton John's "Levon" blasting through the window. As soon as Asher and Willow got into the back seat of the car, Rosie put on a pair of comically large pink iridescent sunglasses and rested them precariously on her nose so you could still see her eyes.

"Pizza's at home," Rosie explained, anticipating Willow's and Asher's hunger. "But tonight, we are eating with Elton . . . I hope you're ready."

Willow could see that Rosie was ready. She was wearing her favorite Elton John T-shirt. It had a huge saturated but now a bit faded image of Elton belting from behind a piano, eyes squeezed with passion. Willow could imagine her mother with a similarly scrunched face, lip-synching into a banana microphone while dancing on the couch.

Willow smiled, and then boogied along to the tune of "Levon" as the wind whipped through her hair. She looked at Asher, who was doing the same head bob to the beat.

Yes, Rosie, Willow and Asher were all ready to eat with Elton.

As soon as Lili Von came to a stop in the driveway, Rosie dashed into the house while Willow and Asher collected their backpacks, and then made their way through the front door. Rosie had her hip resting against the wall and a silver sequin vest dangling on her left pointer finger and a big necklace with a glittered dollar sign hanging from her right. She immediately wrapped Willow in the vest and placed the necklace over Asher's head. Rosie wiggled her hand and wrist up into the air and turned her nose toward the ceiling like she was onstage in front of thousands as the music started to pulse in the air.

"There are more clothes upstairs in the dress-up drawer in the closet. Go add to your outfits, and then we'll dance!"

Willow and Asher looked at each other with wide eyes and openmouthed smiles, bursting with excitement. They turned and ran for their mother's closet.

A strange pause.

"Don't go in the top drawer though," she yelled after them.

They never heard their mother saying words like *don't.* And they already knew where the dress-up clothes were. They had done this one hundred times.

"All the fun clothes are in the bottom," Rosie shouted warmly after they completed their way up the staircase, hopping two steps at a time.

When Willow and Asher reached their mother's closet, they pulled sequin shirt after sequin shirt out. They held them up against their bodies and posed in the mirror. They opened the bottom drawer and swapped sunglasses and hats and boas. They threw any uninteresting articles of clothing up into the air and let them float onto the ground. And so quickly, Willow was lost in the magic of the evening.

But then, without her mind telling her to do it, Willow's fingers wrapped themselves one by one around the translucent knob of the top drawer her mother had asked her not to open.

And while Asher tried to walk in a pair of red patent leather stilettos, Willow slowly pulled on the drawer. But before Willow could get a full look of what was inside, there was a slapping crack that startled everyone. Rosie's long fingers were wrapped tightly around her daughter's wrist.

Rosie and Willow looked at each other, both stunned at the strangeness of this interaction. When Rosie and Willow touched, it was always soft and warm. But not this time. This was harsh and scary and unfamiliar. Their eyes stuck there, locked intensely. They could all hear the rolling of bottles and scattering of something as the drawer was forced shut. But before any more tension moved through the moment, Rosie looked side to side, smiled and said, "You're it!" as if they had been in the middle of a game of tag all along.

Willow giggled and chased after her mother.

But there was a red mark on her wrist from her mother's tight grip and a seizing uncertainty about those things rattling around in that drawer. But everything quickly turned back into fun.

After an hour jumping up and down on the couch to "Bennie and the Jets" and feeding each other pizza, Rosie sank into her seat quietly.

"I think it's time for bed, noodles," Rosie said languidly.

But Willow didn't want the night to end. And she requested a viewing of *Blazing Saddles.* It was her mother's favorite movie. Rosie looked at Willow, and then rocked to her feet to put the movie on. There wasn't reluctance. But there wasn't excitement. And watching her mother listlessly turn the television on with limp fingers made Willow's tummy turn again.

Willow turned her attention back to the movie. She never understood all the jokes, but she always laughed when Mom did. But tonight, Rosie never cued anyone to laugh. They just sat on the couch, quietly scooping ice cream into their mouths.

But Willow remained confident that the couch dancing would ignite when it was time for Lili Von Shtupp to sing "I'm Tired." It was their favorite part of watching the movie, flopping around like they were actually tired. They would all loosen their legs and arms and slowly tip over onto the pillows, only to get back up and act wobbly all over again. And they would laugh, and laugh, until they ended up in one big pile of fake tired in the middle of the couch. And, for the best part of the scene, Willow, Asher and Rosie would huddle up together and yell along with Lili Von as she said she was "pooped." It was their favorite part and they couldn't get through it without giggling and giggling straight from their bellies.

But tonight when the familiar scene of Lili emerging from the red velvet curtain in her black dress came on, and Willow took her position standing on the couch, Rosie looked the real kind of tired with her head leaning on a pillow and her eyes only half-open. But still, Willow and Asher did their flopping. And when Willow whipped her head around to yell out, "I'm pooped," she expected to be joined by her mother. But Rosie's eyes were completely shut and her small thin body was limp against the cushions of the couch. Without even letting Lili Von Shtupp finish her song, Willow turned the television off and put a blanket over her mother. She ushered Asher up to bed, then came back down and kissed her mother delicately on the cheek. She didn't want to wake her.

And then Willow went upstairs to her own bed in her own room. She fell asleep slowly in a pair of pajamas that didn't match her mother's.

Willow's eyes burst open and her heart stopped at the loud crack of lightning followed immediately by booming thunder. She gripped onto the edges of her sheets and braced herself for another loud sound. She could hear the frozen rain slapping angrily against the roof again. At the second lightning crack, Willow leaped out of bed and dashed downstairs to find her mother, who was still asleep on the couch.

"What is it, noodle?" Rosie asked in a raspy, just-woken voice as she stretched her arms out warmly for her daughter, who was standing nervously by the wall.

Already Willow could tell that her mother, although sleepy, was back to her normal vibrancy. Her normal level of attention to Willow's needs.

Willow barreled into Rosie's arms and tucked her head into her mother's shoulder.

"*Ooo,* is it the storm?" Rosie asked behind a little bit of a chuckle.

Willow nodded her head but made sure to keep it pressed against her mother's warm body.

"It's just a bunch of water, baby! Nothing's gonna hurt you."

Rosie peeled her daughter off her chest, held her by her shoulders and looked her straight in the eye.

"I've got an idea. I think we can get unscared of this thunderstorm thing. Yeah?"

"Okay," said Willow, who was filled simultaneously with fear and trust and excitement.

Rosie lit up.

"Okay, sit tight for just a second. I think I have something that will do the trick."

Before there was even another loud crack or boom from outside, the room had filled with a familiar song. It was Prince's "Purple Rain."

Willow followed her mother upstairs, and then Rosie started digging through the costume drawer in her closet. When Rosie emerged, she was holding a strange-looking pair of sunglasses. The lenses had been popped out of the thick black rims and replaced with purple translucent paper that was taped sloppily around the edges. Rosie bent down next to the bed and slid the glasses gently onto her daughter's face. And just like that, everything magically turned purple. Rosie picked her daughter up underneath her arms and carried her to the window.

Willow was a little too big and Rosie a little too small for this, but it still felt so right.

They looked out the cold window together. They looked at the still-icy air with thick rain slashing through it.

"Check that out, baby. That's purple rain,"

Rosie said to her daughter in a warm whisper.

And it was. Big purple sparkling drops of water filled the sky. And when the drops met the ground, they turned into large purple sparkling pools of water. And when the lightning cracked and the thunder boomed, they only served to enhance the drama of Willow's private purple storm.

It was beautiful. It was magic. And Willow was in awe of the purple sky. And of her mother for turning it that color.

Willow felt herself sinking into the scene. She felt herself become mesmerized by it right there in her mother's arms. Willow's muscles relaxed. Her heartbeat slowed, and her shoulders fell.

Right there in front of the window, Willow's mother was her mother again. And Willow felt a wave of energy surge through her as she squeezed her arms against her mother's chest.

"Okay, noodle. We're going out."

And before Willow could understand what her mother was saying, Rosie had already dashed down the hallway with Willow still in her arms, and her daughter's little body bopping up and down at her hip as she held her purple glasses desperately against her face to keep them from falling.

Rosie pushed the back door open, set Willow down, tossed off her Elton John shirt, stepped out of her loose gray pants and ran out into the cold purple puddles.

Willow watched her mother's bare bottom wiggle toward the bare trees on the periphery of their backyard. Willow couldn't remember if she had ever seen her mother so naked before. She watched the way her mother's hips moved side to side as she ran from one puddle to the next. She watched her breasts bounce freely up and down. She watched her curly hair stick to the sides of her wet cheeks. Willow wanted her body to move like that. She wanted her soul to be free like that. So Willow took off her nightgown and joined her mother in a naked dance in the purple moonlit rain at midnight.

The freezing winter rain kissed Willow's skin on its way to the ground. It soaked her in happiness.

There Willow was, nose red and fingertips white, drenched in the cold, drenched in her fear, but feeling only happiness. There Willow was in her purple-lensed glasses, unscared of the storm. And entranced by her mother. Swept up in her love.

Rosie picked up her daughter's cold slippery body and hugged her closely.

Then as Rosie carried Willow inside, their wet skin slid against one another's, but they felt all the more connected for it. And when they went upstairs, Rosie ran a warm shower for Willow and told her to meet back in Rosie's bed to finish *Blazing Saddles* once Willow had dried off and gotten back into her pajamas.

"Wear the pink ones with the bunnies," Rosie said through a wink. "I'll wear mine too."

Willow loved these nights with Mom. Tucked in her bed. Tangled up. Time extending indefinitely. Warming each other. Loving each other. Wearing the same pajamas.

But when Willow slipped back through her mother's door after her shower, Rosie was already sound asleep on her bed. Naked with her wet hair still stuck to her cheeks and wet clothes scattered across the floor. She hadn't even made her way under the covers. Willow nudged her cold bare shoulder back and forth.

"Mom. Mom," Willow whispered.

No response. No movement.

"Mom. Get up."

No response. No movement.

"I want to watch the movie." Willow was now rocking her mother's body back and forth, then quickly and desperately.

Still no response. Still no movement.

"MOM!"

Something was bursting inside of Willow. She wanted her mother awake. They were supposed to be watching a movie. And Rosie always did everything perfectly for Willow. And she had already fallen asleep once tonight.

"Mom? What about the movie?" Willow whimpered, pressing on her mother's shoulder even harder.

"Please just wake up. *Please.*" The salty tears running down Willow's cheek felt nothing like, tasted nothing like, the rain that had dripped down them only a few minutes ago.

Rosie peeked one eye open and pulled her daughter in toward her.

"No more movie tonight," Rosie said, still not fully out of the grips of sleep. Or haze. Or something else entirely. "I'm too tired for a movie."

And even though Rosie had closed her eyes and rolled over, and even though Willow still had tears flowing out of her, Willow curled around her mother like she always did. She placed her knee over her mother's thigh. She rested her arm across her mother's tummy. She let her heart fall against her mother's chest. And as she felt her mother's chest rising and falling, her heart slowly beating, she realized that this was the first time she ever heard her mother really say no.

And then Willow thought she heard her mother add, "I'm always too tired," through another sleepy, breathy mumble.

Even though Willow didn't feel scared of the rain anymore, she was having trouble falling asleep. And even though there was still magic lingering around in the air, Willow's tummy turned at her mother's broken promise. Mom never broke her promises. And never fell asleep too early. And never didn't laugh during *Blazing Saddles.* And always tickled Willow's arm.

But things had changed. Now she knew it for sure.

And the thought of a change in her mother terrified Willow. All the way down to her bones.

She didn't know this mother who had become too tired. Too tired to dance on the couches? Too tired to watch a movie? Too tired to get in pajamas? Too tired to mother? Too tired to love?

Questions burned inside Willow.

Was her mother really tired? And what was

rattling around in that drawer that her mother didn't want her to open?

23

Six Years Ago

When Rosie walked into the backyard, she was overwhelmed at the sight of Rex pushing Willow on the tire swing. Overwhelmed at the perfection of the scene. Overwhelmed with love. Overwhelmed with the idea that she didn't want to be anywhere else in that moment.

Rosie had spent her life in perpetual motion before Rex. She moved from city to city without any thought. She bounced from job to job. She had many boyfriends but never considered a future with any of them. She buzzed around bookstores and cafés and boutiques. She explored every cranny of her world with full interest and full openness. She absorbed it wholly and let it fill her up. And then she would let it go — most of the time — as quickly as it came. But this moment, watching her husband pushing her daughter on the swing had almost made her want to stay still, here, for the rest of time. Stay here, in the backyard with her husband and daughter, for the rest of time.

Of all the good things Rosie was able to uncover behind Rex's harsh exterior in their relationship so far, gentleness was not one of them. Over time he had been thoughtful and attentive, instead. But never gentle. Not until Willow. He was so, so gentle. Watching Rex pushing Willow delicately on the swing showed Rosie just how gentle he could be. Just the perfect amount of gentle push to make little Willow feel like she was flying. It made Willow smile a big toothless smile as her wild hair covered her little face. His broad hands against her tiny back, pressing her through the air.

Rosie wanted to cry at the beauty of Rex's bigness next to Willow's littleness. At how the happenings of this instant defied the very laws of the universe in which big overpowers little. But not in Rosie's new world.

In her world, big could be gentle to little. And little could be so happy in the hands of big. And with this new knowledge, this new truth, Rosie's heart was warmed. And even though when she turned around, her house was still filled with white walls and her paintbrushes were still tucked away in a white drawer, Rosie felt fulfilled.

When Rosie saw Rex hand Willow a purple Pixy Stix when she got off the swings, Rosie was certain about the choices, the compromises, the sacrifices she had made coming to Virginia. Because everything was perfect here.

And it would only get better.

Rosie placed her hand on her big swollen belly as she felt the new baby twirl around inside her. She could do this again with Rex. She could live like this with Rex.

She was thrilled about it.

But the birth of her son two months later brought Rosie a depression that was equal and opposite to the elation she felt with the birth of Willow. It was chemical, and it consumed her immediately.

As the nurses held her cooing infant, Rosie's mind zoomed right into the future with that baby. There was the intimate terror about the sleepless nights and the raw nipples. There was the impending frustration with the manacles of her diaper bag full of bullshit things required to satiate a baby's needs — pacifiers and bottles and formula and toys and wipes and diapers and powder and lotion. Things that didn't bother her with Willow, but daunted her now. Rosie enjoyed things, but hated to be encumbered by them.

And then there was the baby, itself. Asher, himself. With his big blue eyes and a full head of blond hair that couldn't possibly have been created by her genes or formed in her body. When she had looked into Willow's eyes for the first time, she could see an extension of herself. It was so clear in the way Willow looked and the way she felt when Rosie looked at her. It was nothing like the way she felt when she looked at Asher. Blond-haired, blue-eyed Asher. Rosie felt every inch of her body tense up when the nurse tried to place him in her arms for the first time. She crossed her arms and turned her head away until Asher was gone from the room. Rosie shouted after the nurse to double-check the name tag before she brought him back into her hospital room again.

Dr. Winthrop told Rosie that it wasn't unusual for women to experience these feelings after childbirth. "Up to fifteen percent of women experience postpartum depression," she said in a tone that could have been used to describe a sunny January afternoon. Nothing to get too upset about.

But Rosie was very upset about it. About wanting out, out, out of this life. Out, out,

out now. Out and away from Asher and Willow and Rex. Her need to escape boiled up inside her so fiercely. And everyone could see the waves of raging heat seeping from her every pore. Especially Rex.

But, even still, Rex was kind to Rosie after Asher's birth.

When Rosie insisted on sleep, her husband lay awake with his cooing infant through the night. Asher didn't cry much, but he was noisy. Rosie could tell through the bedroom door that Rex found his son's gargling and spitting and squeaky noises so endearing as he rocked him to sleep in the hallway. And Rosie could tell that her husband could see through the ajar bedroom door that these same sounds grated against his wife's ears. Because when his son excitedly kicked his feet and looked at his mother, Rosie just quietly turned away. When Rosie refused to breast-feed, her husband prepared Asher's formula and fed him in the rocking chair that he had built from scratch as a present to his unborn son five happy months prior. And when Rosie didn't want to leave the house, her husband took Asher for long walks around their quiet neighborhood with the white fences, crisp lawns and dark windows.

Rosie said thank you to Rex many times.

She said it warmly. She would even place her hand on his back, and say thank you right to his face. Because nothing would change the fact that she still wanted out, out, out. All the time.

Often her daughter would crawl into bed with her listless mother and snuggle right up next to her. Willow would bend her little body to fit her mother's, then just rest there. All wrapped around her mother. And Rosie would force herself to kiss her daughter on the head, then go back to her tense stillness. But still, Willow stayed there tangled in her mother.

Rosie was in her usual position on a Sunday morning, lying in her bed listening to the sounds of her home. Listening to all the annoying sounds of motherhood. Asher spitting formula. Willow accidentally stumbling on her way down the stairs. Cheerios scattering across the floor. Rex rummaging through the pantry. These sounds. They were making her insides crawl.

But just as Rosie was going to press her pillow against her ears to muffle those grinding sounds, the sound of her daughter on the piano wafted up. One careful note at a time. And another. And another. Willow was fumbling her way through the notes of

Elton John's "Bennie and the Jets." She thought of Rex in that piano bar all those years ago. So handsome. So talented. So full of soul.

Rosie was preparing her body to get out of bed to see Willow when another, more capable set of notes flowed through the house.

And then suddenly, her house was filled with the beautiful, heartening, delightful sounds. Her husband's talent and her daughter's fumbling in perfect concert. Rosie watched from the top of the stairs as these sounds were created. Her mouth formed a smile for the first time in many months. Rosie wondered if there was a light at the end of this tunnel, after all. If once she reached the light, she could stay in it.

But Rosie would never be able to stay in a moment indefinitely. She knew it now more than anyone.

24

After school that Thursday afternoon, Willow and Asher waited for their mother to pick them up for pizza at Lanza's. Rosie, with a sparkle in her eye and warmth in her voice, promised an adventure.

When she stepped outside to the pickup circle, Willow tied her knit hat around her chin as the cold began to bite. And then she helped Asher slip his eager hands into a pair of mittens. Willow sat down on the curb with her backpack still on and her bony knees tucked toward her chest for warmth. Willow pulled a Pixy Stix that she had found in the seat of the bus earlier that morning out of her backpack, tilted her head back and poured the purple crystals onto her tongue. She stuck her tongue out and crossed her eyes to get a glimpse of the purple sugar dissolving. And then she opened her word search book and pressed Play on her CD player to welcome the safe tunes of Elton John into her head.

As dusk started to fall and a chill began to make its way into Willow's bones, her tummy turned again. She looked at Asher, who had a smile and a pink nose as he timed himself running from the edge of the curb to the doors of the school.

Then suddenly the sky was entirely purple and fuzzy and everything was cold and quiet outside of Robert Kansas Elementary School.

As the cold bit down harder, Willow couldn't help but wonder what was taking her mom so long. Where she was. The question swirled all around her as she sat on that curb.

And then the bright headlights of her father's car speared through the hazy air and his shiny black car curled around the contour of the pickup circle.

"Hop in, guys," Rex directed from behind the half-rolled-down window.

Everything stayed quiet for another half moment outside of the empty school in the empty twilight.

"But it's Mom's night," Willow blurted out from the sidewalk. She stamped her black Converse sneaker into the concrete in reaction to the unexpected change of plans.

Willow didn't know it, but she was invoking her father here. The desire, the visceral need, to adhere to the rules. It was just that Willow only liked the rules that got her to her mother's house. To her mother's bedroom with matching pajamas and *The Twilight Zone* on the television as she fell asleep. Not the rules of the morning checklist. Not the rules that forced her to practice piano when she would rather be sitting in her beanbag chair with Prince playing over her headphones. Not whatever rules Rex was invoking now to bring his children to his house when it was supposed to be her mother's turn. When they were supposed to be at Lanza Pizza. When they were supposed to be drinking soda and playing pinball. But no matter how unjust, no matter how upset it made Willow, Rex's rules always got to supersede his daughter's. They always did. It maddened her. Now more than ever.

Asher ran toward the car with his backpack bouncing up and down behind him. He was indifferent to whose back seat he was getting into. Indifferent to whose house he would play with his action figures in later. Indifferent to what he ate for dinner. Indifferent and happy.

But Willow refused to move from the curb.

Knees still tucked into her chest. Now shivering.

"We're switching nights, Willow. Hop in."

"But Mom didn't say."

Willow wasn't ready to leave that curb. She wasn't ready to relinquish the idea that Rosie and Lili Von would be roaring around the corner soon to pick them up. Because Willow wanted her mom. And she wanted her dad to know that she wanted her mom. She wanted him to know that he was breaking her rules. And that it was breaking her heart. That it always broke her heart.

"Willow, it's getting late. Would you just get in the car?"

Her father's exasperation was apparent, but Willow sat firmly and tensely on the curb.

"Willow, please."

As Willow rocked herself back and forth on that curb, staring at her father, debating whether or not to get in his car, she got scared. Scared that she had lost her mother. It was a feeling she had experienced up in the branches of that willow tree. And on the couch watching *Blazing Saddles.* And after the rainstorm. But now, on the cold curb of Robert Kansas Elementary School, it felt so real. And it tugged and pulled on every muscle and organ and fiber in her body.

Willow had no choice but to give in to this new reality as she dragged her feet into the back of her father's car.

When they parked the car at her father's house and went inside, Willow left a warm puddle of urine on the seat.

As each second, minute, hour, day and nighttime checklist passed, Willow's panic and worry and confusion intensified. And she wanted all of those awful creeping feelings to just go away.

Willow pulled out her word search book to distract herself. But when she looked at the page, she only saw a mirror into her own loneliness. She pulled out a box of crayons and doodled around on some construction paper. But there was no one there to see a sheep when she had really just drawn one big scribble. No one to tell her to add some orange here or some green there.

She lay down in her bed, put on her headphones and closed her eyes while she let the sounds of Prince and then Elton John and then Fleetwood Mac flow through her ears. She pretended she was at her mother's house dancing around and letting love flow through her heart. But it wasn't enough to imagine it. She wanted it to be real. She needed it to be real. But no matter how much Willow willed for her mother to come home that night and that weekend, Rosie never came.

So every night, after Rex turned out the lights and told his daughter to go to sleep, Willow got up and sat by her bedroom window and stared off into the woods behind her backyard. She tried not to blink as she waited to see a flicker of her mother's flashlight. But the sky was just dark and thick and stale.

Willow grabbed the telescope that Dad had set up and twisted it toward the window. She pressed her eye into the back of the tube and scanned the blurry woods. And then she tilted her telescope toward the sky. Mom was somewhere. Somewhere out there. On this earth or in the stars. But out there.

And when Willow began losing the battle against the weight of her own eyelids, she shuffled back into her bed and wrapped herself tightly in her covers. She tickled her own arm, trying to slow her heartbeat. She held her pillow over her mouth to muffle the sound of her crying. She tried to think of her mother dancing around in a fringe vest, hair swaying wildly. But as soon as the vision would come to Willow, it dissolved back into darkness.

That darkness in her mind, that void in her body, left Willow with sadness in her blood as she went to sleep. Which left Willow with a puddle of urine under her waking body every morning.

On the following Sunday morning, after the third puddle appeared on her sheets, Willow went into the bathroom to get a towel. She caught a glimpse of herself in the mirror. Her usually clear brown eyes were red from crying. Her eyelashes were covered with a white dusting of salt from her dried tears. And her wild brown hair was even more frayed than usual after three nights of tossing and turning on her pillow.

Willow wondered if she would look like this for the rest of her life. If her face, her hair, her eyes would be stuck like this. If her whole body, her whole being, would be stuck at Dad's house. In Dad's world.

She wondered if Dad would start to love her now. She wondered if he could love her at all.

She wondered if she would grow to love Dad now. She wondered if she could grow to love him at all.

She didn't know the answers, but she knew she needed love from somewhere.

Willow's new reality was starting to set in.

Mom was gone and Willow was starting to unravel. But Asher was the same Asher. The same bright eyes and toothless smile. The same silky blond bowl cut and skip in his step.

If there were ways in which he carried the damage around, Willow didn't see them. And watching him smashing two action figures together under the kitchen table made her realize how lucky Asher was in his simplicity. How Asher could find love and happiness in any place and anything. Bugs on the sidewalk. A cartoon character. A room full of toys. An empty box. Mom. Mom's house. Dad. Dad's house. Mom's butterfly kisses. Dad's slight nod of approval.

Part of Willow wanted to live finding happiness everywhere too. She wanted to live open to all sorts of love. She wanted her heart to fill with all sorts of love. But it didn't work. She didn't like Dad's kind of love. She didn't like the chore charts and nighttime checklists. She didn't like his broad shoulders and the intensity between his eyebrows. She liked Mom's kind of love. She liked the kisses and singing and candy and little surprises on the bus. She couldn't help it.

But, even still, when her father ducked

under the table, took her brother by the hand and guided him into the backyard for a game of catch, Willow wanted to cry. Or maybe grab a baseball glove herself.

Everything looked so nice out there on the manicured grass of her father's backyard. Father and son in baseball caps and jackets throwing a frayed old ball back and forth. Asher's big leather baseball glove was way too large for his tiny hand. It dwarfed his entire body. And every time the ball would fly out of her father's hand and into Asher's glove, Asher's entire body would teeter back and forth under the sheer force of Rex's pitch. But as soon as the ball was under control, Asher would fill with pride. He would arch his back and roll up onto his toes as if he had been catching baseballs for years. The forced casualness was endearing even to Willow, who was quietly shaking with jealousy.

Asher reached into his mitt, pulled the baseball out of its clutches, cocked his arm back and looked up at his father. And Rex repeated the throwing motion again and again and again for Asher. He demonstrated a full-shouldered follow-through and the precise turn of the wrist required for an optimal pitch. He'd flick his wrist up and down to ensure that the end of the throwing motion was reinforced in Asher's mind. And then Asher mimicked his father's motion, launching the baseball straight into his father's hand.

Rex tucked his glove into his opposite armpit, ball still swaddled in there, and shook his hand around dramatically. Like he was relieving the sting of the fastest fastball ever thrown. She could tell her father was faking it, but Asher swelled with pride all over again.

Willow could see so clearly what was happening out there on the grass. Rex had told a small lie pretending his hand hurt, but he was giving a gift to Asher with that lie. The gift of a proud father impressed by his son. And Willow could see that the lie was worth it. It was connection. It was love. It meant something. Something important.

And even though Willow couldn't hear anything through the window, she could see her father's lips moving as he imparted something worthwhile and true to his son. It was making it a little hard to breathe. She wanted something too. She wanted love. She wanted it so bad. She needed to breathe it in. It was her oxygen. She was suffocating without it and there her father was providing a bounty of it to her brother.

But Willow and Rex were separated by a

glass window and so much more. So Willow just sat there, aching for love and trying to catch her breath.

The sensation was brand-new.

Because this time, that ache for love was directed at her father. All throughout Willow's life, her mother had loved her so much there was no space for anything else. But right there, forgetting to miss her mother and watching this shared moment between her father and her brother, Rex and Asher, father and son, made her want her father's love too.

Made her crave it.

Because once you taste that first crystal of Pixy Stix on your tongue, you want to pour the whole rest of the pile on top. Even if it isn't your favorite grape flavor.

When Willow walked away from the window, her chest came to a stillness. She missed her mother all over again. She missed her all the way down to her bones.

She was burning up with questions.

Where was she?

Where was her mother?

Did it have anything to do with what was rattling around in that drawer?

25

Five Years Ago

Even though there were glimmers of hope over the last few months, with every new day, Rosie felt more and more like she was existing underwater. When Asher cried to be fed, or Willow asked for crayons to color with, or Rex asked how the day was, Rosie only heard blubbering, echoing sounds. Even moving her legs to walk downstairs or her arms to pour water into a glass met with an unrelenting resistance. Blinking even felt like too much energy to muster.

And while Rosie was dull and listless on the outside, on the inside she was panicked. Panicked about the state of her motherhood, her marriage and her health. She knew the ugliness she saw in front of her was all a delusion, but she could not escape the rage she felt encompassing her whole entire life. Her life and her children and her husband.

Rosie's brain and heart rattled inside her body. They clanked around in her skull and beneath her ribs until she hurt. She just lay in her bedroom for hours and hours staring at the walls and listening to the gushing sounds of her own syncopated heartbeat. She saw herself in her mind's eye swiping the picture frames off her dresser, tearing the curtains off the poles, dragging her uncut fingernails down the walls until they were peeled to shreds. She hated these twisted fantasies. She was tortured by them and she wanted them to stop. She wanted them to stop so badly. But they were always there. She knew how lovely her life was, but she just couldn't stop the dark visions from tearing the whole thing to the ground. And the more she tried to push the dark thoughts out of her mind, the more they crushed in on her.

One solitary afternoon, when she couldn't endure the harrowing pulse of her organs any longer, Rosie picked up the bottle of Vicodin that had been sitting in her bathroom cabinet since Rex's minor surgery a few months prior. She opened the orange tube, tapped a tablet into her hand, rolled the tiny white pill between her pointer and thumb. She remembered the feeling of calm that kind of white pill induced all those years ago on her couch. The tingling relaxation. The sinking tranquility of her bones. The quiet in her mind. The kind of peace Rosie yearned for. The kind of peace she needed.

And so, without hesitation, Rosie put that white pill plus one more onto her tongue and swallowed.

And within just a few moments, the tingling began.

Finally, her body and mind slowed. Finally they eased. There, lying alone on their king-size bed, Rosie felt like she had submerged herself in a warm bath. She found herself on the receiving end of a kind embrace. With Vicodin in her blood, Rosie felt safe in her own body and mind for the first time in months.

Still, though, the listlessness continued. And the hours alone in her bed extended. Because, now, instead of her depression, it was Vicodin melting her muscles, her bones, her mind. But at least she had a quiet mind and, though drug induced, she welcomed this state of being with open arms.

And surreptitiously, with equal openness, Vicodin welcomed Rosie's affinity for her high. Vicodin coiled around Rosie and squeezed her so tight she was unable to move. Unable to parent. Unable to do much of anything at all. Except lie there alone and breathe.

Until she couldn't even do that.

It was hard for Rex to see how much his wife tensed up in loathing at the presence of her son. And he didn't understand it. He didn't understand how sweet, kind, helpless Asher could fill Rosie with so much anger. He didn't understand how her blond-haired, blue-eyed, cooing baby could fill her with so much sadness.

How could Rosie lock herself in their room staring at the walls when her two children were downstairs? How could she pull away from her children when they needed her? How could she pull away from her husband when he needed her?

Rex knew that his wife was overwhelmed. And that it wasn't just with parenthood. It was with life. And Rex thought he understood that. Because Rosie had always breathed in every bit of life around her. It was what he loved so much about her. The acute interest in every single cranny. Her fixation on the invisible, infinitesimal, human-to-human forces flowing all around her. The need to explore the smallest, most seemingly insignificant things in the world. The things that everyone else just skipped right over. The image on the T-shirt the guy across the street was wearing. The detailing on the facade of a house. The mural hidden in the alley peeking out from behind a tarp. The smell of spring rain compared to fall rain. The way two birds in flight intersected one another. The orientation of the bow in Willow's hair. The softness of the socks that covered Asher's feet. All of those teeny, tiny things that stacked up on top of one another until they were all too much to handle. Because Rosie's delicate lungs, her delicate body, did not have the capacity to take in all that life all the time. Nobody's did. And so, as much as Rosie filled up in her life, she would have to empty it all out too.

And right now, the Rosie he was looking at was empty. Morning after morning. Night after night. But how much longer would it take until she filled up again? Until he had his wife back? Until his daughter had her mother back? Until his son could meet his mother?

Rex was getting tired. He needed Rosie. And he needed help. Help changing diapers and cutting up chicken into teeny, tiny pieces that his daughter could handle with a fork. He needed help cleaning Lucky Charms off the floor when Asher would adorably sweep them off his high chair. He needed help remembering to freeze Asher's favorite Batman-themed teething ring. He didn't know how to braid Willow's wild hair. Or that he should always have three extra pacifiers on hand. Or which brand of mashed bananas or pureed yams Asher would like best. He didn't know to arrange Willow's vegetables in the shape of a face on her plate to get her to eat them. Or which spots under her arms were the most ticklish. He didn't know which scent of bubble bath calmed Willow down before bed. Or which Mozart composition would soothe Asher before a nap.

Those were things mothers were supposed to know. Those were the things that Rosie had been so good at. Throughout her whole life. And with the birth of his daughter five years ago. And Rex was trying. Really trying. But he was not a mother. And he was not Rosie. He would never be in tune to these things. These little details of life that Rosie was always so in touch with. These little details that would make his children feel so loved. Rex couldn't do it like Rosie could do it. No matter how much he tried.

With the little he could offer his wife while she was in this state, Rex just rubbed Rosie's back tenderly. He kissed her goodnight lovingly. He didn't call for her to help him even when both Willow and Asher were crying. He didn't act frustrated when she refused to have sex. Or talk. Or even blink. And he didn't protest when she said she wasn't going to join the family for dinner once again.

But when Rex saw that Rosie had made her way through his bottle of Vicodin, he knew this was bigger. Bigger than that one joint Rosie smoked in front of him back when they were in Manhattan. Bigger than his brand-new house with the front lawn for the kids to play in. Bigger than not coming down for dinner. Bigger than his marriage. Bigger than any choices he had ever made in his whole life.

Every fiber of his body ached with sadnesss for the wife he may have lost. But every synapse of his brain fired simultaneously with determination for the father he wanted to become. A father that would do anything to protect his children.

Rex dug deep into his soul before pulling one of the keys to 299 East 82nd Street out from the back of his drawer. He held it tightly in his fist and walked delicately into his and Rosie's bedroom, where he knew he would find his wife wrapped in stillness lying on their bed. He gently knelt beside their bed on one knee and pulled Rosie's hand into his chest, pleading for some acknowledgment from his wife. Pleading that she might surrender to help.

"Rosie," Rex whispered. "We need you."

Rosie stared at the ceiling.

"I know you are in pain here. There are places we can go."

Rex's throat tightened as he placed the key to their apartment in New York into Rosie's palm. She slowly curled her fingers around it and turned her face toward Rex. Rosie's eyes met Rex's deeply. There were tears climbing onto her eyelashes, not yet ready to slide down her cheeks. But still, her face and body were still. Rex willed Rosie to sit up and kiss him. Willed her to sit up and say, "Let's get out of this place." But she said nothing.

"I kept our apartment, Rosie. I kept it for us. I kept it for you."

Rosie's tears were falling now onto her otherwise motionless cheeks. His cheeks and chin were wet with them. But there were still no words.

"Please, Rosie. We can go. We can all go."

Rosie turned her eyes back toward the ceiling and slowly uncurled her fingertips to drop the key back into Rex's lap.

Rex's chin sank into his chest as he felt the slight weight of the key hit his legs. As he felt the overwhelming weight of his circumstances hit his heart. He realized that he had been crying too.

Rex didn't want to accept Rosie's refusal for help. Refusal for optimism. Refusal for a happier future. He picked up the key, stood up and looked down at his wife, his Rosie whom he barely recognized. His Rosie who didn't want any of the things she used to want out of life.

Rex placed the key from his lap on Rosie's bedside table so she would know the apartment, her old life, a better life, would always be there for her. That he was always there for her.

Rex walked toward the door and without even turning back to Rosie, he said, "Then it has to be rehab."

Rex walked out of the room, closed his eyes and exhaled before reaching back to close the door behind him.

As he did, he heard Rosie speak. Her voice was weak but clear.

"I won't go, Rex. I can't. And I won't," Rosie said.

And as Rex shut the door, he knew she was right.

Rex walked down the hallway away from their bedroom; he felt his hands and ears and belly warm. A new fire, a new anger, grew inside of him. He wanted to shake his wife. He wanted to grab her by the shoulders and shake every ounce of hurt out of her. He wanted to put his face in hers and yell at the top of his lungs. Tell her to move. In any direction at all. He wanted to grab her wrists. He wanted to grab them tightly and tell her that she had to try. Had to make a sacrifice. Any sacrifice. In any direction at all.

But Rosie had told him plainly that she couldn't. That she wouldn't. And Rex wasn't capable of tugging it out of her. He was never capable of tugging enough out of her.

26

Rosie stood right there at the forefront of Willow's mind every day she was away. Every minute of every day for the last four days. She stood there in a floral-printed dress, waving her hips and arms and blowing kisses at her daughter. And then she dissolved away.

As Willow and Asher played Marshmallow City, Willow wondered if her brother was thinking about the same thing. But when she looked up from her sticky hands to read Asher's mind, she had no idea what her brother was thinking.

The scene in Dad's kitchen was so familiar. The two of them on Dad's tiled kitchen floor sticking toothpicks into marshmallows. Then sticking those marshmallows onto other toothpicks. Then those toothpicks into other marshmallows. Doing this until large toothpick-and-marshmallow towers were erected. Arranging the towers across the kitchen floor until a marshmallow metropolis formed. Lining the black-and-white-speckled kitchen tiles with mini marshmallow roads and mini marshmallow walkways with toothpick streetlamps.

It was a game they used to play upstairs in Asher's room until Dad found out that Asher had been hiding marshmallows under his pillow and sneaking them before bed.

It was a game they used to play loudly and energetically. They would debate over the appropriate orientation and height of a tower. They would ruminate over which color toothpick to use for which building. They would dispense Asher's action figures throughout their city to inhabit their towers and their streets. And Batman would wave to the Hulk as he walked down a marshmallow pathway. And Superman would share a toothpick-lined room with Rambo.

But today when they played with their toothpicks and marshmallows, everything was quiet. In Marshmallow City and in Dad's kitchen.

Willow broke the silence when she looked up from her marshmallow-and-toothpick cube and asked her brother, "Where do you think Mom is?"

Asher snapped his eyes to meet his sister's. His big, blue, wholesome eyes. And now also his swollen marshmallow-stuffed cheeks.

"I don't weally know," he said. The marshmallows were pressing their way out the corners of his mouth as he spoke.

While Asher tried to swallow the marshmallows in his cheeks, Willow tried to swallow Asher's nonresponse and return to erecting her towers. But Willow wasn't ready to end the conversation. She wanted, needed, wanted to talk more.

"But what if you just had to guess or something?"

Asher stretched his neck up, and then dipped his head and scrunched his eyes as he swallowed the white marshmallow bolus in his mouth. He wiped his lips with the back of his hand and stretched his spine to answer his sister.

"What if she, like, took a twip into space?"

Asher lit up at the sound of the fantasy he created.

"Yeah. Maybe she went in a wocket ship."

Asher's whole body started to levitate at the idea. His eyes floated upward and his earlobes rose. He smiled a gummy smile and stuck another marshmallow into his cheeks. Willow could tell that Asher had considered this recently created story of where Mom was a genuine possibility. And that he was beginning to create a catalog of questions in his mind that he would ask Mom about her adventure in outer space when she came back. Asher's optimism about their mother's return almost made Willow smile a little. It almost made her smile enough to allow the belief to seep into her too.

No, her mom wasn't in a rocket ship in space, but yes, her mom would be coming back. And yes, she was probably just having an adventure. Maybe even in New York City. An adventure she would share stories about when she returned, if she returned, when she returned.

So as Willow stuck another toothpick into a marshmallow, she went on guessing, hoping, guessing when and where that might be.

But still, that turning in Willow's stomach, that longing in her bones, would not go away. But she knew, hoped, knew it would all end soon.

With each additional passing day without her mother, all the tiny things in Willow's life hurt even more. Things inside of her father's house and also outside of it. Bus #50. Patricia and Amanda. Her long, empty lunch table. The taunts in Sharpie on the bathroom wall. The crying. The bed-wetting.

The days without her mother. The nights without her mother. All day. Every day.

The next day, when Willow boarded the bus home to her father's house, she unpeeled the duct tape on the seat, willing there to be Pixy Stix lodged in the stuffing. Needing there to be Pixy Stix lodged in the stuffing. She needed some sign that something, someone, was there for her. To comfort her. To refill her even the littlest bit with the love and attention she had been missing all these days without Mom. She tapped her hand around inside of the seat. Nothing. She dropped her shoulder and pressed her arm deeper underneath the thick green vinyl. Nothing. She pushed her shoulder and her arm until it couldn't go any farther. Nothing. She moved some stuffing out of the way and tapped her hand all around. Still nothing.

Nothing. Nothing. Nothing.

Fury exploded from inside of her immediately. Pure, raging, all-consuming fury. Willow yanked piece after piece of stuffing out of the seat and thrust them down to the floor of the bus. She flung herself back and forth against the back of her seat. She growled and flailed while she did it.

And nobody on the bus noticed. Not the

fourth grader in the seat next to her. Not the group of fifth graders in the back of the bus. Not even the bus driver in the seat in front of her.

Willow stomped off Bus #50 with a big gray cloud around her and walked down the long driveway toward her father's house. She didn't want to go in there. She didn't want to see Dad. She didn't want to do her homework. She didn't want to set the table with the bread plate on the left and cup on the right. She didn't want the afternoon checklist. Or the scary spiral staircase she always tripped walking up. She didn't want broccoli for dinner or to drink her whole glass of milk. She didn't want any of it.

And so she started running. She passed her big brick house and ran through the backyard toward the woods. Her backpack jerked around and she stumbled on her way. But she kept going and going. Passed newly sprouting tree after tree. With the naked late-February air scraping her cheeks. Her own breathing became heavier and faster as she ran. It cooled her throat and lungs. Her breath and her legs had escaped her control. They were just vehicles propelling her into a new place. A new state of mind. A new state of being that belonged only to her. An intensity of presence. A hyperawareness of body. A new sense of self, free of distraction. Free of thought.

When Willow's body finally stopped moving, she looked around. She was in the middle of the woods. And she was alone. And somewhere entirely new. With new sounds and new sticks and new stillness and new silence. Because it was so far beyond the thirty-seven and a half steps to the tree house. And so far from anyplace she had ever been before.

Willow took her book of word searches and purple gel pen out of her backpack, and then leaned up against the trunk of a tree. She rested her back against it while her fluttering lungs and heart slowly came under control. As she kept her focus on uncovering words and drawing big ellipses around them, she felt more calm and safe than she had in months. With just the stillness of the trees and the lifelessness in the woods, Willow felt more herself than she had in months.

A few drops of rain trickled from the gray sky. And then her fingertips moved from pink to white. And then her nose and ears started to sting. And an inky black started to take the sky. And then, suddenly, the urge to be inside took Willow. The urge to be warm and to be watched over. By anyone.

She thought about her father inside. Probably thinking about his daughter. She thought about the kitchen table that probably had a plate of dinner waiting on it. She wanted to be sitting behind that plate. Even if there was broccoli on it.

Willow pressed herself off the tree, wiped the traces of crumbling bark from her back and retraced her shallow muddy footprints back to Dad's house. She was surprised to feel relief at the big brick facade and heavy front door. The same brick facade and heavy door that had made her muscles tense up so many times before.

She rubbed the light dusting of frost from the front window and pressed her face toward the cool glass. She could see straight into the living room. A movie Willow didn't recognize was playing on the big television above the mantel, and Willow saw the back of her father's head peeking above the couch and his shoulders bouncing up and down with laughter. She saw the back of a woman's head, as well. A thin blond head. And then she saw her father's fingers caressing that thin blond head. The same fingers that never touched Willow at all.

The same fingers that had dripped with blood when her father cracked that vase and told her to get upstairs.

The same fingers that stuck straight out in anger after Willow tried to tell her father about her one good day at school.

And the fury that Willow thought she left on Bus #50 when she ran into the woods bubbled up inside her again. It made her cheeks hot and her ears ring. It made her jaw tighten and her temples flare. She expected to be missed. She expected that someone ached about her absence the way she ached about Mom's.

Willow stared through the window, willing her father to turn around. Willing him to see her out there underneath a crying sky without a hat. Willing him to see her with a red nose and red ears. Willing him to look outside his window and inside his daughter. Inside to how angry she was. Angry at him. Angry at Mom. Angry at everyone. Angry at everything.

But, no matter how much Willow willed it, Rex didn't turn around. So she watched her father watching his movie until the cold and her hunger were too much to bear. She walked in through the back door and straight up the stairs without stopping at the kitchen table, without saying a word. Her feet immediately went into tiptoe formation on her way up those back steps. It used to feel so good, so exciting, keeping her feet arched, keeping invisible, as she made her way across those steps. But now it just felt lonely. And when Willow made it into her room unseen, she slid herself under her comforter and gave her pillow a tight squeeze. She was grateful to be in her bed even if nobody knew she was in it.

She placed her right ear against her sheets and brought her pillow from her chest to her face. Then Willow cried and cried into that pillow hoping it would muffle the sound. The sound of her own tears had become maddening and she wanted to sleep. Her body and her eyes wanted it too. But even after a couple of hours in her bed alone and tired, her heart was awake. Burning and grieving. Grieving and burning. Creating so, so many tears. And although after some time that night Willow's tears dried up, she was still left with an ache. And the exhaustion of that relentless ache. She didn't want to be a ghost in this home. She wanted to be seen and heard and hugged and loved. And even if she couldn't get all of those things from Dad, she at least wanted him to know she was there. So she untangled herself from her sheets and pillow and shuffled across the house to her father's bedroom.

She heard a rhythmic hum rippling from

behind his closed bedroom door.

Good, Willow thought. *He's here.*

So Willow brought her hand slowly to the doorknob. She turned it cautiously, and then stepped delicately into his dark room. There was no one in his bed, but the way the sheets were twisted and warm, she knew that Dad had been in there recently.

"Dad?" Willow called quietly into the empty room.

"Dad?" she whispered a bit louder as inertia carried Willow across the bedroom.

"Dad?" she said again when she neared the mirror-lined entrance to the bathroom.

All of the lights were on and the rhythmic hum had turned into a steady moan.

When she reached the bathroom, the first thing Willow saw of her father was his bare ass contracting and relaxing. And then she saw his naked back. And then she saw that woman's naked arms splayed across the mirror as her long fingers clenched on to the wall, vying for anything to grip. She saw that woman's tousled blond hair waving around wildly. And that room of mirrors created infinity, infinity, infinity of all of it.

Willow stood frozen at the image of her naked father and that naked woman in the mirror over and over and over and over and over again. Pushing themselves into, and then out of, and then into each other over and over and over and over again. There was infinity and infinity and infinity and infinity of these two fleshy, glistening bodies pressing into each other quickly and harshly. And no matter where her eyes moved, there was more of it. A new view of it. A different angle of it.

Eyes right. His gyrating hips. Eyes left. Her bouncing breasts. Eyes right. His hand on the inside of her thigh. Eyes left. Her ankle hooked around his. It extended indefinitely and indefinitely and indefinitely and indefinitely in the mirror. And even when she closed her eyes, the sound of skin slapping together, and the smell of something acetic, forced the vivid image right back into her head.

And when Willow finally managed to unstick her feet from the floor, she scurried out of her father's room and quietly but shakily closed the door behind her. Once Willow made it to the dark and quiet hallway, she crouched over her knees, squished her eyes shut and breathed deliberately until she was as close to calm as she could be. She slid back to her room and then under her comforter. Willow gave her pillow a tight squeeze and was grateful for her bed for the second time that night. Even though, still, nobody knew she was in it. Even though there was no safe place for her mind to wander.

So Willow just turned and turned in the darkness of her bedroom with her fingers tight around her covers. She turned and turned as she tried to sleep, but the vision of her father and that woman, sweaty and entangled, pressed ruthlessly against the back of her eyes.

As she lay in bed, Willow heard a creaking sound of footsteps in the hallway and her body tensed up even more. She pressed her eyelids together and forced her body into stillness. She wasn't ready to see her father. Even if he was dressed. Even if he didn't have blond hair wrapped around his knuckles. She squeezed her eyes again as a voice slid around the door and into her room.

"Willow, awe you awake?"

Willow exhaled at the broken *r* sound. And then she rolled over to the door with her eyes open. Even in this darkness, she could see her brother's silky blond hair wiggling on top of his head as he bounced into her room.

"Yeah, Ash. What are you doing up?" Willow asked as she sat up, her muscles finally relinquishing the tension that had forced them to be so stiff this last hour.

Asher hopped into his sister's bed, steadied himself on his knees and bounced up and down with his hands on the headboard. "I don't know. I couldn't weally sleep. Wanna play something?"

Willow smiled and shuffled out of bed and over to the telescope next to her window. Willow pushed the left window pane open, and turned the black tube toward the stars. A refreshing winter chill barreled through the window and dived into her lungs.

"All right, Ash. Let's do it. Constellation game?"

Asher took one last bounce on the mattress and joined his sister at the window.

She loved playing this game with her brother; carving out patterns in the stars, naming new constellations, detailing their origin stories. She loved scanning the sky for new connections, new shapes, new tales. Creating a new world out there in the vast inky darkness.

Willow peered through the telescope and out into the star-glittered night sky.

"I got it!" Willow almost-whispered after only a few rotations of the telescope. She helped her brother find the same cluster of stars that she had identified. And Asher nodded and took his place on the floor as he looked up at his big sister, ears, eyes and heart wide-open. Willow began her invented story.

"That's Lipina. She is a big, big red pair of lips," Willow said in a deep, soothing tone, ready to sink into her tale.

"I thought it looked kind of like a butt."

"Asher!" Willow gasped with her eyebrows pushed up, trying to fight a smile.

Asher chuckled behind his fingers as his sister dropped back into her tale.

"This is NOT a butt. This is a pair of lips. And her name is Lipina. And once a year, all of the other constellations in the sky line up for Lipina's kisses."

Asher popped up again. "Oh, is it like the gwoss wet kisses fwom Mom? I bet no one would line up for one of those!"

Willow smirked and thought about all those times Mom would force her big red lips into Asher's cheek. How she would swirl her face around and around as Asher giggled and winced. How as soon as Mom would pull away, Asher would vigorously rub his palm against his cheek in a futile attempt to clear the thin layer of saliva and bright red footprint of her kiss.

"Well, I don't know if they're wet kisses but they are the most special kisses in the whole entire universe. Because if Lipina kisses you, you will have eternal happiness."

"Does etewnal mean you tuwn awound and awound?" Asher asked, finally engrossed in Willow's story.

"No, it means you have it forever. It means anyone who gets a kiss from Lipina will be happy forever."

Asher nodded slowly with his chest forward and wide eyes.

"But first, before any kisses, the other constellations have to do a dance for Lipina. And you only get a kiss if she likes your dance. And the other constellations only get one chance. So you have to make it perfect."

Willow almost lost herself in her vision of that crest of stars when Asher got to his feet, rolled his elbows around by his ribs and twisted his hips back and forth.

"Think I'd get a kiss for this dance?"

Willow laughed at her little brother wiggling around in his too-big T-shirt in the middle of the night.

"I don't know, Ash," Willow said through a chuckle. "You'll have to ask Lipina if you meet her."

Asher abruptly stopped his dance and grabbed the telescope.

"Okay, my tuwn" he said, wiggling in front of Willow and pressing his big blue eye into the back of the tube.

He tilted the telescope up into the sky as Willow sat down in her beanbag chair. Asher swept the telescope back and forth across the sky, slowly and deliberately. Another gust of winter wind swirled around the room as Asher pulled away from the telescope.

"Hewe's one," Asher said with an unforeseen solemnity creeping up in his tone.

Willow stood up to look into the telescope and see what Asher had found. There were four white glistening specks huddled together in the sky. She sat back down on her beanbag and looked at her little brother. His body was still and his words were earnest as he crafted his explanation for the way those four bright stars came together. How each of them used to live in a different part of the sky. How they all used to like different things. How they all had different favorite colors and books and movies and candies. How they wore different clothes and ate different snacks.

"Until one day, gwavity changed. Like a vowtex. Like magic. And then all those staws ended up wight next to each other. And, at fiwst it was bad. And they fought for a little bit. About what books to wead and what movies to watch. But then one day, one staw gave the other staw a Pop-

Tawt to twy. And even though the staw didn't want to twy it, he weally liked it! And then they all stawted twying new snacks and books and movies. And evewybody liked evewything they twied."

Asher exhaled in his place. His words had been spinning out of him so quickly until this sudden pause. He looked at his sister.

"And then they all loved each other," Asher concluded slowly with a glimmer of wisdom in his eye.

And Willow nodded. She nodded and smiled with a closed mouth at the world Asher explained to her. A world she knew so well, and then not at all. At the world she hoped she could live in one day.

"Yeah, and now they are fouw staws that awe in one little gwoup out thewe hugging!" Asher said a little too loudly as he jumped up out of his story and back into his impish self.

But before Willow could take her second turn at the telescope, she and her brother heard heavy stomping in the hallway outside her door.

There was a moment of electric eye contact, and then Willow jumped under her covers and Asher dived straight under the bed. Even though Willow's eyes were squeezed together, she could feel her father's eyes on her back. His suspicion radiating.

Willow opened one eye, just a sliver, to see whether Asher had made his way into hiding. She could see his white socks peeking out from beneath the bed frame. She could see his toes wiggling excitedly. Or maybe anxiously.

Willow pressed her eyes closed again at the sound of the slow, creaking, deliberate pressure of a heel and then a toe, and then a heel and then a toe, moving across her carpet.

And then Rex crashed through the silence.

"Gotcha!" he shouted as he bent down.

Willow's eyes popped open as she sat up to find her father's hands around Asher's ankles. His sock-covered feet were squirming in his father's strong, broad hands. Twisting under his taut knuckles.

Rex pulled Asher's little body from underneath the bed and up into his chest. And then he took those same strong, broad hands and shook them over his son's chest and belly until Asher was giggling uncontrollably.

Asher eked out three words between vibrating breaths so full of laughter.

"No."

"Mowe."

"Tickles."

Rex pulled his hand away and scooped it under his son's back as he turned to exit Willow's room.

"Well, that's for making all that racket in the middle of the night, ya little sneak."

Rex gave his son one last tickle on his belly and then carried Asher out the door.

The last thing Willow saw before closing her eyes again was the shadow of her father kissing her brother as they dissolved into the darkness of the hallway. And the jealousy of it made her bones ache, right down to the core of them.

27

Four Years Ago

For over a year now, Rosie had been in a nearly catatonic state. There was the depression, and the Vicodin, and then some poisonous cocktail mix of the two. Rex couldn't even tell the difference anymore.

For the first few months, Rex felt his call to duty. He prepared bottles of formula for Asher. He got Willow dressed in the mornings. He made sure Willow and Asher had toys to play with and movies to watch. He kissed his immobile wife goodbye every time he left the house, even though most days he didn't even receive a smile in return. He rubbed Rosie's back in bed until she fell asleep. But then the seesaw tipped. Rex grew weary. He was tired and exhausted and teeming with it. First at his wife. But then at himself. He knew this day would come all those years ago. He knew he and Rosie were mismatched. How they were always tugging at things within the other. Tugging at things the other didn't want yanked at.

Where to live. Where to eat. When to speed up or slow down.

And as quickly as Rex inhaled Rosie all those years ago, he exhaled her back out. He could continue being a father, but could not continue being a husband. Especially not in these circumstances with those drugs involved. Especially after Rosie had refused help. He was certain of this. And once Rex Thorpe was certain of something, his mind could not be changed.

Rosie felt Rex slipping away, but she could not move to do anything about it. The depression, and then the Vicodin, and then some vicious mix of the two, had sunk its nails too deep into her. And the grip was tight in every second, every interaction and every cranny of her world.

And when the family went to Lanza Pizza one typical Tuesday evening for dinner, this fact had become so apparent, so blaring, so bright, so harsh, that neither Rex nor Rosie could ignore it anymore.

As soon as she walked through the door of her favorite pizza place, Rosie headed straight to the orange booth in the back and let her head fall into her arm. No request for crayons for doodling. No big cup for cream soda. No hug for John behind the counter. No quarters jingling in her pocket for the pinball machine.

And while Rosie twirled the pepper shaker with her middle finger and ignored her pizza, Willow scribbled away quietly and Asher pounded a meatball into the table. And her husband just sat there. Watching it all quietly unravel.

She remembered how in the early months of her depression, Rex would stare at her boldly. Urging her to move. Urging her to eat, to dance, to inhale, to do something. But tonight he just stared down at his pasta, defeated.

In that moment, Rosie knew her marriage was over.

And still, when Rosie got into the front passenger seat of the car on the way home from dinner, she wanted to turn to Rex and kiss him so deeply. But the thought of moving her neck was too overwhelming. So Rosie continued staring vacantly out the window. She listened to the tune of "Leather and Lace" fill the car and silently thought of the afternoon that Rex interrupted her dancing to this same song at Blooms Flower Shop. And then her memory silently shifted to the evening she and Rex first danced to

"Leather and Lace" in their first apartment in New York City. To the moment she hung her tarnished golden locket on the wall as a tribute to just how much love was in that room. And then her thoughts silently shifted to how much love had to have been lost to get to where they were today.

Rosie was on the verge of full heartbreak when she heard Willow mumbling every other word to her and Rex's song from the back seat. It warmed her breaking heart.

Rosie was simultaneously so full of love and so full of Vicodin as she listened to her daughter fumbling through the chorus. She was full of wanting to hug and kiss her daughter, but so unable to act. So full of wanting to kiss her husband, but so unable to move herself to do it.

A tear danced on the tightrope of her lower eyelid and dripped down her cheek. But neither Rex nor her children could see it. It was just Rosie up there on that island of her front seat. Rosie and her high and her one tear.

It was so simple and so true. Their marriage was over.

Rex reached over and put his hand in Rosie's lap and continued to stare straight ahead at the snow-dusted road. He reached over and squeezed her leg, like he knew it too.

28

When Willow opened her eyes the next morning at her father's house, she couldn't help but think that she might never see her mother again. It had already been nearly a week. She ghosted through another day at Robert Kansas Elementary School. Through another afternoon at her father's with word searches and her CD player and completing her checklists. Until, that evening, the doorbell rang and it was her mother. Rosie looked as lively and cool as ever in her slightly tattered knee-length floral-printed dress and red lipstick.

Asher burst past Willow and hugged his mother's slender leg without even a pause.

"Hi, Mommy!" he cheered through a toothless smile.

Rosie stretched her arms out for her daughter with Asher still wrapped around her calf.

But Willow still had sadness, confusion,

anger, hopelessness, frustration and longing in her heart and in her blood. And she was not ready to relinquish that sadness. That anger. That confusion. That hopelessness. That frustration. That longing. All of these terrible, terrible feelings that had been swirling around inside of Willow for the past week.

Willow stood there in the doorway of her father's house trying to digest what it meant that her mother was standing right in front of her like nothing happened. Trying to decide how to feel. What to say. She wanted to untether the questions that were stuck in the back of her throat and just blurt them out. She wanted to ask so many things. So many big, important things.

Where were you?

Why did you leave us here?

Why didn't you tell us?

Why did you fall asleep on the couch?

What were you trying to say to me up in the willow tree?

Where were my Pixy Stix when I needed them at school?

What are those things in your drawer you didn't want me to find?

But the questions were stuck. And Willow was all quiet.

So Rosie stole the silence.

"Oh, get over here, you noodle," Rosie said casually to her frozen daughter. And Rosie tilted her head to the side and looked straight at Willow's eyes while she said it.

And so Willow did. She hugged her mother like she was asked but she did it with open eyes. And as Willow got into the back of her mother's car, her fears stuck with her. Fears that she'd had somewhere deep down for some time but were now illuminated. Fears of a life without her mother in it. Fears of an existence where no one understood her. Fears of a life without her mother and her mother's love. Fears that allowed her to rebound right back into Rosie's love as the sounds of Prince flowed through the car.

But when her mother made a left turn instead of a right out of Rex's street and Willow felt adventure coming, she couldn't help but fill up with excitement. An excitement that allowed love to take over all those icky things inside of her. And as love took back over, as Rosie took back over, all the sadness, the anger, the confusion, the hopelessness, the frustration, the longing disappeared. It was so easy.

Willow looked over at Asher to see if he had similarly sensed adventure, but he was just clicking his feet together and watching his shoes light up.

Willow looked up at Rosie but could only see her mother's eyes in the rearview mirror. They looked big and full. Now she knew for certain that an adventure was coming.

"Mom, where are we going?" Willow asked, trying to shout over the music.

And Rosie tilted the rearview mirror down to meet Willow's eyes and get a clearer view of her children, prioritizing the view of her children's faces over the view of the cars traveling on the road behind her.

"Yeah, Mom. Whewe awe we going?" Asher chimed in though he wasn't sure why.

When Rosie rolled down the windows and sped up without an answer, both Asher and Willow lit up, certain they were in for an adventure. They bounced up and down in the back seat of Lili Von and let their mother bring them back into her life.

"Where are we going? Where are we going?" they chanted in staccato and in unison as the car sped up faster.

"Where are we going? Where are we going?" they continued, now pounding their palms on the leather seats to the beat of their own chant.

Rosie joined in on the same choppy cadence. "I know where we're going. I know where we're going." She honked the horn to that same beat.

And then, through a deep belly giggle, Asher forced out a "TELLLLLLL USSSSSSS!" with a screeching volume and enduring breath that surprised everyone in the car.

Rosie stopped the car on the side of the road, turned around and opened her big brown eyes as wide as they could go.

"Hang on to your hats and jackets. We're going to the beach."

"HOORAY!" Willow and Asher rejoiced in unison out the open windows while they swallowed the wind and swayed their hands above their heads to "1999," as the taste of salt took over the cold air.

And when they got to the edge of the sand, Rosie pulled her noisy blue car with its googly eyes to a stop. Willow and Asher were already out of the car and sprinting around the shoreline. They looked like two windup toys with their legs zipping around beneath their hips. Rex had wound them so tight with homework checks and chore requests while she was gone, and they were finally releasing it all right there on the sand of Sandbridge Beach.

Willow and Asher chased each other to the top of the dunes and fell into the sand with their arms extended. And when they saw their mother walking toward the water, they rolled down the dunes without caring about the sand in their hair and their shoes and their pants. They ran across the beach and caught up with Rosie. And Willow got right up next to her mother and watched her red toenails sink under the cold sand and reveal themselves again as they walked closer and closer to the water. Farther and farther from everything else.

Rosie handed Willow and Asher each a kite and made eye contact and smiled with each one of her children as she did. She instructed Willow and Asher to hold the spool in their right hands, the string in their left hand, and then to run, run, run as fast as they could. To go, go, go and feel free. Rosie jumped up and down and cheered after them as they ran down the empty beach.

And as Asher took off, the wind scooped effortlessly underneath his kite and lifted it right into the early twilight. But Willow's little stumble caused her purple kite to dip straight into the sand. She threw her body down in frustration as she watched Asher's kite wiggle around high in the sky. And then Willow looked up at her mother. Up at her mother, who was looking right back at her lovingly.

And soon Asher's legs got tired, and after Willow buried her kite entirely underneath the sand, Rosie taught her children how to find the perfect skipping stones. "Flat and long," she said as she rubbed her fingers across the smooth stone she took out of her bag.

Willow noticed that the way she caressed that stone was the same way she tickled Willow's arms. Kindly. Gently. Deliberately. She noticed how her mother touched that stone, a thing without any feelings, a thing she just met, a thing that should mean nothing to her, in the same way that she touched her daughter.

But, even still, Willow walked down the beach as the cold water washed over her toes and back into the sea. She bent down, felt a stone, tossed it aside, took two steps, bent down, felt a stone, added it to her pile, took two more steps, bent down, felt a stone. She felt happy and calm in the monotony of it. Happy and calm in the presence of her mother again. But when she picked her head up to return to her mother and Asher, it was just sky and sand and ocean and her pile of rocks. No Asher. No Mom.

No Mom.

No Mom.

No Mom.

No Mom.

She dropped all the smooth stones from her arm and ran back in the direction she had come from. She stumbled and splashed with every other step. And when she arrived at the parking lot, there was still no Mom. No Asher. No Mom. No Mom. No Mom. No Mom. No Mom. No Mom. Just more sky and sand and ocean.

Willow froze in her place. Toes buried in the cool sand. Hair twisting in the ocean breeze. Heart in a knot. A warm puddle formed below her and she stared at the empty beach.

No Mom.

No Mom.

No Mom.

No Mom.

But after only a few long seconds, Asher and her mother emerged from behind the dune where they were gathering their own handfuls of stones. Willow and Rosie made eye contact. And for a second they were both frozen in their places in the sand. Frozen until Rosie saw Willow's wet purple leggings and winked and skipped back toward the car.

When Rosie reemerged from the trunk, she was carrying an extra pair of purple leggings, a few logs and a brown paper bag full of s'mores fixings. And then, like magic, Willow was sitting in dry purple leggings in front of a roaring fire with a golden marshmallow drooping from a stick perfect for roasting. Rosie pulled out her secret s'more ingredient, bacon bits, and the three of them licked their sticky fingers as the sun dropped behind the horizon.

And then, when the purple twilight succumbed to near darkness, Willow looked up at her mother and her eyes said so plainly, *Let's go home.*

And so they did. They drove straight home. To Rosie's home that Willow had missed so much.

And as soon as Willow walked through the front door, she inhaled the smell of the walls. The patterns of the wallpaper. The glow of the lights strung around the windows. She felt safe and taken care of when she was back at Mom's. And as soon as her mother kissed her on the mouth before they all walked upstairs, Willow felt all of the love that she had been missing wash over her again. She felt all of that unadulterated, concentrated, rejuvenating, specific, manic love. That kind of love that her mother, and only her mother, could give her.

And even though Willow washed the sand off her toes all alone in her bathtub, and Mom didn't invite her into her bed, she still fell asleep almost happy. Happy because she was back at Mom's. But not entirely happy because it was so eerily quiet all around. Not entirely happy because she was all alone in her bed with no idea what kind of pajamas Mom was wearing.

29

Four Years Ago

It was Rex's idea to tell Willow and Asher about the divorce on a sunny Saturday morning. Rosie would have preferred to enjoy the day first — take a walk, have a picnic, skip stones. But Rex had already decided that he wouldn't be sacrificing any more for Rosie. So, with Rosie already in tears, he invited Willow and Asher into their bedroom to talk.

And while his children sat quietly and attentively on the edge of his bed, Rex told Willow and Asher that he and Rosie were getting divorced. He took out his notepad and moved through the list of things the parenting books had told him to say. The list of things that would ensure his children properly understood and digested the news. He told them how they would still get to spend lots of time with their mom and with their dad. That they were still a family, just a different kind. That they still loved their children very much. How nothing would change that. How Mom had already found a new house to live in. How they would take turns visiting each house. How everything would be okay.

And when Rex finally turned his attention away from his yellow lined notebook paper, both of his children were completely still. Except for the meandering streams of tears flowing from their wet eyes. They were completely still until they got up from the edge of the bed and pressed themselves into Rosie's arms. It was Rosie and Willow and Asher in one pile of tears and love and sadness. And it was Rex alone tearless with his notepad.

Willow was only six and Asher was only two, but Willow understood that things were changing. That everything was broken. That it was going to hurt. That it already did. As Rosie rubbed her children's shaking backs, Rex caught Willow looking at him from over his soon-to-be ex-wife's shoulder. There was something undaughterly in her eyes. Something beyond sadness or confusion. Something loveless. Something hateful as she stared, stacking an invisible wall of bricks around her father. Stacking and stacking until a big solid wall was formed. A big solid wall that kept her mother inside, and her father outside.

Rex knew intimately what it was like to be in a brick-protected world where only Rosie's love existed. He knew it felt so good in there. But he also knew how awful it was when that love stopped. How hard it was to get out once those tall brick walls were created. He knew how inevitable it was for that love to end. But still, he watched his daughter stack, stack, stack those bricks. And it broke his heart.

Rosie eventually peeled her children off her, and Willow and Asher returned to the edge of the bed. Rex flipped to the next page of his notepad, scanned it and then began explaining the logistics of the arrangement. Mondays, Wednesdays and every other weekend with Dad. Tuesdays, Thursdays and the other weekends with Mom. And as Rex went down his list for Willow and Asher, Rosie, tears dripping from her eyes, continuously repeated, "We love you guys so much," in the background. Willow nodded slowly while Asher looked down and twisted his toes around anxiously.

When Rex finished his list and his children left his bedroom, he noticed a warm wet puddle where Willow had been sitting. Rex recalled that parenting books said something about this too. How loss of bladder control was common for children who were feeling like they had lost control in other arenas of their lives. It was something Rex could understand. Understand and solve with more books, more structure. Rex understood how Willow had lost control of lots of things sitting on that bed. Her bladder and her heart. Her heart that was splitting in two.

But the parenting books didn't say anything about a six-year-old with a heart torn in half like Willow's. With a heart already taken by her mother. The parenting books didn't tell Rex how to snatch up pieces of her heart before it was lost. And Rosie didn't have to read any books to know to grab all the pieces of her daughter's heart that she could right there in that bedroom. Because in every moment, happy, sad and in-between, it was Rosie's nature to do just that. To take Willow's heart and keep it next to her heart all the time.

30

Willow's mother winked when she told them she would pick them up from school even though it was Dad's night. "I want to make up for some lost time with my noodles," she said as she waved goodbye through the window.

The image of another night at Mom's was the only thing getting Willow through the day at Robert Kansas Elementary School. She counted down the hours until she would be at Mom's again. And she couldn't help but smile a full red-lipped smile when she met Asher at the pickup circle and took position on the curb with her word search to wait for Mom. Willow watched Amy and then Sarah and then Greg and then Erin and then Annelise hop into the back seat of their parents' cars while she and her brother waited and waited. Asher was occupied with an overflowing anthill while Willow was half-attuned to her word searches and half kept an eye on the entrance to the pickup circle. But when Asher reached boredom and sat down next to his sister with his chin in his palms and his elbows on his lap, Willow started to worry. And her tummy started to turn. And her bladder started to tickle. It was cold and it was getting still and dark.

"Please. Not again," Willow said so quietly into the air. She could see a cloud of her breath on the tips of her lips as she said it.

But then Willow heard the familiar roar of her mother's car approaching just as the tingle of anxiety in her belly was reaching her chest. She saw the big googly eyes on the front of Lili Von coming around the bend of the pickup circle. There she was! She knew Mom would be there. Willow couldn't keep the corners of her mouth from turning up as she stood up excitedly with her word search book in her mitten and waited for the car to gently stop right in front of her on the curb. But Rosie's car continued speeding toward Willow and Asher, swerving wildly between opposite curbs. And without slowing down, the two front wheels leaped over the curb, and then came to a screeching, jerking stop. For a moment, everything was so still. The twilight, the school, the car, the street. Willow, Asher. Their eyes wide. Everything was still except for the pink-haired troll swinging back and forth from the rearview mirror.

Rosie lifted her heavy arm and waved slowly at her children with just her fingers through the windshield until they were ready to move. And Willow and Asher made their way into the back seat without any help with their backpacks, or kisses on their cheeks, or questions about their day. As her children got in the car, Rosie massaged her temples. And the eerie quiet around her endured until the grumble of the engine picked up again. Rosie silently put the car into motion and resumed the pinballing from curb to curb. And as Rosie turned out of the pickup circle, the sharp torque of the car thrust both Willow and Asher toward the right window. Their seat belts had barely enough time to tighten around their chests.

As Willow regained her position in her seat, she reached over and squeezed Asher's hand. She squeezed it tightly as she looked straight out the windshield at the road ahead. Willow watched trees and cars and the yellow lines of the street pass as fear clawed its way up one rib and then the next and then the next, creeping its way toward her heart.

And when Asher, Willow and Rosie pulled into the driveway, Rosie dragged her shoes and walked into her house without a kiss or a hug or a story or a song or a plan for dinner. She pulled her feet up the front steps and let the door creak closed behind her.

Willow helped Asher with his backpack and walked into a quiet house. She poured a bowl of Lucky Charms for her brother and then herself, but neither of them said a word even though they were both thinking about crayon colors as they watched their tinted milk turn colors.

The same fear that was climbing up her ribs in the car, the same fear Mom had nearly vanquished at the beach with her kites and her stones, had its nails all the way inside Willow's heart again. Could it all go away, Willow thought, if she were to just go upstairs and ask her mom to come down and cook dinner, or do the Time Warp, or paint the walls, or squish tomatoes, or put food coloring on her vanilla ice cream? It would all be so easy, Willow hoped, willed.

So, with her heart in the talons of fear, Willow walked up the stairs, concentrating on each foot on each step, and slowly made her way to her mother's closed bedroom door. She pressed her ear against it before walking in. There were no sounds, but she could feel her mother breathing in there. Feel her mother slowly inhaling and exhaling. But when Willow entered, she walked into an empty quiet room with an unmade bed and a burning candle. She moved slowly through her mother's room to the door of her closet. And when Willow peeked her head around that door, she found her mom.

She found her mom lying on the floor with one arm twisted unnaturally at the shoulder and her legs bent out. She found her mom with her underwear exposed and her bangs splayed messily across her forehead. She found her mother with her eyes shut and her chest rising and falling slowly but fully. Willow tried hard to swallow as fear tightened around her throat. She shook her body into motion and went to get two pillows from her mother's bed. And then she placed one under her mother's ear and one in the space on the floor next to her heavy head. And then Willow dragged the heavy comforter from the bed into the closet and tucked the edges underneath her mother's sides.

She returned for Asher and the two of them watched TV together until Willow ushered him into his bed and tucked the sheets around him in a similar fashion. And then she returned to the floor of her mother's closet and pressed he body into her mother's until she could feel her mother's heart beating against her. Willow let herself drift into sleep, but could not ignore for one more second the fear that was swaying back and forth.

31

Four Years Ago

Although it was Rex who first vocalized the desire, the need, for the divorce, Rex was crushed when Rosie moved out of their home. His heart broke when he watched her toss her dresses into a cardboard box labeled "clothes." Even though she did it without folding them. And Rex's heart broke when Rosie sprinkled her paint-brushes into that same box. It broke when he watched her butt swaying as she pushed that cardboard box into the back seat of her bizarre blue car. It broke when he watched that car drive away, and Rosie waved out the window with her left knee peeking out.

And it broke all over again when he turned around to his home that had now become just a house. It broke when he realized that without Rosie's paintings, he was left with bare walls. And that without Rosie's record collection, he was left with a quiet home.

And that without Rosie, he was less.

It was almost as if Rosie took all of Rex's good with her when she moved out of their house. Because all this time, without Rex knowing it, Rosie had been on one end of a seesaw holding down a boulder. She was sitting there, thus enabling Rex to soar. But when Rosie got up off that seesaw, Rex hit the ground so hard. He hit the ground so hard he didn't know if he would be able to get back up.

Rex called his old friend Roy as he sat at the foot of his now-empty bed. "Remember how I told you Rosie would be trouble?" he said. "I think I'm the one in trouble now."

And Rex was right because without Rosie, Rex hardened. His shoulders pushed up toward his ears. His eyebrows furrowed and his upper lip crinkled. His bottom teeth twisted and his jaw jutted out. He chewed his Bubblicious gum so hard that his temples flared.

All this heartbreak, all this loss, all this sadness, all this anger began oozing out of him as he writhed around on the ground. On the ground and in pain without Rosie. It oozed out of him and enveloped him in a dark and stormy cloud.

Anyone, everyone, could see it from a mile away. Especially Willow.

But Rex knew of nothing better than to sink into the parenting books and proven coping mechanisms. "Be big and strong," the books told him. Big and strong he could do. Always. "Your children will be feeling a loss of control and structure," he read. "You need to restore structure for them, even if artificially," the book said. And Rex complied.

The next morning when he woke up, Rex taped a to-do list of morning activities on his daughter's and then his son's doors. It included teeth brushing and face washing. Made beds and folded pajamas. Brushed hair and tidy outfits. Things all children could do. Rex stared at the space on the page at the bottom of the list. "Family Breakfast," he added. He stared for another moment before reversing his pencil and erasing the word *family.* But the grooves in the page were still there. Staring right back at him.

Rex promptly retraced the indents with the tip of his pencil. They were still a family. Rex, Willow and Asher. A family. One part of one family. And a family of their own.

While Rex struggled after the separation, Rosie flourished. Because without having to sit on that seesaw, holding that boulder for her husband, Rosie felt free again. And the instant Rosie drove down the driveway and past the boring white fence Rex loved, and out of the quiet neighborhood he chose, Rosie felt empowered to take control of her life. To re-create a world she loved. Re-create a love where she could love. To re-create a world wherein she could love herself. And Willow. And Asher. Even if it were here in the quiet suburbs of Virginia.

She tossed all of the pill bottles she had sneakily acquired through the years into a drawer in the depths of her closet and wiggled her way out of Vicodin's grip immediately.

The simultaneous release from her husband, that house and those white pills enabled Rosie to breathe again. So fully. So deeply. So happily.

Rex had inadvertently deprived Rosie of oxygen for so long. Rex wanted to live a life with rules. And a lot of them. He wanted bedtimes and classic books and the television off. He had read every parenting book in the library while Rosie was pregnant, and this was what they told him his children needed. Structure, regimen, consistency. And Rosie let Rex do all of these things while she silently disagreed.

She kept quiet in her belief that there wasn't any one thing all children needed. She had trusted Rex and his parenting books enough to keep quiet about her belief that each child, each person, was different and, accordingly, needed different love. So Rosie just silently prepared to be a mother who would listen to and act upon individual quirks and preferences. She had done this so naturally with all people. But she would do it with particular kindness and attention for her children. She wanted them to have fun and feel free. To be themselves and be happy. And she wanted to be fun and free with them. She wanted to be herself and be happy with them. She wanted to be coloring and singing and making a mess. She wanted to be watching movies and listening to records. She wanted to be playing dress-up and putting on makeup. Yes, she wanted to be herself. With her children next to her. She wanted all of them soaking each other up all the time. She wanted all of them filling each other with love. So much real, specific, nuanced love. And she was manic with life and energy when she walked her children into her new cottage with ivy growing up the side and peeling wallpaper on every wall. She was so happy, and so reenergized.

She gushed with it. And she was so excited to swaddle her children with it.

So when her children came to see her new home for the first time, she filled the house with sugary snacks and Prince albums. And she allowed all those things to flow and flow indefinitely in her home. She allowed her children to see and do everything in that home. She showed them all of the things she loved. Elton John and Fleetwood Mac. *Blazing Saddles* and *The Rocky Horror Picture Show.* Allowed them to sing and dance and feel free. She gave them glitter and face paint and makeup and clothes to dress up in. To feel silly in.

She hugged them and kissed them at every chance she got. She gave them so much love. So much of the most Rosie kind of love.

When Rosie noticed that her children's bodies had become exhausted with fun, she invited them into her bed to love and hug and kiss them some more as they fell asleep. That night, there in Rosie's bed, all twisted up and happy with her children, it occurred to Rosie that her divorce from Rex was the best thing that ever happened to her. She was herself again. Dancing, singing, laughing, making art and, most importantly, loving her children again. Loving them wholly.

In her heart and in her head. In her bones. She could feel it moving through her. And after many years without any of that, she was so happy to have it back.

But as Rosie's eyelids fell heavy and she drifted off to sleep, she wondered if these feelings could endure. Because even Rosie knew that she was still just a ballerina pirouetting across the stage. Everyone loved to see her dance. But when she got offstage, her feet were covered in blisters. And no matter how much Rosie loved to dance, those blisters hurt. They hurt so much she might eventually have to stop dancing.

32

When Rosie picked Willow and Asher up from their father's house, she didn't even get out of the car to greet them with hugs and kisses. There was no music playing and the windows were locked shut. Willow had to tug on the car door twice to get it to close without Mom's help.

When Willow felt the car roll over the asphalt, the claws of fear dug deeper into Willow's heart. Again. And as Willow looked out the window and out toward the dusting of snow on the road, she put her hand over her brother's in the quiet back seat of Lili Von. Again.

When Willow and Asher got to their mom's house, they asked if they could play outside even though it was cold out. And they were ushered out to the driveway by a listless and lipstickless woman who barely resembled their mother. Willow wiped her red lipstick off with the bottom of her

T-shirt as soon as she noticed her mother's bare lips. And then Rosie dragged a bucket of chalk out of the front closet and dumped the contents at her children's feet on the cold asphalt.

"Why don't you draw something for Mom?" Rosie mumbled as she turned around to shuffle back into the house. The sounds of her mother's shoes scraping against the ground grated against Willow's ears and broke her heart. Her mother used to float. But this woman, dragging her feet like that, didn't look anything like her mother. Willow watched a stranger in a bathrobe make her way into her home one slow and labored step at a time.

By the time Willow had turned her attention toward the blacktop, Asher already had blue chalk all over his face and hands. Willow crouched down, picked up a purple piece of chalk and started writing out her name in big rounded letters. As she pulled the chalk across the asphalt a purple powder swirled around her hand and landed delicately on the ground. Even though the cold was nibbling at her nose, Willow felt at peace outside with the chalk in her hand. The repetitive motions of drawing the lines of her name over and over again. The smooth vibration on her hand. The brisk air filling her lungs. The calmness around her.

But the distant sound of a car rumbling quickly toward her interrupted the quiet stillness. Willow snapped her head up and noticed that Asher had done the same. It was their father's car roaring around the bend.

As Rex's sleek black car came to a quick stop on top of Willow's and Asher's doodles, all of Willow's organs started to rumble. This wasn't right.

"Hi, Dad!" Asher said while Willow stood there frozen.

Go away! Get out! Get out of here! Willow willed with her mind as she stood rigidly in her place.

Rex got out of the car with determination between his eyebrows.

And then he said, "Get in." And he said it firmly. With a shakiness in his words.

Asher tilted his head to the side in gentle perplexity. But Willow was already boiling. "No," she yelled. She yelled it as she stomped her right foot down on the asphalt.

"Willow, get in the car. Asher, you too," Rex insisted curtly.

Asher took a hesitant step toward the car but Willow refused.

"NO!" Willow screeched as she thrust her arms down by her sides and tightened her eyes. Everything bad was coursing through her voice and her body. Fear. Confusion. Anger. Sadness. Vulnerability. Protectiveness.

Smallness. So much smallness.

Without another pause, Rex scooped Asher up in his arms and yanked on Willow's rigid shoulder. But Willow refused to move her feet.

"NO! NO!" she yelled as Rex dragged her rigid body by the arm. It was so visceral, holding her arm out stiff like that. But her scrawny body was no match for Rex's strength. For Rex's bigness. So much bigness.

"Mom! Mom!" Willow yelled and yelled. The words scratched against her throat and they thrust themselves into the cold air.

"Get off me!" Willow howled as she tried thrashing her way out of her father's grip. "Get off me!" she howled again.

Rex had already forced his daughter into the back seat of the car and wrapped her in a seat belt. But Willow continued thrashing and yelling and yelling and thrashing. She tried ripping the seat belt her father had buckled around her straight from her chest. "Get off me!" she screeched again and again and again. She thrashed some more, and then yanked and yanked on the door handle that had been child-locked from the front seat.

"MOM!" Willow yelled again at the closed icy window.

But no one was answering her cries.

"MOM!" she yelled as forcefully as she could at the glass.

"MOM!" she yelled again, pushing her words as far as she could.

"MOMMYYYY!"

As Rex's car started to roll way, Willow saw her mother nonchalantly pressing her palm against the front door to open it.

"MOMMYYYY!" she yelled again, pressing her own hand into the cold glass.

She watched her mother slowly scan the scene out there on her driveway. She watched her mother slowly digest everything happening out there on top of her chalk drawings. She watched her mother try, but too slowly, to put all of the pieces together. And then she saw her mother's big brown eyes fill back up. With life. With terror. With rage. With horror.

Rosie met her daughter's big brown eyes, bulging with fear. She saw her daughter whipping her wild hair wildly around. She saw her daughter's seat belt tightening around her chest as she tossed her body back and forth. And then Rosie leaped to a run behind the moving car.

But Rosie was too late.

Willow turned around and pressed her hand on the cool glass of the back window again. She had finally become still as she watched her mother chase the car down the street. She watched her mother run and run and run until her legs gave out.

By the time they made it back to her father's house, Willow was depleted of her voice and her tears. And she fell asleep in her rigid bed at her father's house with the taste of emptiness on her sheets.

As Willow completed her checklist the next morning, not a word was mentioned about Rosie. Not a word was mentioned in the whole house at all. And Willow helped Asher with his hat and mittens, and then walked out of the big heavy door, and then walked down the winding driveway, and then boarded Bus #50 with nothing but her mother on her mind.

As soon as Willow took her spot behind the bus driver, she peeled the duct tape back on her seat and dug into the hole, willing a gift from her mother to be waiting in the depths of the green vinyl cave. And there it was. Two more Pixy Stix. Two tiny purple cylinders of relief. Two skinny purple tubes of love. Willow clutched the Pixy Stix close to her chest, and then placed them delicately into her backpack. She wanted them for recess. Yes, Pixy Stix and Prince and a word search and thoughts of Mom.

It would be okay.

And when Willow got to recess, she did what she always did. She ignored the rest of the kids in Robert Kansas Elementary School, running and swinging and playing and laughing. She ignored the rest of her classmates with the jungle gym and the slide and the soccer ball and the basketball hoop. She ignored the rest of her classmates with their friends. So many friends. Because the only things Willow ever had at recess were her CD player and her word search book. And it was usually enough to fill her head and heart. She had the sounds she loved. The sounds that reminded her of Mom's house. The sounds that reminded her of dancing around and dressing up and feeling happy. The sounds of feeling loved. And with those headphones, she could drown out all the other sounds of the playground. She could drown out all the other sounds as she scanned the page of her word search book. She would stare at the mess of letters until a word emerged.

But today when Willow leaned her back

against the brick exterior of Robert Kansas Elementary School with her legs stretched across the blacktop, she realized she didn't have her word search book. It was left in the entranceway at Mom's because she didn't have any time to pack when Dad came to steal her like that. And when she put her big purple headphones on and pressed Play on her CD player, no sounds came out. She twisted the cord of her headphone. She pressed the play button over and over and over again. She jammed her finger into it and shook it around. She turned the silver contraption over and saw the red "low battery" light blinking menacingly. There weren't going to be any sounds at all. Willow slammed the CD player onto the pavement. She slammed it again until it was in pieces. Until it was as shattered as she was.

Willow tore open her Pixy Stix and inhaled the purple crystals as her racing heart slammed against her chest. But she was still as sad and lonely and frustrated and confused as ever. There was a limit to what those Pixy Stix could do for a breaking and raging heart.

Willow closed her eyes and tried to slow her breathing. She loosened her jaw and tried to slow her mind. But she couldn't drown out the sounds of laughter whooshing by. The swishing of feet through the grass. The screeching of a bouncy ball on the pavement. And then, so clearly and loudly above all the other sounds, there was the soft scraping of chalk against the blacktop. The click of the chalk hitting the hardened asphalt, and then grating against it.

And as soon as she heard that familiar sound, Willow was so viscerally taken back to the moment she was drawing big purple letters on Mom's driveway yesterday. She could feel the granules on her fingertips. She could taste the powder on her tongue. And all of a sudden she was right back there on Mom's driveway with Dad's car roaring around the corner. With Dad pulling on her arm. With her seat belt pressing across her chest. With the car door refusing to open as she tried to get out. With Asher's big wobbling tears. With her words scratching against her throat. With Mom running down the street. With Mom's legs giving out on the street.

But before Willow could get her bearings, before she could come back to the reality that she was just sitting on the blacktop at school, Willow's fear had clawed its way back up her throat and made its way out of her mouth.

"GET OFF ME!" Willow screamed at no one.

"GET OFF ME!" Willow screamed as she sat there with her eyes closed, tossing her body back and forth.

"MOMMMMMYYYY," she shrieked.

"MOMMMMMYYYY," she shrieked and shrieked and shrieked on the blacktop of Robert Kansas Elementary School.

Willow flinched aggressively when she felt a hand on her shoulder. But when she opened her eyes, it was Mrs. McAllister. And a group of fifth graders were standing in front of her with their hands over their mouths in shock. And there was a pool of urine in Willow's purple leggings. As Mrs. McAllister walked Willow inside, the urine dripped down her legs and pooled around her socks. But all Willow could think about was getting to have pizza with Mom later that night. She ignored the warm urine and focused on her pizza. Yes, pizza would be good. It would be perfect. It would be like it always was. With soda and cheese teeth and cheese earrings and quarters for pinball.

And with thoughts of her evening with Mom, and when her legs had slipped into the fresh pair of purple leggings from her cubby, Willow's heart slowed to the same steady *tick, tick, tick* of the second hand of the clock in Mrs. McAllister's room. She watched as the second, and then minute, and then hour hand of the clocked moved to three forty. And when it did, Willow did the same thing she always did. Smiled a big full smile, went to get Asher from his classroom and waited for her mother at the pickup circle.

And for the first time Willow could remember, her mother and Lili Von were waiting right there as soon as she and Asher got outside. No waiting. No fear. Just Mom. Everything was already so, so much better.

And without an explanation of what happened outside the day prior, Rosie drove her children straight to Lanza Pizza after school. She even stayed on the proper side of the yellow lines in the road.

As they pushed through the glass door under the neon Pizza sign, Willow waved at John and Rosie shuffled to the counter to accept her crayons and three paper cups. But when Rosie walked over to the soda fountain and pressed her empty cup into the cream soda dispenser, nothing. Rosie aggressively whipped her head around to John behind the counter and sharply asked, "Where is it?"

"Oh, Rosie, we had to get rid of the cream soda. You were the only one who ever drank any!" John chuckled a bit with one hand over his overhanging belly, expecting an undoubtedly charming response from his most loyal patron.

"You're kidding me, right?" Rosie came back combatively.

As Rosie's words left her lips, Asher tugged on his mother's long skirt, and then held his cupped hands out for a roll of quarters.

Rosie looked down at her son with an unfamiliar crinkle in her upper lip. "Asher, I don't have any quarters. Go sit down."

"Oh, man!" Asher said as he dropped his shoulders and walked away.

Rosie immediately turned her attention back to John. "Seriously though. You're kidding, aren't you?"

John just looked at her. Perplexed at the response. Perplexed at the anger behind it. At the grumbling in her voice. Perplexed that Rosie Collins, whom he had known for so many years as a beautiful orb of pleasure, was so unpleasant.

Rosie whipped her head around a second time, now toward her two children, who were perched on their knees and sliding the salt and pepper shakers across the orange tables.

She grabbed her son and then her daughter by the hand and pulled them out the door by their arms, leaving their paper cups empty and the pepper shaker on its side.

"Mommy needs her cream soda," Rosie said as she walked her children hastily through the parking lot. Asher turned around and waved to John through the restaurant even though he was stumbling over his feet as Rosie dragged him across the asphalt.

That night, Willow and Asher got their pizza and Rosie got her cream soda. But it was a frozen cheese pizza with no toppings and they ate it while sitting on the couch in silence. And the cream soda was in cans, and they each sipped it quietly through a straw until Rosie announced that it was time for bed. And then Rosie dragged her feet up the stairs as her children followed behind her.

When they nearly reached the top of the staircase, Rosie lifted her knee lazily to complete the final step, but crumpled onto the carpet instead. Her small body hit the floor and her head followed quickly behind. And then Rosie's narrow limbs were in a twisted pile on the floor. Willow and Asher stopped and stared down at their mother. Afraid to move. Afraid not to move. Afraid to talk. Afraid to stay quiet.

But then Rosie untied every morsel of tension in the air when she picked her head up and laughed. She laughed and laughed so hard that she snorted. And that snort caused Asher to laugh, which caused Willow to laugh. And, just like old times, Willow and Asher and Rosie were in one big jumble of laughing on the floor. And in between clutching her elated tummy filled with giggles, Willow noticed that Mom had tears running down her cheeks. And there wasn't any way to tell whether these were happy tears or sad tears.

Willow fell asleep quickly that night to the resonant echoes of her mother's laughter in her mind.

But when she woke up the next morning, Willow saw blue walls instead of pink ones. And a wicker dresser instead of the wooden one she and her mother had doodled all over with Sharpie markers. And it didn't smell like Mom's or sound like Mom's either. Because it was her father's. Her father's sheets and blue walls and cold carpet. Willow turned out of bed and stumbled downstairs in a sleepy blur to find her father sitting sturdily by the kitchen table.

"I'm so glad you're home," Rex said to his daughter without blinking.

Yeah, right! Willow thought but didn't say as she poured herself a bowl of cereal.

Yeah, right that he was glad. He didn't even like her. How could he be glad she was home? And what did he mean by home, anyway? This wasn't home. Home was, would always be, at her mother's.

As Willow listened to the sound of her own crunching cereal, she wondered whether anyone would mention the kidnappings. Whether anyone would explain to her why they were happening. How many times she would expect to be at Mom's and end up at Dad's.

She wondered whether she was safe anywhere.

Safe for sleeping or for living.

Willow decided not to wash out her cereal bowl and put it in the dishwasher before leaving the house for school.

She was sick of her father's rules.

33

6 Months Ago

Rosie sat cross-legged on the floor of her closet with her head in her hands. She couldn't believe this was happening again. That she was finding her thin fingers wrapped around the handle of that drawer more times than she could count in the last few months.

It had been so good for so long. Until the last few months, Rosie had been certain that she was categorically out of her depression. And she had celebrated. She swept her children right up in her tornado of love in lockstep. She swept them right up in her tornado of love and paint and toys. Of candy and soda. Of crayons and dancing and singing. Of silly noises and costumes. Of sneaking her children out of school to go to the candy store. Of spontaneous trips to the beach to watch the sun take over the sky. Or to sink out of it. Her tornado of waking up in the middle of the night to gaze into the stars and make up stories about them. Her tornado of snuggling up in matching pajamas before bed. Of hugging and kissing and kissing and hugging. Of everything. So, so much of everything. She loved it. Loved everything.

But as it always did with Rosie, everything quickly became too much. And even though Rosie so thoroughly, deeply, maddeningly enjoyed seeing, and hearing, and smelling, and feeling, and loving as deeply as she could, here she was, fingers around the handle of that drawer, exhausted of everything.

Her life had too much candy, and soda, and paint, and toys. Too much dancing and singing. Too much Willow and too much Asher. Too many trips to the beach and waking up in the middle of the night. Too much snuggling and hugging and hugging and snuggling.

She had done all she could to hold those feelings off in the last few months. And at first it was really just a moment or two. A pill here. A pill there. An extra minute in the bathroom with the water running as she sat on the lid of the toilet and wept. A couple more pills. An extra five minutes in the shower rinsing her tired skin while her children watched a movie downstairs. A couple more pills. An extra hour in bed after she heard the first sounds of her daughter rustling in the kitchen downstairs. But as of late, it was bigger. So much bigger.

She found herself so relieved when she would drop her children off at Rex's on Sunday nights. She would return to her home, head still spinning, and do her best to let her bones sink into her couch. She needed to exhale after breathing all that life into her lungs. She needed to exhale so badly. But her body couldn't rest. And neither could her mind. Another handful of pills for that too.

Rosie was panicked there on the floor of her closet. Panicked at the thought of sliding too far down into another valley. It caused more energy, more feelings, more things to swirl around in her tired body and mind.

Rosie unlocked her grip and rocked herself back and forth. But the small white pills in the top drawer of her closet began to chirp. Rosie plugged her ears and breathed in and out and in and out. But she could still hear those pills so readily offering up their embrace. And she could still feel the sadness in her belly or her throat or her mind creeping in. And it only made those pills shout louder. Louder and louder and louder and louder and louder. And louder.

Until she yanked that drawer open and slipped one, and then another, and then another white tablet into her mouth. She cried full tears as she did it again. She cried full tears because Rosie knew what this meant for her children.

She had become unfit to parent. Unable to craft little notes to leave in Willow's lunch. Unable to swing Asher around by his arms. Unable to dance to *The Rocky Horror Picture Show.* Unable to meet Willow in the tree house. Unable to stay awake during word searches or *Blazing Saddles.* She hated it every time she fell asleep too early. Every time she didn't hug her children hello. Every time she didn't cook them dinner. Every time she couldn't allow the forces of her love to flow effortlessly out of her and wrap themselves around her children in the most beautiful perfect loving embrace.

But it all fell away as the tingling of the Vicodin slithered around in her blood.

34

All day long at Robert Kansas Elementary School, Willow dreaded returning to her father's house. Because no matter how sad or detached her mother had been for the last couple months, Dad had been all of those things but worse for years. He had been cold and mean when she wanted to watch her TV show and he said she could only watch for fifteen minutes. He was cold and mean when he slammed that vase on the fireplace. He was cold and mean when he dangled her favorite purple socks over his head on Sundays for The Box. And he had been cold and mean when he turned her lights off without giving her a kiss goodnight. And he had been cold and mean when he didn't notice Willow standing in his bedroom while he slammed his naked body into that naked woman. He had been cold and mean when he took her from Mom's without asking. He was cold and mean when she woke up this morning in her bed, and he hadn't told her how she got there. He was cold and mean when she left for school this morning without a word about Mom.

And Willow dreaded how cold and mean he would be when she got back home from school today.

But when Willow and Asher walked into the kitchen late that afternoon after school, Dad was wearing an apron and had bowls, and spices, and vegetables, and all sorts of pots and pans waiting on the counter. They were scattered awkwardly across the marble counter.

Asher stopped abruptly at the newness of the scene at his father's.

"Awe we gunna do SCIENCE?" he asked as his blue eyes darted around the countertop and his fingers swirled around the edges of the assorted bowls.

Rex stood in place in his unstained apron as his chef's hat sank over his forehead. Rex raised one of his thick eyebrows at his son.

"What?" Asher said, giggling a little bit. "It looks like an expewiment!"

"I thought we'd try cooking tonight, kiddos," Rex said as he forced a smile. "You know, have some fun. The farmer's market just opened for spring and I got us some veggies to cook with. What do you think? Should we give it a whirl?"

Now he was looking at Willow. Straight at her. His look begging her to say okay. Begging her to try. To try cooking with her father. To try forgiving him for what was happening. To try loving him. Willow had given those same begging eyes to her father before. While riding on her bicycle. While attempting to kick a soccer ball. While swirling her blue-ish purple-ish milk around in her cereal bowl. She knew what it was like to want love so badly that your eyes asked for it. She looked up at her father and let her eyes reply, *Okay, Dad.*

So Willow slid into the apron draped over the counter and let her father tie the strings around her back. Because Willow saw the same thing her brother did. This *was* an experiment. An experiment in bringing Rosie's kind of love into his home. An experiment in bringing the creative, exciting, free-flowing love Rosie brought to them all the time. An experiment designed to see if he could provide this kind of love for his children too. The kind of love he knew they liked. An experiment designed to see if Willow and Asher could absorb this kind of love from their father.

But out there on the table was Rex's kind

of experiment. With all of the ingredients so meticulously measured and placed into separate vessels. The cookbook open to the recipe page that had been recently highlighted. Everything so sterile and organized. But, when Willow noticed that Rex had taken the Don't Touch sign down from the side of the table, she decided to press a smile though her teeth and read the first step from the splayed-open cookbook on the other side of the counter.

And Rex guided Asher's hand as he placed already-chopped onions, and mushrooms, and peppers into a pan. And Willow mixed exactly two cups of ricotta cheese, and exactly two cups of mozzarella cheese and two large grade A eggs in a bowl. And they watched Rex meticulously layer pasta, and then cheese, and then vegetables, and then pasta, and then cheese on top of one another. He didn't want Willow and Asher messing up the ratios, he said. And then Rex placed the tray of lasagna into the oven and set the timer for exactly forty minutes.

Asher pressed his face against the oven for at least twenty of those minutes. And he licked his lips and made slurping noises while Rex quietly cleaned the dishes and Willow quietly set the table.

Willow hadn't known cooking could be so

structured. So serious. So silent. But for tonight, it beat her lonely word searches on her lonely beanbag chair.

And when the oven timer dinged, Asher held a fork up next to his face and stretched his eyes so wide. Rex tilted his head, looked straight at his son and tapped the final highlighted direction of the recipe three times.

"We have to let it cool for fifteen minutes, Ash. It says it right here."

Asher frowned dramatically, lowered the fork to his side and slumped over his plate.

And when exactly fifteen minutes passed, Rex sliced the lasagna into a perfect four-by-three grid and served each of his children the dinner they had made with their father.

"GWOSS!" Asher shouted and spit his mashed-up mush of pasta and cheese and vegetables from his mouth onto his plate. He marched over to the pantry and grabbed a bag of Parmesan Goldfish and shoveled its contents into his mouth.

Willow waited for Rex to shout. To force Asher to finish his dinner anyway. But he didn't. He just stared down at his plate and forked bite after bite of bland lasagna into his mouth. The pasta wasn't good.

All three of them knew it.

With a growling tummy, Willow jammed

her fork into her rectangular pile of lasagna and looked forward to the next Spaghetti Sunday.

When Spaghetti Sunday rolled around, Willow had to face the truth of what was in front of her. Because up until now, the formidable wall of denial she had built was so high Willow almost couldn't see over it. But tonight, her mother's emptiness stared her right in the face over several cartons of uneaten Lo Mein from the Chinese takeout place around the corner.

Earlier in the evening, unprompted, Willow had donned her favorite apron and helped Asher into his. They raced each other upstairs, bumping elbows and laughing the whole way up to get their mother.

"Spaaaaaaghetti time!" Asher shouted when he reached Mom's door. But the door was shut. Again. Willow tried twisting the knob but it stuck rigidly in its place. Again.

"I ordered Chinese," Rosie forced out from the other side of the door. But she spoke straight from her throat, too tired to put any diaphragm behind words. "It should be here soon. Go play. I'll meet you down there in a minute."

Asher nonchalantly slid down the railing but Willow lingered. She pressed her ear to the door. She couldn't decipher any sounds but she could feel her mother's tears saturating the air. She could feel the damp depression of the room behind the closed door. It had happened. The fear had its way with her heart. And now, in front of that closed door, Willow's heart was torn in shreds by the claws that had been progressively sinking themselves deeper and deeper into her.

Rosie joined her children at the table for dinner, but only in body. She swirled her soy sauce around with a chopstick as she leaned her head on her arm. There was nothing left of the mother she used to be inside of her.

Asher stuck his face into a pile of white rice and sat back up with several grains stuck to his face. "Rice fweckles!" he shouted, revealing his big tooth gap. Willow looked over at her mother. This was the kind of thing Mom loved. Used to love. The kind of thing she would laugh about, and then replicate on her own face. The kind of thing she would do every subsequent time rice was put in front of her.

But Rosie didn't react at all. Even Willow could see there wasn't a thing in this world that could bring a smile to her face.

And without intending to, Willow absorbed her mother's sadness from across the table. And she sat there in her seat at the kitchen table as her mother pushed a single grain of rice from one edge of her plate to the other. Over and over and over again. Over and over and over again until she went upstairs and slipped under her empty sheets.

Willow fell asleep in her bed slowly and in tears but woke up suddenly to the clicking of the first rain of spring on her roof. She felt her full bladder pressing against her belly. “Don’t go,” Willow pleaded with herself audibly as she felt her bladder swell. “Please don’t go.” But before the fear of the storm was going to cause Willow to wet the bed again, she unraveled herself from her covers and ran to her mother’s room. The purple glasses would help. She burst through the door to Mom’s bedroom. But her mother’s bed was empty and uncharacteristically stiff. The sheets were still ruffled and the pillows were still scattered, but there were no signs that a body had been curled up in there. And the pillow had no indent to indicate a head had been pressed into it. It was all so firm and cold. So unlike the bed that Willow had tucked herself into next to her mother so many times. But at the sound of another wave of rain drumming on the roof, Willow wrapped herself in Mom's taut sheets and squeezed her eyelids shut. Even though she was alone in there.

Thoughts began to orbit and then swirl so fast Willow was dizzy with it. Dizzy with the knowledge that things were never going to be the same with her mother.

I need those glasses.

I need Mom.

I need those glasses.

I need something.

From anyone.

Something.

Anyone.

Something.

Anyone.

I need those glasses.

I need Mom.

I need those glasses.

I need something.

From anyone.

Something.

Anyone.

Willow's bladder pulsed again as she lay frozen in her bed, afraid that any movement might shake the urine loose. "Don't go," Willow said to herself, now more forcefully. "Please don't go." And thoughts of her mother continued to swirl all around until she fell back asleep.

But before she even drifted into another dream of her mother the way she used to be, Willow half woke up to a pair of strong hands sliding gently underneath her back. She forced one eyelid open a crack. It was her father. Curling her up in his arms. Draping her wrists over his shoulders and around his neck. Pressing her cheek into his chest. Willow's body was still heavy with sleep and she let her dad carry every ounce of her weight. Her torso bounced up and down with the steady cadence of her father's steps.

From Rosie's bedroom doorway to his car in the driveway, Rex carried Willow so gently and so lovingly. And for that same distance, Willow allowed herself to be carried. Feeling that gentleness. Feeling that love.

As Rex placed her delicately in the back of his car, Willow felt her father's lips on the top of her head. A little kiss. A little, gentle, loving kiss. Willow smiled and drifted right back into sleep with her seat belt resting on her chest and her head on the warm leather of the car seat.

35

Three Months Ago

Nothing special had happened the day that Rosie decided that she wanted to start over. But she made a decision that she wanted to be the old Rosie. The old Rosie with Willow and Asher next to her.

And she made a plan for doing it that did not include this house or Rex or anything in Virginia. A plan that would take her back to that apartment in Manhattan where she was once so happy. Where she felt love in Rex's arms. Where she felt love with Willow in her belly. Where she envisioned what her family would look like. Where she hung that locket on the wall and expected to be that happy forever.

Rosie was so excited about her thought, so resolute in making it real, that she drove straight to Robert Kansas Elementary School to share it with her daughter. To tell Willow all about the new life they would have. Rosie would finally use that key to 299 East 82nd Street. The one that Rex left on her bedside table years ago. That key Rex left beside her in her saddest moment. That key that promised happier times again once she had the courage to start over.

But when Rosie saw her daughter's wobbly legs running toward her through the backyard of the school, Rosie's insides churned and her resolve broke. She knew the old Rosie was gone. She knew she could never make it back to 299 East 82nd Street no matter how much she wanted to. She knew it even as she once again led Willow up into the branches of that willow tree and told her daughter she would take her with her to that apartment. She couldn't stop her words from flowing out of her body and into Willow. She couldn't stop wanting it to be true. Willing it and saying it and saying it and willing it. She wished everything she said would just stay there up in that tree with her daughter. That she could keep Willow and those words hidden by the cold leaves.

Rosie knew that her fantasy was irresponsible. And she knew that sharing her fantasy with her young daughter was even more irresponsible. But she ached for the Rosie in that fantasy. She ached for it in her blood.

In her marrow. And saying it out loud breathed life into it. Infused it with attainability. But the whole fantasy was just that, a fantasy. No matter how terribly irresponsible it was to say those things to her daughter, it still warmed her heart to share them with Willow in that tree.

It still warmed her heart when her daughter believed in it. When her daughter believed in her. When her daughter wanted to go with her. When her daughter listened to her and hugged her and told her she loved being up there with her mother.

Rosie knew she shouldn't have said those things, but she wanted another chance at effervescence. She wanted another chance at immortality. And even if her spirit might not be recovered in this world, it could still be celebrated by Willow somehow, somewhere.

But by the time Rosie got back home a couple hours later, her fantasy turned into guilt. And that guilt turned into another three white pills sliding down her throat even though there was only another hour until she had to pick up her children from school at the end of their day. And once the Vicodin was coursing through her blood, her fuzzy mind couldn't stop her from driving all the way up onto the curb of Robert

Kansas Elementary School.

She knew it was all so bad. She knew she was spinning out of control.

The next day, while she waited quietly at home before picking her kids up from Rex's house, Rosie promised herself that she would never again drive high. Especially if her children were in the car. And she promised herself that she would never parent while she was high. And she pulled herself off the couch and marched upstairs with the intention of flushing every last white pill down the toilet.

She opened the top drawer in her closet, twisted the cap off the translucent orange tube and dumped a handful of pills into her palm. She balled her fist so tightly, so intently around them, and walked into her bathroom toward the toilet. She balled her hands so tightly in her hatred of those little white pills. Her hatred of the damage they had caused her. To the damage they had caused her marriage and her husband. The damage they had already caused her children.

But on the way, she caught herself in the mirror and looked straight into her own eyes. Straight into her tired, vacant eyes.

And then she watched those tired vacant eyes fill up with tears as she dropped four white pills into her mouth. She fell into her bed and let the tingly high overtake her arms, and then her legs, and then her fingertips, and then her eyelids. And then she stood up, pulled her feet across the carpet of her bedroom and then across the wood flooring of the staircase, and then the asphalt of the driveway, and got into her car.

Even though she was stoned.

Even though she promised herself she wouldn't do this.

Even though she wished none of this was happening.

Rosie drove to Rex's house to pick up her children.

Rex had already made sure that Willow and Asher had packed everything they needed for their mother's house when Rosie pulled into his driveway and honked the horn twice.

"Be good for Mom," Rex said as he let his children out the front door, all the while quietly hoping that their mom was going to be good for them.

Rex expected Rosie to give him the coy wave from the front seat she always did. He expected her to tip her oversize sunglasses down onto the tip of her nose and say, "Hey, Rex." He expected her to get out of the car and hug her children. He expected her to get her red lipstick all over their cheeks when she kissed them hello. He expected her to take their bags and toss them casually into the trunk and drive away with Prince vibrating through the speakers.

As Willow and Asher maneuvered themselves into the back of Rosie's car, Rex's insides twisted and his face started tingling. Something wasn't right here. Something wasn't right with Rosie.

He watched Willow tug the heavy door twice before she was able to get it to close. And then Rosie began to drive away. And as she did, one tire rolled onto the cobblestone edging that lined the driveway before the car swerved back onto the pavement.

Rex knew exactly what it meant when he saw his ex-wife's car moving like that. He knew how Rosie talked, and walked, and sounded, and drove when she was high on those little white pills. And this was it. This was exactly it.

Rex's chest tightened and he lost his breath. His ears got hot and his fingers tingled. His jaw tensed and his spine straightened. The divorce had already brought so much anger, so much sadness into Rex's body. But the sight of Rosie driving stoned with his children in the car filled him with a fiery rage. It burned through his whole entire being.

He would do anything to keep his children from drowning in Rosie's wake. From suffering one more ounce. He would do anything at all. Anything at all to save them.

And for Rex, anything at all meant brute force. Of body and soul and will.

36

As Willow opened her eyes, she was comforted by the idea that she knew what she would see. Those blue walls. That wicker dresser. The gray lattice carpet. The set of lacy throw pillows on the floor next to the bed.

But today, when Willow's eyelids separated and she inhaled the morning, all of her senses filled with something new. There was an unfamiliar airiness around her. There were pale yellow walls and light wood floors. There was a light salty breeze rattling the old windowpanes. There were thin white curtains undulating freely in the wind.

Willow rubbed her eyes in an effort to bring some clarity to the scene. But those yellow walls, that salty taste in the air, that creaky wooden bed. They were all still there. She peeked her head out the window and saw ocean. Blue, swirling, rhythmic ocean. Willow made her way down the thin staircase cautiously. Her left knee buckled and she tightened her grip on the wooden railing.

There was Dad, posed at the kitchen table with his steaming coffee. Right leg crossed over left in a nearly familiar scene. But as Willow scanned the room, all the differences revealed themselves immediately. There was already the breeziness and the lightness of the walls. But there was also a pile of eggs and a game of Candy Land poised to be played on the kitchen table too. Willow rubbed her tired eyes again and when she lifted her hands, Asher had already popped his head out from underneath the table.

"Finally!" he shouted, shoveled a forkful of eggs into his mouth and moved the plastic orange Candy Land figure to its starting position block. Willow took a seat at the table and looked at her father, and then at Asher, and then at her father, and then, without any questions, moved a purple plastic figure next to Asher's and slipped into this new kind of morning with Dad. This new kind of Wednesday morning with Dad in a T-shirt and breakfast on the table. With board games and open windows. With the April air swirling around her. With the sound of waves tumbling onto the sand.

There were questions Willow almost

wanted to ask. *Where are we? How did we get here? Why are we here? Are we going to school? Where is Mom? How long will we stay here?*

But as she pulled her first card from the stack in the middle of the game board, she let those questions slip out to sea with the receding tide she could see from the kitchen window. Willow didn't want the moment to unravel. And there was a sense that the lightest tug on any loose string could unwind this precariously woven but beautiful moment her father had crafted.

The three of them turned over game cards and counted spaces until Asher made it to the Candy Castle at the end of the board. And all the way along, they giggled over setbacks and fortuitous color jumps. Over Gramma Nutt and her peanut brittle house. Over Lord Licorice and his sharp chin. Over Mr. Mint and his candy cane legs.

And Rex and Willow and Asher all swirled around in their laughter and happiness. They allowed themselves to be enveloped in each other's laughter and happiness. They allowed themselves to stay so present in it. And when the game was over, and it was about to get quiet, Dad kept the fun flowing. Kept the love flowing.

"Want to head down to the beach?" he

asked casually and hopefully. "It's usually just warm enough in April."

Willow nodded her head and her wild hair bobbed around. Asher exposed the big gap in his teeth with a full smile.

But then Willow's chin sank down. "But I didn't bring a bathing suit," Willow said to her father. He was always disappointed when they weren't prepared.

But today was different.

"I got 'em right here for both of you," Rex told his daughter. And Willow noticed how her father's chest puffed out at these words. She noticed how his chest puffed out at what fatherhood could also look like if he were just a little bit less demanding of structure and perfection. If he were just a little bit more open to fun. A little bit more willing to love freely.

Asher and Willow cheered and dived into their bathing suits and then the ocean. The water still had some of its winter chill in it, but it felt so good as it first shocked, and then soothed Willow's skin. There was splashing and diving and toes covered in sand. There were boogie boards and breath-holding contests and cartwheels. There was fun. Unadulterated wholesome all-consuming fun.

And when Willow and Asher had wrinkled

fingertips and salty hair, Rex held one towel open at a time and wrapped his son and then his daughter in the warm cotton. They shuffled through the sand back to the house, pulling one foot in front of the other. And when they reached the blue wooden door with the chipped paint, both Willow's and Asher's feet were caked in sand.

Rex stood by the door and stared down at his children's toes. Willow looked up at her father and waited for his instructions to clean off her feet before coming inside and messing the carpet. But instead, her father pressed gently on her shoulders until Willow was sitting down on the front steps, and then bent down and used a wet towel to wipe the sand from Willow's feet. He held her ankle and patted around gently until her feet were clean. He did it with such focus and such precision. They were traits that Willow had always seen in her father, but she had never felt the love behind them. But here, outside this house at the beach, she saw how Dad could take care of her. How he could be gentle. And warm. And caring. And kind. She saw how he could get sandy toes so clean.

And when there wasn't a single grain of sand left on Willow's toes, Rex pressed his daughter's feet together and kissed them decidedly. And when Rex picked up his head, he and his daughter locked eyes. And just for that instant, they locked hearts too.

And for this day, and six more days at this house at the beach, Willow, Asher and Rex created a new and magical world. Here at this house at the beach, Asher didn't spill anything or forget to tie his shoes. And Willow didn't stumble or wet the bed. And Rex didn't yell into his phone or ask his children to keep quiet.

Instead, here at this house at the beach, it was seven full days of ocean and beach and corn on the cob. Of sand castles and spotted handstands. Of board games and sea glass. Of sweatshirts on the top and towels wrapped around the bottom.

They were all a new version of themselves in that old house breathing in the salty air. And on the drive away from the beach, it was impossible to say whether Willow or Asher or Rex could live as their new selves back at home. But for at least these seven days, each of them could have almost envisioned the three of them living happily ever after.

37

1 Month Ago

Rex's organs twisted and gushed as he picked up the phone to call his ex-wife. To call her and tell her that it had to stop. To call her and tell her that she had to stop. To tell her that he wouldn't let her around their children when she was like this. Stoned like this.

It broke his heart to think of Rosie without her children. Her children without their mother. But this wasn't their mother.

Rex said these things to Rosie as gently and kindly as he could.

"When they're in my world, I get to make the rules," Rosie came back sharply before Rex could even finish his plea. But there was an airiness, a detachment, in her voice that Rex didn't recognize. Rex had seen Rosie frazzled, even untethered, a few times in their relationship. And she had been frazzled and untethered in precisely the way she had been in every other facet of her life. Wholly and fully. But not now. Not in these words. Not in this new state. She sounded so far away.

"Rosie, your rules don't get to be that there are no rules. It's not fair to them," Rex said as gently as he could. But his disappointment, his desperation, his exasperation was thinly veiled.

There was silence on both ends.

"It's just not fair, Rosie. You need to do better here. You need to, Rosie."

More silence.

"You just need to."

Rex said it, urged it, with all of the kindness he could muster.

And then Rosie moved so quickly to tears.

"I love them, Rex. I love them so much."

All Rosie's anguish, and sorrow, and hopelessness was pouring out of her eyes and straight through the phone. Her suffering coursed through his veins and clung to his heart.

And then his ex-wife asked so simply, so innocently, so naively, "Isn't that enough?"

And then Rosie fell into full sobs.

"Why can't it be enough?"

And then Rex, invoking all the love he still had for Rosie, said something so plain, and so true. But so difficult.

"No, baby. It's not enough. You need help, Rosie," Rex stated calmly, plainly and warmly. "But it needs to come from you. You need to get yourself help."

There was a moment of thick, sticky silence.

"Okay? Can you do that, Rosie?" Rex said into the phone.

He held his ear to the phone. And then, through breathless whimpers, Rosie said, "I need some time away from it all. I'm sorry."

When Rex opened his mouth to ask what it meant, there was just an empty dial tone on the other end of the phone. He hoped his plea had been enough.

"I'm sorry too," he said into the empty telephone.

As Rosie pressed the phone into the receiver, she knew everything that her ex-husband just said was true. She could taste it in her tears and feel it in her heart. Because, for months now, sadness had been seeping out of her every pore. In every moment of every day.

And it was relentless.

And it spilled all over everyone and everything around her.

And it was too much for her babies to soak up. She knew they had already become saturated with her sadness. Especially Willow. And Rex was right, it wasn't fair at all. She had to be better. But she couldn't be better.

Because early in her sadness, Rosie had the sense that it could dry up. That if she cried enough tears, released enough pain, that eventually there might be none left. So she would allow herself days and days crying in her room. Sometimes within moments of Willow and Asher smiling at her feet, she would poise herself for happiness. She would dry her eyes and try to put on some red lipstick. She would pull out a sparkly vest or play "Little Red Corvette" as loudly as her speakers would go. But no matter what, it was always straight back to sadness. Straight back to listlessness.

Rosie knew, and so did her children, that her sadness was an endless repository. Her sadness rose up in her faster than she could pour it out. And the more that sadness flowed out of her, the more sadness had filled up inside of her. She was drowning in it. And her kids were too.

The more she felt sad, the more she retreated to her room. And the more she retreated to her room, the more Vicodin pills she swallowed. And the more Vicodin pills she swallowed, the more guilt she felt. And the more guilt she felt, the more she felt sad. And the more she felt sad, the more she retreated to her room.

Rosie knew Rex was right. She needed help. She needed it if she wanted to survive.

So as she admitted herself to Clareton Rehab Center, she thought about the vicissitudes of her whole life. With those little white pills and everything else. She wanted to rid herself of them.

And in meeting after meeting, counseling session after counseling session, she described how there was so much love and then none of it. So much life and then none of it. How she had already hurt Rex so badly with her ups and downs. How she couldn't bear the idea of hurting her children with it too. How she couldn't keep filling up her children with love, and then draining them of it. How she couldn't keep allowing them to absorb her love. And then her sadness. And then her love again. And then her sadness again. It would hurt them too much.

She explained that she never intended for it to happen that way, but it did. That she saw the future for her children in which she filled them with love, and then wrung them out with sadness over and over and over again. That it was so unfair to them. So, so unfair. Mothers were supposed to mitigate their children's ups and downs. Not cause them.

She asked, begged, for help getting rid of the ups and downs. But it was right there at Clareton Rehab Center, in meeting after meeting, and counseling session after counseling session, that she realized she would always be this way. She wished she wasn't but she was.

She wished she hadn't spent her whole life loving something, and then hating it. Wearing it every Saturday night and then letting it sit in the back of her closet. Eating it every day for lunch and then never again. Going there every afternoon and then, all of a sudden one day, avoiding it entirely. Loving Rex so much, and then withdrawing from him. Filling Willow and Asher with her life, and then wringing them dry.

She wished she had never tried those pills. She wished she had never had those pills again. She wished she'd had the strength to move back to New York. She wished she had never had those pills again. She wished she could resist the temptation to contact the dealer who made it so easy to buy more pills whenever she thought she had resolved to stop. Again and again and again.

Rosie wished she could take her whole life

back so that she could be a better mother now.

She wished she could be helped. But all of this was just part of the pattern. A pattern of being away at rehab or stoned behind a locked bedroom door. Over, and over again. A hopeless pattern of up and down and up and down. In and out of pills. In and out of happiness. In and out of rehab.

Her children needed to be loved in a way that was steady. Steady and sustainable. Her children needed to be loved in a way that was better than the way she could love. They needed to be loved by Rex. And Rex alone. She felt an overwhelming certainty that Rex was with Willow and Asher now. Protecting them, caring for them. Bringing them happiness. What a relief it must be for her children to find that peace without her.

Rosie knew she needed to be out of this terrible cycle.

She knew all these things as simple truths.

And so Rosie stood up with more energy, more conviction, than she had stood up with in months. And she walked out of Clareton Rehab Center. And straight back to her bedroom.

38

When Willow and Asher got back from the beach and returned to their mother's house, it was mostly quiet all the time. Sometimes there was the clanking of spoons in cereal bowls. And sometimes there was Asher accidentally knocking a wave of cookies out of the box. And sometimes there was Willow bracing herself against the wall after a stumble. But it was mostly just quiet.

As Asher played with his action figures underneath the breakfast table, Willow looked around at her quiet world. At the quiet kitchen. The quiet kitchen without her mom in it.

It had never looked messy in here to Willow before, but it did now. The cabinet doors were left open. There were empty cartons on the counters. There was a lazily tied garbage bag tilting over in the middle of the floor. There were stains on the tiles and dirty plates stacked in the sink.

It was all a big mess here.

In the kitchen and everywhere else.

Willow reached into the cookie jar where lunch money was usually kept, but it was empty. So she spread peanut butter and jelly over white bread for both herself and Asher. She wrapped tinfoil around the sandwiches and placed them into brown paper bags. And then called out for Mom.

"Mommy!" Willow shouted from the bottom of the stairs, gently requesting for her mother to come down and bring them to school.

"Moooooommmmmyyyy!" Asher joined through a giggle. Asher bounced his knees and hollered from the bottom of the stairs toward the second floor.

But Willow knew her mother wasn't going to come down.

"Stay here," Willow told Asher and walked slowly up the stairs, holding the railing the entire way.

Mom's door was closed, but Willow turned the knob anyway. The gold handle stayed in place. Again.

"Mommy?" Willow whispered to her mother with her mouth on the door.

She wasn't sure if the sound would move through it, but she sensed a need for quiet.

"Mommy, are you in there?"

More quiet.

"If you're there, please come out."

Willow closed her eyes and willed it to happen. She willed her mother to open the door with her Elton John T-shirt and red lipstick on. Ready for fun. Ready for love. Ready to bring her and her brother to school. Willow willed it with every fiber in her body. She willed it from the bottoms of her unreliable feet to her longest twisting curl.

Willow turned her head to put her ear against the door. And although she heard nothing, she knew her mother was in there. She could feel her breathing. Breathing amongst her tangled sheets.

Willow could have banged on the door or jerked on the knob or yelled louder, but she didn't. There was a solemnity in the air. A quiet calm. Eye of the storm calm.

Willow turned around, went downstairs, grabbed her brother's hand, and they walked to school.

39

Rosie heard her daughter's jagged footsteps approaching her door. "Mommy," Willow whispered innocently.

"Mommy, are you in there?" she heard her daughter say, but Rosie couldn't bring herself to respond.

"If you're there, please come out," Willow continued so gently.

It was breaking Rosie's heart picturing Willow outside her locked door in her purple leggings. It twisted her insides picturing Willow with her ear against the door with her wild hair and backpack full of CDs. It suffocated her heart picturing Asher downstairs bouncing up and down with his backpack already on.

But still, Rosie remained immobile. Immobile and entwined in the sheets of her bed. She lay still in her bed until she heard her daughter shuffle away.

When Rosie heard the front door squeak

closed behind her children, she felt ready for the pain of her failure as a mother to stop.

She felt ready to give Willow and Asher the steady, better love they deserved. The good, whole, love she knew Rex could give to them. Because Rex was smart and true and kind when it mattered. He was disciplined and determined. He was thoughtful and willing. And he was all of those things all the time.

Rosie knew she had stolen his children's love with her candy and effervescence. With her singing and splatter paint. But she wanted to give it back. She wanted to give it back to the man who could love his children the way they needed to be loved. Wholly and steadily. Responsibly and with stability.

Rosie grabbed a purple pen from next to her and in neat rounded cursive, Rosie wrote a note for the three people in the world she loved most.

My Willow. My Asher. And also my Rex.
I love you oodles and oodles and noodle poodles.
I am sorry for all of it.

— Mom

And with this note resting on her bedside table, Rosie let an avalanche of pills slide from her hand into her mouth.

She swallowed the pills — and then they swallowed her.

There was a moment of calm before all her muscles contracted.

Rosie let out a delicate gasp that no one was there to hear.

And she did it as all the love in her heart — past and present — released into the universe.

40

After school, Willow and Asher waited and waited for their mother on the curb of the pickup circle. Again. Willow did her word searches and Asher hopped around the pavement trying not to touch any cracks. Again.

Aside from the sporadic squeak of Asher's shoes against the blacktop, the school had already gone quiet for almost an hour when Rex pulled up in his sleek, black car. Again.

A sense of fear bubbled up in Willow. Her body still tensed at the sight of her father's car. At the thought of being forced into it. At the image of her mother running hopelessly down the street behind it. How it had been so hard to breathe in that car. With her seat belt pressing against her chest and her heart twisting behind ribs and her lungs trying to keep up with her tears.

When Willow saw her father through the closed front window of the car at the pickup circle, she was finding it hard to breathe all over again.

Willow waited for her father to roll down the window and tell her to "Get in." But instead he just stared vacantly out the windshield. It was a look she didn't recognize in him. And between that empty gaze and the pallor in his cheeks, something felt wrong. Something felt bad.

Asher hopped into the car as Willow dragged herself into the back seat. Asher buckled his seat belt and activated his light-up sneakers by knocking them together, and then so casually asked, "Whewe's Mom?"

Willow straightened in her seat and prepared for her father's response.

But Rex didn't say a word as he focused only on the yellow lines of the road being swallowed up by the front of the car.

The silence had become thick and viscous, but Willow waded through it.

"Yeah," she said. "Where's Mom?"

But still, Rex couldn't bring himself to respond.

And there was just more silence. More thick, sticky, gooey, heavy silence.

But Willow couldn't stand how that silence clung so heavily to her skin. How it seeped down into it and oozed over her ribs. How it engulfed her lungs and then her heart until once again, she couldn't breathe.

She needed an answer. She needed an explanation. She needed words. She needed sounds. If that thick silence stayed in her lungs any longer, she was going to suffocate. If that viscid silence surrounded her heart any longer, it was going to stop beating.

"Dad," Willow said sternly, "I asked you where Mom was."

Willow pressed her palms into the leather seat. She demanded him to answer her. She willed her father to answer her. She willed it and willed it until he did.

"She's not coming," Rex said, and then paused. "She's dead."

The whole world did one whole spin, and then everything stopped.

And then, just like that, the silence returned. The sticky, gooey silence. The heavy, viscous, unapproachable silence. And just like she thought might happen, Willow's lungs stopped taking in oxygen and her heart stopped beating as she sat there drowning in silence.

Drowning in sadness. Drowning in sorrow.

Willow reached over and squeezed Asher's hand without looking. They both cried silently, still buckled up in the back seat of their father's silent car.

No noise. No eye contact.

No love. No warmth.

No permission to mourn.

41

The days following Rosie's death were a hazy blur for Willow. A solitary, aching, hazy blur. It had twisted Willow's insides to see her mother without lipstick. To see her mother without ideas. Without energy. To find her asleep when she wanted to watch a movie or play her word searches or have her arm tickled. It had twisted Willow's insides to look at her mother and see a ghost. To see a body but not see anything real or true inside of it.

But, as Willow lay in her bed at her Dad's house, the physical loss of her mother was excruciating. Because up until now, there was still a shell there for Willow to wrap her body around. To wrap her mind and heart around. To curl up next to and feel against her chest and arms and legs. But now there was nothing. Just hollow crevices and throbbing bones. Just holes and empty spaces.

And even though it was emptiness, the

weight of it was profound. It sat on her chest and constricted her throat. It pressed against her ribs and stiffened her shoulders.

She felt it at school and at Dad's house. At her lunch table and her kitchen table. In her bedroom and in the classroom. She felt it when the sun rose and when the sun set. She felt it everywhere. In everything. Inside Willow's body and outside in the world around her.

Everywhere.

All the time.

All the time.

Everywhere.

But still, nighttime was the hardest time.

Willow would lie in bed with her knees tucked up toward her chest. She would press her ear into the sheets of her bed and hold a pillow over her mouth to muffle the sound of her crying. She couldn't bear the sounds of her own sadness.

But no matter how badly she wanted the tears to stop, they poured out of her in relentless waves. They dripped and then spilled and then poured and then gushed out of her in the darkness of her bedroom. Her chest expanded smoothly, and then contracted with short, choppy, syncopated exhales. And then there was more and then more dripping, spilling, pouring, gushing tears.

Willow would wake up in the morning, not remembering how she'd managed to fall asleep, and drag her feet downstairs with a face salty with dried tears.

Rex would be sitting there with his coffee like he always was. And he would turn his neck around at the sound of his daughter dragging her feet across the kitchen. And then he would look at her. Look through her.

And when Willow would meet his eyes, her emptiness and loneliness would wash over her once again.

What would it be like to live with Dad? All the time. With everything bad.

What would it be like to live without Mom? Without love. Without everything good.

She asked herself these questions over and over and over again.

42

Rex thought that the worst day of his life had already happened the day he got the call and learned that Rosie had died, but today at the funeral it was so much worse. The sea of black clothes. All of the tears and choppy exhales. All of the hugging and mourning and hearts broken for Rosie. All of the hearts breaking for Willow and Asher too.

Rex was dizzy with it.

He thought of his children as Rosie's friends — so many of Rosie's friends — walked up in pairs of two, arms tightly linked, toward her casket. As they bent over and kissed Rosie's lifeless cheek. As they ran their hands across her still-curled bangs. As they stood over her body and wept.

Rex was dizzy with that too.

He took three short strides toward Rosie's casket, and didn't know if he could make it all the way. He didn't know if he could see her body that used to be full of life, so empty of all of it.

He felt a gentle hand on his back and continued toward the mother of his children. He traced his finger along the smooth mahogany of the casket and looked at Rosie. Pure, tortured Rosie. He stared at her eyelids and willed them to open. To open and end all of the hurt in the room. To open and look back at him. To open and tell him how to be a father to his children. How to be a mother *and* a father to his children. How to be better. But there was only stillness. So much stillness. So much harsh and rigid stillness.

As Rex stood there and looked over Rosie, he remembered how he used to wish that Rosie could find stillness. That she could stop twirling and vibrating and just be. And there Rosie was, still at last. It broke his heart.

As he turned away to return to his seat, he wished that he had someone waiting there to hug him. He inadvertently wished that that someone was Rosie. And then he wished for Willow and Asher. He wished he could wrap himself around Willow's small bones and big hair. He wished he could find calm in Asher's red cheeks and big eyes. He wondered if his children could hold him up.

But then he was reminded why they weren't there. He didn't want Willow and Asher to have to see their mother lifeless like that. He didn't want them to see someone who was once so warm and full of life, so cold and lifeless. Someone who was once so alive, so dead. So blatantly, crushingly, oppressively dead. He didn't want them to have that terrible image to carry around in their little minds.

He didn't want them to see their father with red eyes or weak knees. He didn't want them to see their father so powerless.

He didn't want them to see and feel again all the things they already knew they lost.

Instead, he called Roy and asked if he could come down from New York and stay with Willow and Asher. And Roy said he would without a question.

Rex thought he knew what he was doing. He thought he was doing the right thing.

43

When Willow woke up and walked downstairs to find Roy on the couch, she knew it was an unusual day. "Hey, Willow," he said casually, but with a tension in his shoulders. "Your dad asked me to watch you and Asher while he was out."

"Oh," Willow responded with an equally forced levity, and then went to find Asher playing in the next room.

"Where do you think Dad went?" she asked her brother, knowing he wouldn't know either, but might be able to comfort her anyway.

"Pwobably just to get us a toy," Asher responded, not looking up from his action figures. And Willow smiled.

But when a few hours later Rex pressed through the big heavy front door of the house wearing a black pin-striped suit with a silk black tie, Willow confirmed the day was unusual indeed. Rex never wore a suit and tie on the weekends. And what was Roy doing here from New York, anyway?

Willow watched as her father walked directly into his office with his chin on his chest and eyes tracing the floor. And then she watched Roy follow him in there with a comforting hand on his shoulder.

Willow followed a few steps behind them and pressed her ear against the sliding office door.

"Roy. It was awful. The whole thing was fucking awful."

"I'm so sorry, Rex. I am so sorry."

"I don't even know how to talk about it . . . All of these people — all young like us — crying and holding each other. A funeral for a thirty-six-year-old woman is a tough thing. That's something you don't ever expect to experience . . . I wish I didn't have to see it, live it. It was awful. Rosie, the love of my life. My ex-wife. The mother of my children. The mother of my children, Roy. Dead at thirty-six."

A brief pause. Willow couldn't see it but imagined Rex was cradling his own head with his hand.

"Holy shit, Roy. I can't believe it. I really can't."

Another moment of quiet.

"Thank you for coming down and watching the kids," her father said through a tight throat. "Thank you for just being here."

Willow imagined Roy standing over him with that same hand on his shoulder.

"Of course, buddy," Roy responded.

What Willow had heard was entirely and viscerally maddening.

Her father had neglected to tell her and Asher about their mother's funeral. It was her mother. Her mother's funeral. She wanted to be there. She deserved to be there. She needed it.

Willow found her hands shaking and her head spinning. She felt heat in her ears and pressure in her throat. And then all of a sudden, her crotch was wet and warm. She stood outside her father's office with urine sliding down her legs until it was absorbed by her socks.

She wanted to be there to say goodbye to her mother.

She wanted to see her with her red lips one more time. Even if they were attached to a cold and rigid body and lying in a casket.

Even if she looked nothing like, felt nothing like, the mom she remembered.

44

Rex told Willow and Asher they could stay home from school for two weeks after Rosie died. And then he told his children that it would be best if they could "return to normalcy."

But this explanation meant nothing to neither Willow nor Asher. For Asher, *normalcy* was a word that had not yet entered his vocabulary. And when Rex looked at Asher for a reaction, Asher just smiled his genuine and toothless smile and continued banging his action figures against one another. And for Willow, normalcy was not something she could return to. She had never been normal, and neither had the world around her. She had never even aspired to normal.

Rex looked at Willow for a reaction, but she just whipped her body around and walked away. He didn't understand her. Not at all. Not before and definitely not now.

When the two weeks were over and Rex dropped his children off at school that morning, Willow could see the awkwardness in the air all around her. She knew everyone had heard the news about her mother. She knew everyone was talking about the news behind cupped hands in the hallways.

This was undeniable when, as Willow walked through the front door of Robert Kansas Elementary School, Patricia and Amanda, with matching blond hair, matching pink skirts and matching pointers, extended those fingers directly at Willow.

Willow's knee buckled and her black Converse squeaked against the green linoleum. But she just readjusted her backpack and kept on walking as she turned heads more than she ever had before. Because the girl with the dead mom was back at school.

As more time passed, Willow noticed that there were two primary responses to the girl with the dead mom: sympathy and fear. And Willow had to deal with the sympathizers and the fearers over and over and over again.

The sympathizers were the group of moms with black cars and white T-shirts. And also some teachers who previously ignored Willow, even when she had her hand raised and the correct answer on the tip of her tongue. And also the lunch lady who previously refused to give her an extra cookie even though she gave one to Jackie Milham, who was only two girls in front of her in line.

The sympathizers ran right over to Willow with waving arms and forced frowns. They bent down in front of her with creases in their foreheads and the corners of their lips turned down, but not a trace of empathy in their eyes.

"We are so sorry about your mom," they would say. The volume of the "so" was an eight.

"If you ever need anything, you call me anytime, okay?" They said "anything" at a ten. And then they would draw Willow forcefully into their chests and rub her back in big rounded circles.

And it was all crap.

Willow saw how these women looked at her mother when Rosie would turn the corner in her Lili Von. She knew what they thought about the bright blue color and the googly eyes. She saw how they shook their heads disdainfully when her mother turned the music up and rolled down the windows. She saw how they rolled their eyes when her mother knocked on the classroom door and said, "I need Willow for *ummm* an appointment."

Sympathy had caused the histrionics of falling arms and melodramatic frowns, but Willow would have much preferred quieter empathy. Eyes that actually had sadness in them. A hug that actually meant she could call anytime. From anyone. Anyone at all.

And then there was everyone else. And everyone else was a fearer.

They were the rest of the teachers and staff at Robert Kansas Elementary School. All of the other fifth graders in her class. Even Alexandra, who she thought might be a friend after she helped her with her necklace. Willow could feel all of their stares burning into her. All the time. When she was sitting or doing her word searches or eating her lunch. Or even just breathing.

And when Willow would turn around, she would catch the fearers staring into her, unable to blink. And maybe it was because they had never known someone who had been so close to someone who was now dead. Maybe it was because they expected some sort of physical manifestation of grief. A face that twisted with sadness. A big black band on her arm to commemorate her loss. And even though Willow knew those things didn't exist, the fearers scanned her body for it relentlessly.

Fear had caused them to stare intensely at Willow when she was doing the banal activities she had always done. But Willow would have much preferred a warmer empathy. Someone to ask "How are you?" Or "Are you thinking about Mom today?"

Or anything. From anyone. Anyone at all.

More than anything else, Willow wanted the sympathizers and the fearers to just go away. She wanted it all to go away. But when she thought more about it, Willow considered that those hugs from the white T-shirt ponytail moms still felt good. It felt good to be hugged and cradled for even a millisecond. It felt good to have her back rubbed. It felt nice even if Willow wasn't hugging back. And even it was from those other moms who never really liked her real mom.

45

After about a month, the hugs from the other moms stopped and no one else touched Willow. No one tickled her arm before bed, or let her sit in their lap. No one ran their fingers through her hair or held her hand when she crossed the street. No one hugged her or kissed her. No one even grazed by her in the hallways at school.

It left an insatiable hunger on the surface of Willow's skin.

And without any deliberate thought about it, Willow began to feed that hunger herself. She started sucking vigorously on her arms while her teachers scribbled on the chalkboard. She would fold her arm at her elbow, nuzzle her face into the crease, press her lips into her skin and then suck, suck, suck, like a nursing infant. And Willow sucked her skin so quickly, so rhythmically, so regularly, that her arms were left spotted with raw red hickeys.

And then there was the braiding and unbraiding her hair. All day. Every day. Incessantly. Until now, Willow's curls had been springy and excited. But now, the constant self-touching had caused them to take on an entire life of their own. Each ribbed strand now thrust itself from Willow's scalp in every imaginable direction as if it were trying to escape. And each coil developed its own protective web of frizz. All of the braiding and unbraiding, twisting and untwisting, left a wild knot atop Willow's head.

And then there were the scratches on her left shoulder blade. Rex noticed these even before Willow had. He noticed how his daughter had been nervously hanging her right wrist over her left shoulder and running her nails up and down her back. Up and down, up and down, until her shoulder bled so slightly from those three thin red lines. And even when scabs formed on those scrapes, Willow would scratch and scratch until they fell off and bled so lightly again.

Between the collateral damage of the skin sucking, hair-pulling, shoulder scratching, the red eyes from sleepless nights and the faint smell of urine that now followed her around, Willow Thorpe had turned into some kind of barely recognizable monster.

When Willow walked by her classmates, her teachers, even some strangers, she would catch them wince when they saw her skinny body bouncing and scratching and sucking beyond her control.

Walking down the driveway after another spring day at Robert Kansas Elementary School, Willow noticed that her brother's pockets were unreasonably full. It was not uncommon for Asher to keep things tucked away in the depth of his jacket. Asher was always finding things he wanted to carry around with him. Things he was sure he would play with later even though he seldom did. Funny-shaped sticks. A flattened penny. Strange flowers. Packets of ketchup.

But today, Asher's pockets bulged more aggressively than usual. As they walked through the front door, Willow opened her mouth to ask about the pockets, but quickly decided to keep silent. She didn't feel like talking. So she followed her typical path through the foyer, up the back stairs and into her room. Her bones naturally carried her up there onto her bed with her new book of word searches her father had bought her. And then her eyes naturally started scanning the grid like she did every afternoon. She sank into her big lacy blue pillow waiting to find reprieve in the monotony of circling those groups of letters.

But then there was a knock on the door. And Asher's voice behind it.

"Willow, awe you in thewe?"

"Yeah, Ash. Come in."

Asher pushed his sister's door open and stood there in his green hooded jacket with the bulging pockets.

Willow laughed a little bit. He looked so small, so silly, with those little hands and those big pockets.

"Asher, we're not outside anymore. You can take your jacket off, you know."

Asher thrust his tiny hands into his pockets and started to fidget.

"Well, I had to go to the nuwse in school today because I huwt my toe on wecess. And I saw that she had so many Band-Aids. And when she wasn't looking I took a lot for you and I put thum in my pockets."

"Band-Aids?"

"Yeah. Because your awms. All those things on thum. It looks like they huwt and maybe you wanted some Band-Aids."

Willow felt her eyes filling up with tears. They were tears of embarrassment. Embarrassment that she couldn't contain how much she was hurting.

They were tears of love. Love for her little

brother who wanted to take care of her.

They were tears of relief. Relief that somebody was looking out for her.

Willow was quiet while she looked at her brother in the doorway and tried to swallow the lump in her throat.

Asher was standing there fidgeting. And then he continued talking. "Well, I just didn't know if we had any in the house ow not."

Willow's mind went blank and her whole body relaxed. She looked straight into her brother's clear, warm, loving blue eyes. And he looked right back at her. Into her sad, desperate, writhing brown eyes.

"Hewe you go, Willow," Asher said so simply as he pulled one Band-Aid, and then another, and then another, and then another Band-Aid out of his pocket. He created a big pile of them on the floor. And then took the final one from his pocket and unpeeled the waxy paper.

Willow slowly and silently extended her arm out to Asher. Her thin arm covered in raw red sores. Her thin and needy arm. And she let her brother place one, and then another, and then another, and then another Band-Aid on her.

She watched without a word as Asher was so gentle. So kind. So calm. So sweet.

Willow silently wondered what kind of Band-Aids her brother needed. She wondered what was hurting him.

It must be something.

But when every Band-Aid was stuck on Willow's arms, and their wax paper shells were scattered all over Willow's bedroom floor, Asher smiled and skipped out of his sister's room with his green hooded jacket in hand. His light-up shoes blinked as he made his way down the hallway.

Willow went into the bathroom to look at her new Band-Aid armor in the mirror. She looked ridiculous all covered up in those sticky beige strips that didn't quite match the color of her skin. Those sticky beige strips that Asher applied at random angles all over her arms. And she laughed. She laughed and laughed until she cried big and full tears. Big tears full of sadness and also full of happiness. Big tears full of anguish but also full of hope.

This was the first time she had allowed someone that wasn't Mom to love her so directly. This was the first time she had allowed someone else to care for her. Soothe her. Console her.

And it felt good.

Because for so long Willow had pushed everyone out if they didn't love her, play with her, talk to her, love her in just the way she liked. She wouldn't bend for anyone. But it was a tragic mistake. A mistake so many of the people around her made, as well.

But some of that was starting to wash away. And it was exposing something beautiful and pure.

46

When Rex looked at his daughter, he felt lost. He wanted to help her, to heal her, so badly. But he just didn't know how. He saw the hickeys and the scratches and bloodshot eyes. He washed her sheets in the mornings that were soaked with urine.

He had a sense of the things that would help. A high five for a perfect score on a spelling test. A rub on the back when she walked offstage after a perfect performance at her piano recital. A good-night kiss. A fatherly hug. Any of those things could have reversed every rogue piece of hair and every red mark on her skin. Any of those things could have sent that invisible brick wall between Rex and his daughter tumbling down. But how would he even begin to do these things after all that had happened? After all that space he'd created between them?

Of all the preparation Rex did to get ready

for fatherhood, nothing prepared him to handle this. Any of it. The drug-addicted wife. The divorce. The drug-addicted ex-wife. The ex-wife that his children adored. Whom he once adored and still missed. The sudden and tragic death of that ex-wife. The son — the simple and innocent son — who showed no signs that he had internalized anything that was going on. The daughter who didn't love him. And might never love him. The eleven-year-old daughter who still wet the bed and still had to bring a change of clothes to school. The daughter whose change of clothes was another set of exactly the same clothes.

How was he supposed to know how to tell his children that their mother had died? He thought back to that moment in the car when he just told them plainly she was dead. He remembered the stunned silence, the thickness in the air, then the sound of tears. His heart ached for his children. His heart broke for them. He couldn't even turn around and look at them. Come face-to-face with their sadness. Come face-to-face with his failures.

How was he supposed to know what to do? How to be a father in that moment? How was he to forgive himself for the awful way he shot that delicate news out at them?

And how was he supposed to know that a father should allow his children to mourn at their mother's funeral? He so desperately wanted to spare them from any more pain. From seeing their mother in a casket. But when he found that puddle on the floor where he knew Willow had been standing, he knew his decision to shield them was wrong. He knew too late what a colossal mistake he had made.

But how was he supposed to know how to be a father in those moments? How was he to forgive himself for depriving his children of a critical component of finding closure?

How was he supposed to be a father to his children who loved their mother so, so much? How was he supposed to be a father to his children who couldn't, and shouldn't, be exposed to their mother's flaws? How was he to forgive himself for not doing more? To save his children? To save their mother?

Rex saw so intimately what was happening that morning when he found his children so comfortable in Rosie's bed with their caked-on makeup after what was undoubtedly a night dancing to *The Rocky Horror Picture Show.* He remembered being forced into this ridiculousness himself while living with Rosie in Manhattan — and yet loving every moment of it. He remembered having to wear nail polish and face paint and sometimes a boa, and feeling so uncomfortable in his outfit, but so happy with Rosie sprawled all over him. He could see so clearly that his children were experiencing this same sensation of being swept up and carried away by Rosie's beautiful and terrifying tornado of love.

He knew this tornado so intimately. He knew that now it would be fishnet stockings and glitter blue eye shadow and kisses and love. And that later, there would be pain and aching as she slipped away and took her love with her. Because that level of fishnet stockings and glitter blue eye shadow and kisses and love was not sustainable. Her tornado would always have its aftermath. Its heartbreaking wreckage.

He knew because he himself was left broken from it once. Was still broken from it. And he was scared of what would happen to his children once Rosie's tornado picked up momentum because he knew in his bones what would happen. He should have protected them. But how could he be a father that pulled his children out of the sky? Forced his children to run from their mother's love? But how could he be a father who didn't?

There were so, so many chasms. So many bridges he would have to build from scratch. "How?" Rex asked himself with his chin at his chest. "How?"

As an unfamiliar empathy moved around his body. Part of the sensation hurt, but part of it warmed him. This was a start.

.

As Rex paid more attention to his daughter in the weeks following Rosie's death, he noticed a fire in his daughter he had never seen before. He saw intensity in her eyes. A seriousness in her chin. A firmness in her gait.

There was sadness and anger in all of those places too, but those he understood. Those he expected. The fire and intensity he witnessed were new and surprising. But although Rex knew his daughter was in pain, he swelled with pride when he saw that Willow had these traits running through her. Traits that he valued. Traits that he, himself, contained. It was the most connected he had ever felt to his daughter.

He and Willow had both been so fulfilled by Rosie. They had both been so inadvertently dependent on her special, specific, unique kind of love. And then he and Willow had both had it pulled away from them. Slowly and painfully. They had it taken away just when they needed it most. And in the wake of losing Rosie, they had both hardened. With sadness and anger and hurt. So much sadness. So much anger. So much hurt.

Yet they shared something now. Something so visceral. Something so real.

And then a flood of guilt filled up inside of Rex. Guilt for the way he looked past Willow all these years. Guilt for the way he gave her up to Rosie so shortly after she was born. It was so naive to think that his daughter had no room for his love. Of course she did. He was her father. He just needed to carve out space for it. He had so much love he was ready to give her. He should have tried harder to give it. And his daughter was so young. She would have absorbed it so thoroughly from him. They would have all been so much happier. They could all be so much happier.

And then Rex filled with hope. Hope that there could be a future in which they *were* so much happier. Separately and together. Separately by way of together.

Some changes would have to be made. By Rex himself and by his daughter too. But he was her father and the first step would be his. He was determined in this. Resolute in this. His heart, his whole body, his whole being, felt it so strongly.

It was always known that when Rex Thorpe wanted something, he made it happen.

And he wanted so badly to be better. He needed to be better. So, so much better.

Better than the man who walked away instead of helping his daughter kick a soccer ball.

Better than the man who looked away when his daughter appeared downstairs in her favorite outfit.

Better than the man who was so cold when he told his children that their mother had died. Better than the man who didn't know to invite them to their own mother's funeral.

Better than the man who didn't give his children enough kisses. Enough hugs. Enough love.

Yes, he would be so much better.

More available. More open. More free with love.

More like Rosie.

For the first time in many months, Rex thought back on his ex-wife fondly. He wanted so badly to get through to Willow. And no one knew how better than Rosie did. It was true when Willow was just a little girl and it was still true now. Even in Rosie's death.

Rex closed his eyes, inhaled and thought of Rosie. Admired Rosie. With her quirks and her floral-printed dresses. With her silliness and red lipstick. With her coolness and flowery skin. With her bounce and curly hair. With her special kind of nuanced love that she offered to everyone, everyone, around her. With her special kind of nuanced love that she so beautifully sent straight into the bones, the hearts, of her children. Especially Willow.

He closed his eyes even tighter and channeled Rosie.

Even if she couldn't be his wife, even if she could no longer be Willow and Asher's mother, and even if she could no longer be here at all, he still wanted a piece of her inside of him. He still needed a piece of her inside of him. He had been better with her. Lighter. Happier. Even if it was by accident.

And he could be better again. He just needed a little Rosie. And Willow did too.

47

When Rex put their car in Park in front of their mother's house, Willow's stomach turned. The facade of the house looked as it always looked. The unruly flower beds. The ivy climbing up the brick. The red door with its chipping paint.

Rex turned toward his children in the back seat and handed Willow and Asher two empty cardboard boxes each.

"You can fill those two boxes and bring them back home. The rest of the stuff in the house will be taken care of."

These two simple sentences boiled Willow's blood. They boiled her blood so furiously that she had to grip onto the door to keep from screaming. Willow sat in a silent rage as so many thoughts exploded in her mind.

Put my stuff in two boxes? TWO BOXES?! You want me to fit everything in two boxes, Dad? I had a life in that house. I had toys that

I played with. I had art on my walls. Books that I made notes in. Letters from Mom that I've saved. I had things in that house. Lots and lots of things. And I know that you think the things that Mom and I like are stupid, but I like them. I like my collection of skipping stones and I like all the misshapen bowls that I made out of clay and painted all sorts of colors. I have lots of things that I want to keep with me. Two boxes is not enough boxes for all those things.

Bring them back home? HOME?! You call your house home, Dad? Your house is not home. Your house is a house. Because the air-conditioning is always on too high and you're always saying shh. *Because sometimes you bring strangers into it when you think I am sleeping. Mom's house is home. Because love and laughter were alive in there. And singing and dancing and cooking and art. Life was exciting in that house. In that home. And even if Mom isn't in there anymore, there's still life in that home. It's nothing like your house.*

The rest will be taken care of? TAKEN CARE OF?

What does it look like for you to take care of something, Dad? Does it look like forcing your daughter to empty the dishwasher every night?

Does it look like requiring your daughter to place a quarter in a mason jar every time she says like *or* umm?

Does it look like turning your daughter's bedroom lights off without a good-night kiss? Sometimes without even saying good-night at all?

Does it look like pressing and pressing and pressing your naked body into a woman's body in the middle of your bathroom without noticing that your daughter is standing right there watching it happen? I don't trust you to take care of something, Dad.

I don't trust you to take care of Mom's stuff. And I don't trust you to take care of me.

I want Mom here. I want her here so bad.

Her whole body tensed in the back seat of that car, and then melted at the thought of missing her Mom. At the sight of her house out the car window. And as Willow's heartbeat slowed and her lungs calmed, she relinquished her grip on the door. Rex stayed seated in the front seat of the car as his son and daughter dragged their feet up the driveway and through the front door.

As soon as Willow opened the door, the floral scent of her mother washed over her. Even though Rosie was gone, Willow could still feel her in every cranny of their home. The worn hardwood floors. The paintbrushes in pick-up-sticks formation on the living room floor. The abstract mural on the hallway wall. The half-read, half-annotated books on the kitchen table. It almost seemed as if Mom would walk in any minute and finish her painting or book or concoction in the kitchen. And then Willow imagined it happening. She imagined her mother skating right through the door and picking up a paintbrush like nothing happened. Turning over the book and reading every word to her. Tossing a wooden spoon to her and motioning for her to mix the batter.

Willow spent an hour placing things from around the house into her two boxes. And then removing something she thought she might be able to part with. And putting something new in its place. And then putting the original item back in. And then taking it out again to make room for another something. And then trying to rearrange the makeup and jewelry and books and toys and markers and pictures and purple leggings and black Converse sneakers in her two boxes to make room for more makeup and jewelry and books and toys and markers and pictures and purple leggings and black Converse sneakers.

But there was no combination or orientation of things in those boxes that would have satisfied Willow. And Willow knew that. So after another hour, Willow bent over, turned backward, curved her little fingers over the opened edge of each box and dragged the only remaining relics of her mother she would be allowed to keep down the hallway. As she moved past the white door of her mother's bedroom, Willow couldn't resist the urge to walk in one more time.

The king bed that she had fallen asleep in so many times was still unmade. There were candy wrappers on the bedside table. And two ripped-open Pixy Stix at the top of the pile. The sight of those thin purple-and-white-striped wax paper tubes caused a tightening in the back of Willow's throat. It caused pressure against her heart. Willow felt tears forming. Forming and preparing to drip out of her.

But what would happen if she were to keep crying? Keep feeling sad? Or scared? Or mad? Who would listen to her? Who would hug her?

Without Mom there, Willow knew the answer was no one.

And so Willow, by her own force of will, untwisted the knot in her stomach, waited a moment for the teary wells in her eyes to evaporate and resumed dragging her boxes down the hallway. This kind of independent determination was brand-new to Willow Thorpe. It felt strange as it coursed through her blood, fortified her muscles and strengthened her soul. But she knew she needed it. She knew she would continue to need it. And she let it seep into her as she dragged her boxes all the way down the stairs and out the door.

When Willow emerged from the house, Rex grabbed her two boxes and then Asher's and piled them into the trunk of his car. Then they drove off without saying a word.

Willow sat quietly and tearlessly taking inventory of all the things that she wished were in the trunk of Dad's car with her two boxes. The old chest full of sequin jackets. The pink wigs and floral headdresses. The cowboy hats and fake glasses and feather boas that were in the bottom drawer of Mom's closet. The charcoal drawing hanging on the living room wall that she, Asher and Mom made one day when it was so snowy that you could only see white when you tried to look out the window. The sculpture in the hallway that Willow picked out at a craft fair in a warehouse somewhere that took an hour to drive to one afternoon when she should have been in school. The camera with all of her pictures of the waves crashing against the rocks at sunrise from the time Mom woke her up before even the sun had risen and brought her to the ocean. The silly shaped cookie cutters that made desserts they would eat before they had their vegetables.

Willow wished she could have brought her purple comforter that smelled like Mom's perfume. Or the homemade snow globe with little clay versions of her, and Asher, and Mom wearing bathing suits and waving as little glittery flecks swirled all around them. She wished she could have peeled the paint off Asher's walls and created a secret hideout in the woods behind Dad's.

She wished she could have put that whole house in the back of Dad's car. Every inch of that home, each and every thing that was in it, was a memory. Was a part of Mom, a part of herself. She wanted to live forever in the warm and consuming embrace of all of those things. But with each revolution of the tires, with each tree that passed by in the window, Willow was traveling farther and farther from all of those things. Farther from Mom.

And then Asher broke the silence again. With something both simple and profound.

"Dad, how did it happen? How did Mom die?" he asked while he tapped his light-up sneakers together.

Rex's back straightened and his hands tensed around the wheel. He was quiet for a moment.

"It was an accident," he said.

And then he paused for too long.

"A car accident."

Another long pause. And then an exhale.

And then just another, extending, thick pause.

48

Immediately after his children left for school the next day, Rex dug the old keys out of his sock drawer and called Roy and asked him if he would come down from New York and watch his children again for a couple of days. It was a big favor, but he knew it was important. And Roy was the kind of friend who always did a favor for a friend in need. Roy had checked in on 299 East 82nd Street for Rex regularly over the years, but Rex knew the time had come for him to go up and check in himself.

"Always here to help however I can, Rex," Roy responded genuinely. "I can be down there before the kids get home from school."

As soon as he heard those words, Rex got into his black car and drove all the way to 299 East 82nd Street without stopping. He drove with Willow and Asher and Rosie on his mind and "Leather and Lace" on the speakers. He drove all the way to the apartment he had not visited for years and years and years. To the apartment his mind often wandered to. To the place where Rosie was perfectly Rosie. To the apartment where Rex was a better Rex.

Over all these years, Rex never found himself willing to relinquish that apartment. Especially knowing he had given Rosie a key in case she wanted a retreat. And now, more than ever, he was happy he did. He needed that place now. Perhaps as much as Rosie needed to know it was an alternative, an escape all of these years.

He knew Rosie might not be able to be Rosie in the quiet suburbs of Virginia. The way he knew Rosie might not be able to be a wife without the energy of the city. The things, the people, the movement in the city. The way he knew Rosie might not be able to be a mother without the ripples of the world flowing so wildly around.

And it could not be said for certain whether it was the deprivation of city life or the hormones that rushed through her after the birth of her son or the natural vicissitudes of Rosie's chemistry, but in truth Rosie stopped being Rosie soon after the move. It happened in a way that Rex knew could not be reversed. Not with his embrace or back rubs. Not with his children or his offer to return them all to the walls of 299 East 82nd Street.

Even after Rosie dropped the key in his lap and Rex knew he and Rosie would never move back to that apartment together, Rex could not bring himself to get rid of it. He knew it needed to live on, even if in a faraway dream.

And as soon as Rex took one delicate step through the doorway, he remembered exactly why he had kept it. He had kept it because there were pieces of the Rosie he fell in love with in this apartment. Pieces of her that would be there forever. There were pieces of her in the patterned wallpaper and the mismatched doorknobs. In the intricate crown molding and the rickety heater. There were pieces of her in the mustiness that was thick in the air now after sitting there unused. There were pieces of Rosie in every cranny of 299 East 82nd Street. And keeping the apartment meant keeping pieces of her. And being in this apartment now meant being with her.

He was sorry he hadn't had the wisdom to see it all before — the strength to insist they come back with the children from time to time . . .

Rex walked from room to room with his eyes lightly closed as his fingertips traced the walls. He was feeling for Rosie. Willing her energy, the memory of her, her love to move through him. Willing that energy to be strong enough to enter his heart. Willing that force to be strong enough for him to pass on to Willow.

And then Rex's eyes opened when his fingers were interrupted by a break in the smoothness on the wall. It was the locket he had given to Rosie that first day in this apartment. That first day in the apartment when Rosie first told him about Willow. That day Rosie tacked that locket to the wall as a manifesto to love. To their unlikely beautiful love. To their nuanced and special complementary love.

Rex took the locket into his hands and examined it. He turned it over and over to inspect each scratch. Each bit of tarnish. Each chipped golden edge. He snaked the chain through his fingertips, and then gently moved his fingertips across the engraving on the back.

299 East 82nd Street. Apartment 5.

It was always so special here at 299 East 82nd Street. It still was special here. Because everywhere where Rosie was, was special. And Rosie left pieces of herself everywhere she ever was. Rosie left pieces of Rosie in everyone she ever loved. Even if she was gone.

Rex cupped the locket in his hand, and then pressed it into his heart. He could feel Rosie in that locket. He could feel the locket pulsing. He could feel Rosie's life force pulsing. Giving him love. Giving him life.

It was exactly what Rex needed. And he knew it was what Willow needed too. With Rosie in his heart and his heart guiding him now, Rex felt ready to love his daughter in the way she deserved to be loved. In the way he might not have been able to love Rosie toward the end.

Giving Willow the love of Rosie, the love Rosie stored up in that locket, would be the first step.

The next day, on the way back from Manhattan, when he was almost home, Rex stopped at the bus depot where all of Robert Kansas Elementary School's yellow buses were held. He stopped at the depot like he had so many times already this school year. And he walked over to the dispatcher, Chris, who shook his hand and pointed him the direction of Bus #50 like he had so many times already this school year.

And then Rex slipped two more grape

Pixy Stix into the depths of the front left seat like he had so many times this school year. He tied his "For Willow" note around it. And then he wrapped Rosie's locket around it.

Rex smiled warmly at his gift. Yes, Willow could have a little piece of Rosie to hold on to. And the healing process could begin. The reacquaintance of Willow and Rex through the memory of Rosie. Through the love of Rosie. The reacquaintance of father and daughter through Pixy Stix and an old gold locket.

49

Willow had become a leaky faucet of sadness. She dripped, dripped, dripped with it. It never gushed out in spurts or sprayed anyone around her. It just dripped, dripped, dripped. All the time. It didn't happen in the form of tears or red sores or a wet bed. It just dripped, dripped, dripped out her pores.

And as she took her usual seat on Bus #50 right behind the driver, her sadness dripped, dripped, dripped some more when the silver duct tape on the back of the seat caught her eye. She wanted so badly to peel back the tape and discover a new batch of Pixy Stix. She wanted so badly for her mom to be back in her life. For love to be back in her life. And even though she knew it was impossible, Willow couldn't stop her pointer finger and thumb from pinching the corner of the strip of tape and tugging it back. Willow peered in the hole and thrust her hand into the void as she dripped, dripped, dripped with the expectation of disappointment.

But just like that, the dripping stopped. There was the familiar feeling of those thin tubes of Pixy Stix right there in the seat. And that feeling stopped all the dripping. It dried it all right up.

Two more Pixy Stix.

Two more Pixy Stix!

Mom had left her two purple Pixy Stix.

But how had she left those Pixy Stix?

Was she still alive?

She was still alive.

Mom was still alive!

A rush of the purest happiness and excitement and relief and love jolted through every vein of her body. It jolted through her body and filled her bones and heart. It wrapped around her lungs and her brain so quickly that she was dizzy with it. The whole world did one whole flip and everything was good again.

All of Willow's memories of her mother went zipping into the future. All of the dancing and singing and movies and candy and lipstick that Willow had crystallized in the past projected straight onto a screen of her future. She could barely contain a shriek at the idea that she would have all of those things again.

But where was she? Where was Mom?

Willow pulled her hand and the Pixy Stix out from the hole in the seat. A tarnished golden heart-shaped locket came with the tubes. It was dangling from a tarnished golden chain wound delicately around the two tubes. Willow pressed the locket into her heart. She could feel Mom in that locket. She could feel the locket pulsing. Giving her love. Giving her life.

She felt the same tingling feelings she felt when she had her head in her mother's lap in the tree house. The same feelings of comfort. And relief. And pure, unadulterated, heartwarming happiness.

Where are you, Mom? Willow thought to herself. *Where are you?*

Willow closed her eyes and pressed the locket farther into her heart.

Tell me where you are.

And then Willow opened her eyes and looked down at the locket in her hands. She twisted it around in her fingers and examined every scratch. Every bit of tarnish. Every chipped golden edge. She snaked the chain through her fingers, and then turned it over. She traced her fingers slowly across the engraving on the back. She traced her fingers across it and felt the shallow grooves of each letter.

299 East 82nd Street. Apartment 5.

And Willow's question was answered.

Of course that's where Mom was. She was safe and happy in that apartment in Manhattan she loved. And she wanted Willow to be safe and happy with her there too. Just like she said in that willow tree.

For the first time in months, everything was making sense.

Her mother had been so distant because she was planning her escape. She had left her on that curb at Robert Kansas Elementary School so many times because she was back at her apartment. Getting it ready. Painting the walls and setting up the music. Stocking up on her favorite movies and filling up the kitchen with her favorite snacks. Yes, it all made sense. Why Dad didn't bring her to the funeral. There was no funeral. That phone call with Roy. He had faked it all. He had faked it to get Willow to stay with him in that house in Virginia. But Willow knew better now. And her mother knew better all along.

Willow would find Mom there in Manhattan as soon as she could.

She clutched her Pixy Stix in her fingers, and then tucked them into her backpack. And then she kissed her tarnished locket and tucked it away in her jacket pocket.

And then she pressed her eyebrows together and filled with determination. Determination to get to Mom. Determination to get to love.

And, now, when Willow Thorpe was determined to do something, she made it happen.

It hadn't always been true, but it was now. It was true for Willow as much as it was for Rex.

They had been missing each other's love for so long and they had missed again. Ever so slightly this time. But Willow and Rex, daughter and father, were ready for love and they would do anything to find it. Even if in new places or in new ways.

Willow watched every *tick, tick, tick* of the clock in the back of Mrs. McAllister's class until the end-of-school bell rang and she could go home and tell Asher about all of it. And as soon as she and Asher stepped off their buses and through the big thick door of Dad's house, Willow took her brother by the hand and yanked him into the front closet. Willow's eyes were wide with something.

"When we play hide-and-seek, we don't hide togethew, Willow!" Asher explained slowly and instructively in a noisy whisper.

And without saying anything, Willow reached into her jean jacket and pulled out the locket.

"Ooooooo," Asher said with eyes now wide as Willow's.

But then he said nothing. And within a few seconds, his extended blue eyes shrank back to normal size.

Willow dangled the chain aggressively in front of his face.

"What?" Asher said, still in his noisy whisper.

"Look at it," Willow instructed, turning the locket over to show Asher the address engraved on the back.

"Mom left this for me in the seat on the bus."

Asher's shoulders dropped and his mouth turned down. He welled up with sadness when he thought of his mom.

"Like befowe she died?"

"No. Like now."

Willow expected a burst of excitement for the second time but got nothing but a head tilt from her younger brother in the darkness of the front closet.

Willow continued. "Like meaning she's still alive, Ash. She wants us to find her here. At this address."

Willow now had the locket in the center of her palm, on display for Asher. And she waited for the third time for Asher to share in her excitement.

"Willow, that doesn't make any sense," Asher said as he rubbed his wet eyes.

And then Willow explained everything to Asher. How Rosie had been leaving Pixy Stix in the back of the seat all year. How there wasn't a funeral. How Mom had been planning their escape this whole time. How Mom never would have left them, even if it was an "accident." How they would go to Manhattan and find her.

Willow's belief that her mother was in that apartment gushed out of her. Out of her words and her pores and her bones and her heart.

It gushed out of her so swiftly, so fiercely, that there was no reality anymore.

So Asher did what little brothers have done for all of time. He believed what his big sister told him. And it had nothing to do with the facts and everything to do with loyalty. And love. So Asher let Willow's words into his heart and tacitly but resolutely joined his sister in her plan to find Rosie.

50

And the next day at school, Willow made that plan with the help of the binder full of bus schedules in the library instead of eating lunch. The plan was to walk to the bus stop from their house and take the bus all the way to Manhattan. She studied the times of the buses and turns in the streets. She calculated the timing of each step and what it would require to execute it. A ticket cost two hundred and nine dollars. A second one for Asher took it to four hundred and eighteen. And they would need some extra money for a taxi. And maybe some candy on the way. Five hundred dollars was the number she scribbled in the back of her word search book and settled on. Five hundred dollars to get back to Mom.

Willow thought about how they would get all that money. She and Asher could pool all the money in their piggy banks. And then there was their weekly allowance to count on.

When Willow got home from school, she decided to count up just how far they had to go to reach five hundred dollars.

She wanted to start with what was in Asher's piggy bank. So she walked into her brother's room and watched him as he shook the porcelain pig next to his ear. There was a hollow clank before one dime fell out onto his rug. Asher partly frowned, and then tugged open the drawer next to his bed. He had been spending his allowance every week on action figures from the old toy shop next to the school.

"Sometimes Jack in the candy store even gives me a Blow Pop if I tell him I did all my homewowk," Asher said with pride. Willow did her best to tell her brother it was okay, that she was happy he had so many action figures and sometimes Blow Pops, but, in reality, her insides were bubbling. Because when she looked into that drawer full of action figures, Willow didn't see any of Asher's happiness. She only saw how much longer it would take her to get to Mom. How every plastic Batman meant another ride on Bus #50. Another meal at her long, empty lunch table. How every contorted zombie figurine meant another sleepless night in her cold blue sheets. Another boring plate of string beans and fish for dinner. How every stupid robot, or alien, or superhero meant another stupid, miserable, boring day at Dad's stupid, miserable, boring house.

Willow stormed across the house to count up the contents of her own piggy bank, desperate to figure out just how much more money she would need. And although there was a knob at the bottom of her piggy bank that would have allowed Willow to shake and wiggle her savings out gently, Willow felt like smashing it. She felt like lifting it above her head and slamming it down onto the driveway. She felt like watching all the pieces scatter across the asphalt. She felt like making a mess that maybe she wouldn't even clean up. She felt like making noise. Even if no one else could hear it.

So Willow snatched her piggy bank from the top of her wicker dresser, tucked it under her arm and marched out to her driveway with focus in her eyes and her mother on her mind. And when she got outside, she lifted the porcelain pig over her head and she slammed it down onto the ground.

It barely made a thud as it cracked into five and a half pieces to reveal a sizable pile of bills. Nothing shattered into a million tiny parts like Willow imagined. Nothing erupted into a cloud of white dust. Little ceramic pieces didn't zip in every direction across the blacktop. Out there on Dad's driveway, it was just the chirp of birds, the smell of new flowers, the calm afternoon sun, five and a half pieces of piggy bank and a pile of crinkled bills.

Willow felt the back of her throat tighten and the familiar pressure of tears forming behind her eyes. Ever since that day at Mom's house packing up boxes, her tears almost always stayed stuck right there behind her eyes. They would try to force their way out and run down her cheek, but Willow kept them back there. No matter how much they would relentlessly press and press, Willow held them back there.

She held them back there when she tied her shoes in the morning. And when she took off her jacket and hung it in her cubby. She held them back there when she was walking down the hall to gym class. And when she stared at the clock. Willow held them back every afternoon when she pressed the heavy door to Dad's house open. And when she completed the afternoon checklist. When she retreated to her room with her word search book. And when she set the table for dinner.

She held them back when she swirled her pasta around in its bowl. And when she brushed her teeth and washed her face before bed. She held them back when she slipped under her sheets. But most of the time, when it was late and dark and quiet in her bedroom, Willow couldn't fight the pressure anymore as the tears came. For a moment, they would stop at the hurdle of her eyelids, but when it was late and dark and quiet in her bedroom, her tears would fall down her face.

But here, on the driveway, looking at that five and a half pieces of ceramic piggy bank and that pile of crinkled bills, Willow couldn't hold the tears back as she hoped to get to five hundred dollars.

So Willow sat there, deliberately counting each one of her bills, tear after tear streaming down her face. She picked one up, pulled it straight and placed it in a neat pile. She counted her bills, and then counted them again to make sure. She was relieved to be reminded of the hundred-dollar bills she got for her past birthdays from Roy. "Save it for a rainy day," he told her each time, and then winked. Willow was happy she listened. Four hundred and sixty-four dollars. She didn't have so far to go. And even though she had barely done anything yet, all this thinking, all this feeling, all this dreaming about ways to put her life back together had already started to exhaust her.

Willow placed her elbows onto her knees as she sat legs crossed on the concrete. And let her palms handle the burden of her heavy head for a moment. She let her hands carry the weight of all that thinking and feeling and dreaming and aching.

It had only been a couple of days, and she was already tired of waiting. Because there was only so much happiness a dream could infuse into the day-to-day happenings of a life. The waking up. The morning checklist. The bus ride to school. The empty lunch table. The lesson in American history. The bus ride home from school. The time at the desk with homework. The nighttime checklist. And although she had her plans, and although Mom was in her future, Willow was living a soul-crushingly lonely present. Because she had nothing in her present world but the little steps leading her toward Mom. Nothing else in her present world was getting her through the day-to-day happenings of her life.

With her head in her hands and her eyes closed, Willow didn't realize that her father had been watching her through the kitchen window this whole time.

Willow carried her small stack of dollar bills and few pieces of broken piggy bank upstairs. She knew she needed more money and she knew she needed it fast. She fell into her beanbag chair and thought up ways to do it.

The other kids in Willow's class had always been getting money for things. They sold brownies so that their basketball team could get new team jerseys. They got in shorts and a T-shirt and stood on Main Street offering five-dollar car washes so that their cheerleading team could afford their annual trip to Disney World. When they were in their earlier years of elementary school, these same kids had set up on their front lawn with cups of store-bought lemonade and made enough money to buy new charms for their bracelets or laces for their sneakers.

Willow thought this was something she could do too. Willow, Asher and Mom had baked a billion things together — cakes, and cookies, and pies. And they would always use an ingredient that wasn't listed in the recipe — sprinkles or Reese's Pieces or a handful of Cocoa Puffs. Sometimes they would dye the whole batter a different color with one firm squeeze of food coloring. And while these additions never made their cakes or cookies or pies any tastier, they made them way more fun to eat. That surprise burst of peanut butter when you found a Reese's Pieces in your chocolate cake. Or the unexpected bite of crunchy sugar when you found a sprinkle in your cherry pie. The excitement of eating a bright orange cookie. Yes, her classmates would share in this kind of silly delight. So just like that, Willow's Bake Sale was born.

She opened her box of crayons for the first time since Mom died, left, and scribbled "Willow's Bake Sale" in big purple letters on a big piece of cardboard she found in the basement. She drew a red cookie and a blue cake and a green pie. She scribbled and scribbled with her hair bouncing and her tongue out. She scribbled so hard she had to peel the paper back on the Purple Mountains' Majesty, Razzmatazz, Screamin' Green and Blizzard Blue Crayola crayons. And when she was done coloring in all of her block letters, and all of the cookies, and cakes, and pies, Willow propped her poster up against her desk using her non-scribble-sore arm and stepped back. It looked perfect.

So Willow went downstairs to bake.

It was already almost 9:00 p.m. and her

eyelids were already heavy, but Willow was determined. She pulled her big purple headphones over her hair, placed them on her ears and jammed her pointer finger into the play button. And as "Raspberry Beret" filled her head, Willow bopped her head, tapped her right toe and got to baking. She measured and poured and mixed. She stirred and sprinkled and licked the spoon.

And in no time at all, there was blue chocolate chip cookie batter with crushed up bits of Peppermints in it. And bright green oatmeal cookie batter with Apple Jacks hiding inside. And a flimsy but tasty cherry pie with chocolate chips floating inside. And they were each in the oven coming to life. They were each in the oven bringing her mother back to life. Bringing Willow back to life. They were each in the oven filling the kitchen with the sugary sweetness of Mom's house. Filling Willow's bones with the sugary sweetness of Mom's love.

Willow pressed her nose against the warm glass of the oven and watched her cake and cookies come to life as she daydreamed of her mother twirling around the kitchen holding a whisk at her lips like it was a gold-studded microphone.

The next day when she got to school,

Willow brought her poster and cookies by the principal's office before lunchtime for approval. Principal Rhoads pursed her red lips together and looked skeptically down at the neon cookies. Willow told her about the food coloring and candy surprises, and then was ushered into the cafeteria to set up for her bake sale.

Willow sat in her plastic chair behind her plastic table and cardboard sign as fifth-grader after fifth-grader walked right by her.

They looked at her cookies through the corner of their eye and kept walking. They turned their necks around and scanned over Willow and her treats while sitting on their cafeteria benches. And then they turned back around to their Oreos and Chips Ahoy! neatly rationed into Ziploc bags. Willow gripped the bottom edge of the table so angrily when Freddie Fisher, and then Kara Avett, and then Erin Simmons, and then Ray Callahan walked by. She gripped the bottom edge of the table so intensely that she got strips of plastic under her fingernails. But still, Willow waited and waited for someone to buy something. Anything. Because even one single purchased cookie meant she was a little bit closer to seeing Mom. She waited and waited as the clock *tick, tick, ticked.* She waited and waited as the other fifth graders bit, bit, bit into their cookies. She waited and waited as her classmates sipped the last sips of their juice boxes. She waited and waited and nothing happened.

But with two minutes left of lunchtime, Amanda and Patricia walked toward her table with elbows interlocked, and then stopped right in front of it. They had their straight blond hair styled the same way — tucked neatly into a headband with a bow just to the left side of center. They were both wearing pink skirts and white T-shirts and white platform sneakers.

Willow unlatched her fingernails from the bottom of the table. Her first purchase was coming. She could feel it.

Willow looked up at Amanda. And then Patricia. And then back at Amanda, who was holding a dollar bill. Amanda looked back at Willow, scanned over Willow's treats. And then she laughed one loud laugh and yanked Patricia back into movement.

As Amanda walked away, Willow heard her whisper in her best friend's ear, "I bet you'll get those dots on your arms and start tripping in the hallways if you eat her weird outer space cookies."

And then Amanda and Patricia giggled and giggled as they walked across the cafeteria perfectly in stride.

Willow felt that pressure behind her eyes again. And she clenched her jaw and fists to keep from turning her plastic table upside down and ripping her poster into one hundred teeny, tiny pieces and throwing them all over the cafeteria. After all that planning, all that coloring, all that baking, Willow wasn't a single step closer to 299 East 82nd Street.

And it hurt all over.

Willow Thorpe's Bake Sale was never going to work.

She now realized the flaw in her plan. The kids with the perfectly decorated posters with the perfectly crafted bubble letters and the jars full of cash at the end of the day were not Willow Thorpe. They were kids that other kids, and teachers, and parents liked. They were the kids that played together at recess and had playdates after school. They were the kids who were on the same weekend soccer team and who attended each other's birthday parties. They were not the kid that peed in her pants or had hair that went boing. They were not the kid that tripped in the hallways or wore the same outfit every day or kept a book of word searches in her backpack.

■ ■ ■ ■

She threw away her cookies and thought of new ways to make her money. She wondered exactly what she would have to do. How far she would be willing to go.

51

As Willow dreamed of getting to Manhattan, Willow saw her mother everywhere. In every willow tree she drove by. Every juice box she jammed her straw into. Every word she circled in her book of word searches. Every spoonful of ice cream, which were now few and far between. She missed her so desperately in all of those places. And whenever she felt that pang of missing her mother, she would imagine her mother in a loose-fitting floral-printed dress dancing around her apartment. She would imagine her stirring a big bowl of spaghetti as she bopped her head back and forth to "Little Red Corvette." She would imagine her scribbling in her black notebook with her knees tucked into her chest in a pile of colored pencils. She pictured her doing all the things she used to watch her mom doing.

But as time pressed forward, those full images of her mother started disintegrating in her mind's eye. She couldn't remember exactly how she crossed her legs when she sat on the floor. Or what shade of red her lipstick was. Or whether her hair fell to the right or left. Or what her favorite track on the *Rumors* album was.

Willow had woven together an intricate image of her mother, and now the small pieces of thread were starting to fray. The whole image was falling apart. The whole vision of what it might look like for Willow to insert herself into that image again. And as it all grew fuzzier, Willow began to panic. And from time to time, the hope in her heart would flicker.

But with each drip of doubt, the need to fill in those gaps intensified. Because the only way to have her real mother in her mind again would be to actually feel her. Ring her doorbell, see her face, and then feel her. Willow wanted to feel her. And she wanted to feel her now.

Willow didn't know it, but she got this fiery determination from her father. When Rex and Willow Thorpe wanted something, their blood ran thick with it. Their minds and bodies were taken over.

But Willow and Asher still didn't have enough money in their piggy banks or from their weekly allowance or failed bake sales. But she wanted her mother and she wanted her now. Now. Now. Now. She wanted to see her mother now. She felt entitled to it. And it had been long enough. And the first thing she thought of was the top drawer of Dad's office. The drawer of Dad's office with the ones and the fives he would pull out after Sunday allowance. Surely there would be enough cash in there to make up the difference.

But Rex was always popping in and out of his office. It would be impossible for Willow to sneak in there with 100 percent certainty that her father wouldn't see. So she would recruit her brother. Asher would ask Rex to play a game of catch. And while they were outside, Willow would sneak into that drawer.

But when Willow shared the plan with Asher, he twisted his face right up.

"No way, Willow. I'm not stealing!"

"Well, you won't be stealing, technically. You'll just be playing catch or something," Willow explained hopefully.

"I don't like it. I weally just don't and I'm not gunna do it." Asher folded his arms. He even tried puffing his chest out a little bit.

That accidental *w* that usually warmed Willow's heart had no effect on her.

"Asher, you're doing it."

"No way, Jose." Asher closed his eyes and whipped his head back and forth, blond hair half a turn behind.

"Yes way."

She grabbed Asher's arm while she did it. Asher immediately stopped twisting and looked right into his sister's eyes. He was trying to see what was happening behind them. What foreign things were swirling around in her body. What made her eyes go so wide like that. What caused all those sores on her arms. What had forced her to grab his arm so hard.

But he saw nothing. Just her big, brown, serious eyes.

"Ow, Willow," Asher said, rolling over a lump in his throat. "Why did you gwab me? Why awe you acting like this?"

Full tears were now streaming down his cheeks. They were so full that Asher didn't even have to blink for them to fall over his eyelashes and down onto his chin.

"Why can't you just love Dad? Why can't you be happy hewe? Please, Willow. Please just twy."

Tears. More tears. More big, heavy, wobbling tears. All the way down his cheeks.

"I need you to twy. Please. Dad twies. I see him doing it and you don't even notice.

You just keep on hating him but please just love him. Please, Willow."

Willow didn't know what was coming out of Asher's mouth. And it could not be said for certain that Asher understood the profundity of the things he was saying either. But they were said. And now Willow's heart hurt too.

As Asher sat with his legs crossed on the floor with his wet eyes in his palms, pleading desperately with his sister, Willow realized for the first time that everyone in Dad's house was in pain. Real pain.

But in that moment, Willow thought her pain was the greatest. And she knew a way to end that pain and nothing would stop her.

She scared her classmates. Kept secrets from her father. And today she manipulated her brother.

And with far less coaxing than Willow imagined would be required, Asher, doing what little brothers always do, eventually conceded to his sister. And, just as Willow had planned it, Rex thought he was enjoying the simple pleasure of playing ball with his son while his daughter stole forty-six dollars in cash from the top drawer of his office.

■ ■ ■ ■

On Thursday evening after school, Willow didn't even consider how much she sounded like her father when she tossed a black JanSport backpack at Asher and said, "Put everything you need for Mom's in here." It didn't occur to Willow that, just like there was no amount of things Willow could have stuffed into those two boxes that would make her feel at home at Dad's house, perhaps a backpack stuffed with a pair of jeans, a few T-shirts, a Green Lantern action figure and a blankie wouldn't be enough for Asher to feel safe on his journey to Mom. Or comfortable once he stepped through her door. But Willow helped her brother arrange things in his backpack anyway.

Willow tucked in Asher under his superhero-themed blanket. She kissed him on the softest part of his cheek and rubbed his silky blond hair.

"I'll see you in a few hours," Willow said to her brother, whose eyes were closing.

And then Willow tucked a pair of purple leggings and another black T-shirt with a silver horseshoe on it into the bottom of her bag. She propped her word search book on top of the pile of clothes, and twirled the cords of her purple headphones around her new CD player. She closed the two snaps and tugged on the strings and put all of the cash she and Asher collected into the front pocket.

She looked down at her backpack and felt so ready. So ready to see Mom again. So ready for music and laughing and cooking and singing and hugs and kisses and love. So ready for everything to feel good again.

She thought all about it as she got into bed. But she couldn't sleep.

When Willow's alarm went off at 4:30 a.m., she was wide-awake and staring at her backpack. Her mind had been swirling with logistics all night.

Walk to bus station. Buy ticket. Board bus. Get off at correct stop. Hail taxi. Give driver address. Ring doorbell. See Mom. Hug Mom. Sink into Mom.

Walk to bus station. Buy ticket. Board bus. Get off at correct stop. Hail taxi. Give driver address. Ring doorbell. See Mom. Hug Mom. Sink into Mom.

Walk to bus station. Buy ticket. Board bus. Get off at correct stop. Hail taxi. Give driver address. Ring doorbell. See Mom. Hug Mom. Sink into Mom.

She played out her plan over and over

again in her mind. Every ounce of Willow's being was ready to move, ready to go, ready to burst. She could hardly keep the corners of her mouth from turning up toward her eyes even though they were scrunched closed.

Before her alarm could even make a second beep, Willow was out of bed. She tiptoed into her bathroom and looked at herself in the mirror. Her eyes were large and determined. Her shoulders looked strong. There was finally some pink in her cheeks. She looked ready. She looked different.

With every action she moved through that Friday morning, she cataloged every step, every movement, every breath as she considered that this could be the last time doing all these things at Dad's. The last time turning off that alarm. The last time looking in that mirror. The last time walking by the morning, and afternoon, and evening checklist on her wall. The last time walking quietly down the hallway on the way to wake her brother up. Because in less than twelve hours, she would be at 299 East 82nd Street with her hand around a cream soda and her head against Mom's shoulder.

Willow gently pressed into Asher's room and tapped his shoulder with increasing force until her brother rolled over and opened his big, blue eyes.

"It's time, Asher. Come on, wake up. Before Dad does."

Asher rubbed his eyes with the heel of his hand. He was still gripping his tattered blue blankie between his pinkie finger and palm.

Willow wondered if her brother had the same dreams about waking up in Mom's bed in matching pajamas. She wondered if he was also thinking about what flavor ice cream the three of them would share tonight. Whether he believed that Willow would get him to 299 East 82nd Street. Whether he believed Mom would be there at all.

But Willow had enough belief and determination for the both of them. And after only a few minutes, Asher and Willow were standing downstairs by the back door with their backpacks strapped on. They stared at each other for a moment. They stared at each other and locked eyes as so many things flowed between them. Trust and apprehension. Fear and loyalty. Hope and love.

And then, before either of them could change their minds, Willow grabbed Asher's hand and burst through the door.

Asher turned around and gave a full hand, five fingers outstretched, wave to Dad's house as Willow dragged him along through the presunrise darkness. The walk to the bus station felt long as each of them watched one foot and then the other press into the ground. With each step, it got a little lighter outside. And with each step another few drops of dew evaporated into the spring air. And with each step, their pulses slowed.

Love had prepared their hearts for the journey, but now inertia had taken over their legs.

52

Rex was dreaming of Rosie when he woke up to the sound of Willow in the hallways saying *shh.* And as he turned over in bed, he heard Asher reply with a familiar "sowwwyyy" even louder than Willow's *shh* had been. Rex rubbed his eyes and looked at the clock next to the bed. It was far too early for his children to be awake.

He rolled out of bed and peered over the balcony to find his children walking out of his house with their backpacks on. He could tell by the way they pressed through the door that they weren't going to school. So Rex tied his sneakers and followed quietly behind them. Quietly and slowly fifty yards behind them. Quietly and slowly as the sun came up and the morning dew evaporated. Quietly and slowly and wondering with every step where his children were walking to at this time of the morning. And even though Rex did not know where his children would lead him, he felt assured the journey would help him understand them.

Rex remained perplexed when they ended up at the bus station and Willow stepped up to the ticketing window with a pile of cash in her hand. But when Willow said, "Two tickets for New York City, please," in her tiny, little voice, Rex knew exactly what had happened.

He thought of the locket. He thought of the address engraved on the back of it. He thought of tying it around those grape Pixy Stix. Those sugar-filled tubes that were really meant to say "I love you." The thing he never said to his daughter. The thing he had withheld from his daughter for so long that she thought they were from Rosie. Even after her death.

And it made so much sense now that his daughter thought they were from her mother. The person who did say "I love you" all the time. With her words and her gifts and every teeny, tiny action. The person who gushed with the most manic form of it all the time. All the time until she didn't at all.

And at that moment, it was all understood. It was heartbreaking but it was understood. Rex knew they needed to complete this journey on their own. He knew they needed to get to that apartment themselves. Explore this fantasy, this need, all on their own. But he needed to ensure they could do it safely. And once they did, he could be there for them. Like the father, the man, he wanted to be.

Rex sprinted home and straight into his office, where he checked the bus arrival times into Manhattan. He called up Roy and explained what had happened.

"Can you have someone meet them at the bus stop to guide them into a taxi?" Rex asked his friend anxiously. "I need to be at the apartment when they get there. I need them to get there . . . and think they did it on their own. Can you find someone?"

Roy, the dependable friend he always was, agreed. He would ask his friend Sasha who worked nearby. He would make sure his children got to that apartment. Rex knew that Roy would never make a promise he couldn't keep.

It was all Rex needed to hear before hanging up the phone and packing a bag for himself, and then Asher and Willow. He packed pants and shirts and sweaters. Action figures and superhero T-shirts for Asher's. Even purple leggings and black shirts for Willow.

He stopped in his office and there it was,

the picture of Rosie he kept next to his computer screen. She was standing on the brink of the ocean with a paisley dress on. She was lifting the bottom of the dress so it wouldn't get wet, but the ocean spray was getting to her anyway. She was laughing and bright in her oversize sunglasses. It was a different time. A happier time. For both of them. When Willow and Asher were just a twinkle in their eyes. When love was flowing all around them. Rex turned the picture frame over and opened the back, where he had kept Rosie's note that was found in her room.

My Willow. My Asher. And also my Rex.
I love you oodles and oodles and noodle poodles.
I am sorry for all of it.
— Mom

The note that Rosie left was so carefully written in purple cursive.

Rex thought of that first time he saw that lively rounded handwriting on the card from Blooms Flower Shop. To the first time he felt the hate and love of all time washing over him. To the first time he felt all of those things simultaneously seeping into him and cleansing him. He brought the note to his chest and then to his lips. And then, with a tear in his eye, he placed it back into the frame.

The Rosie that left this note would stay here. In a past life. Hidden behind the Rosie in that picture. Hidden behind the Rosie with sunglasses and laughter and printed dresses and sandy toes. This beautiful, effervescent Rosie hiding the Rosie with pills and pain and suffering. It was how it was all along and how it would continue to be now. It was the Rosie he needed to see there in that picture and in his mind. The Rosie Willow and Asher needed to see too. In their lives and in their memories.

But before he walked out of the house, Rex paused to look at Rosie's photo again. The longer he looked at that photo of Rosie, so happy, so alive, the more that note behind it dissolved into insignificance.

It was nice to have a rare moment of calm, a rare moment of happiness, in the midst of all this chaos of the last few months. Chaos with Rosie. And then without Rosie. And with Willow. And now without Willow.

And, finally, Rex exhaled.

And then got into his car and drove as fast as he could to 299 East 82nd Street.

53

When they got to the bus station, Willow waited patiently at the ticketing window until it creaked open. A scruffy gray-haired man with tattered sleeves sat up in his chair to get a full view of the eleven-year-old girl whose coiled brown hair barely reached the height of the window.

"Where are you two headed?" he asked through a mask of coffee steam.

"Two tickets for New York City, please. The six-thirty bus," Willow said surprisingly confidently. And, for the first time, there was nothing meek or insecure or awkward about Willow as she unrolled the stack of cash she had secured with a rubber band. She pushed the money below the glass pane and accepted her ticket from a man who had seen all sorts of people buying bus tickets to all sorts of places.

And then Willow nodded to Asher, who followed her onto the platform for the bus.

Willow's right leg was vibrating vigorously and Asher's whole body bounced up and down. But when the bus horn sounded and the bright headlights made their way around the bend of the road, both Willow and Asher were still. Still and ready.

The doors opened with a whoosh of air and Willow and Asher walked onto the empty bus and gripped each other's hand, tightly without even looking down at their fingers. They each took a giant step in tandem onto the steps and walked up toward the driver. And with another whoosh, the doors shut behind them and the bus creaked into motion.

Willow and Asher walked down the narrow aisle and took seats next to each another. They placed their hands flat on the light blue patterned seats and let their legs dangle over the edge as they steadied themselves for the ride.

And suddenly, Willow wasn't in the past anymore thinking of what it used to be like when Mom was around. And she also wasn't in the future thinking about what it would be like when Mom was around again. She had become acutely present. The future equal to the past. The past equal to the future. She was so close to Mom as she sat there feeling the excitement of nearing the end of a long and painful road. Feeling the bumps of the tires beneath her legs. Feeling the vibrations of the seats that were way too big for their little bodies too far into a plan that was way too big for their little minds.

Willow listened to her headphones and played her word searches while Asher twisted the limbs of his action figures. Together, they counted blue cars on the highway and alternated between playing rock, paper, scissors and tic-tac-toe.

And then they got quiet. Asher leaned his head on his sister's shoulder and closed his eyes for a nap. And then Willow leaned her head on her brother's head and closed her eyes for a nap too. But they could each tell by the way the other was breathing that neither of them were asleep. They waited nervously and excitedly to get to Manhattan.

And, then, all of a sudden, the road narrowed and buildings stacked up around them. And then, all of a sudden, their farness from home was all so real. It was real in the thick, city air. In the oppressive grayness of the streets, and the buildings, and smoke coming up from the earth. It was real in the density of buildings, and signs, and sounds, and people. It was real in the quickness with which those people stomped through the sidewalks. It was real in the tight straight lanes they moved along in and the black outfits they wore. It was real in the loudness. The flashing lights. The honking horns.

This was a whole different world. Not Dad's. Not Mom's. Not school. Not the beach.

Willow and Asher locked hands and they stepped off the bus into the big terminal. Then they followed a few passengers out the building and stood by themselves on the curb. Willow willed a taxi to stop in front of her and take her and Asher to Mom. But everything was zooming by. Gray and zooming by.

And then a tall, slim blonde woman in a neat white dress tapped Willow on the shoulder.

"You trying to get somewhere, sweetheart?" she asked gently. Maternally.

Willow uncurled her hand and showed the woman the locket with the address on it. And then the woman in white stuck her long and narrow arm out toward the street. A dirty yellow cab pulled up underneath it. She handed the driver a few green bills and told him the address. And Willow watched the woman in white's red nails retreat out the window, and then wave to her and Asher as they drove away.

With every jerky right turn, every red stoplight and narrowly missed car next to them, Willow filled with excitement. She filled so thoroughly that she was ready to burst with it. And when the cab came to a stop in front of a short brown building with a rusted golden number, Willow almost couldn't breathe.

The moment she was waiting for was right in that building. The moment her mother would scoop her into her arms was right behind that door.

54

Rex thought of Willow and of Asher the entire drive up. He trusted they would be safe. What they would think when they saw him. How they would react when Rosie was not there. What they would feel. He thought of Willow. How much she would love the apartment. How much she would be able to feel Rosie's presence there, even if she wasn't there herself. How much he would allow Rosie's presence to wash over him too. How he would love and love and love his children as much as they needed him to. How he would tell them and show them and kiss them every day from now on.

How he was so sorry. For every last instant he was detached. For every last moment he didn't protect his children. And protect them not with force or strength or toughness. But with love. Pure, raw, unabashed love.

He waited and waited and waited in that

apartment for his children to arrive.

And when he heard a knock at the door, his stomach twisted and he lost his breath for a moment.

55

Willow's stomach twisted and she lost her breath for just an instant before she tapped her small knuckles on the door three times. The buzz of the streets faded away and Willow heard movement behind the door. Every inch of her tingled. It tingled and danced and filled right up.

And then the doorknob turned and the crack in the door grew more and more spacious.

And then she saw her father.

Her tall, broad, father looking right at her.

There was so much stillness and so much quiet. So much surprise. So much disbelief.

So much disappointment.

And then, without a word, Willow's father reached into his back pocket and pulled his arm back to the front. He was holding two grape Pixy Stix. And from those grape Pixy Stix hung a typed note that said, "For Willow," in the same font she had seen on those notes for months.

Willow's knees loosened. They loosened more thoroughly than any other time before. Because this wasn't gravity. This was sorrow. And it was all at once and it was overwhelming.

Willow dropped to the floor like a marionette whose strings had been cut. Her legs and arms bent out awkwardly and her chest folded on top of them. She cried. And cried. And cried. She cried loudly and deeply. She cried big, full, wobbling tears until her face was wet with them. She inhaled choppy inhales as she cried some more. And then more and then more.

Her chest bounced up and down on top of her crooked legs as she cried some more. She let her arms dangle next to her as she cried some more. She inhaled more choppy inhales as she cried some more.

And then she felt her father's strong, capable hands under her. The same hands that picked her up and brought her to the beach in the middle of the night. The same hands that had been wrapping notes around those Pixy Stix all this time.

And then her father dropped onto his knees and dragged her body onto his. Her father dropped onto his knees and pulled his daughter's lifeless sobbing body straight onto his strong and sturdy chest.

And Willow let the weight of her body drape over her father's shoulder as she cried more and more and more. Willow felt her father's hands rubbing her back. Rubbing her back from the very top to the very bottom. Over and over again. It was so rhythmic. So steady. So dependable. So soothing. And Willow let herself sink into that rhythm. That steady, dependable rhythm. She let herself be soothed by it. She let herself feel the love behind it.

And slowly, her breathing and her heart hushed. Her chest and muscles calmed. Her tears dried. And then she felt Asher's little hand on her back too. And just as it was about to get quiet, Asher's voice was in the air.

"Can we live hewe now?" he said through that enduring gap in his front teeth.

Willow peeled her chest off her father's shoulder and looked straight into his eyes. His big, brown, serious eyes. And then her father laughed. With full belly and full smile. And it made Willow laugh too. With full body and full heart.

"I think that sounds like a great idea, Ash," Rex said as he rubbed Asher's straight blond hair back and forth.

"I brought your stuff. It's in the other room."

And then Willow sank right back into her father's shoulder. She wrapped her arms around him and pulled them in so tightly. So, so tightly. And her father's arms pulled her in so tightly back. So, so tightly. Willow let herself sink even more deeply into her father's shoulder and closed her eyes. She did it with all the love — past, present and future — on her mind.

56

When Rex opened the door and watched his daughter fall to the ground in sadness, his heart broke. It broke so much it hurt. He scooped his daughter into his arms and let her cry on top of him. And into him. And he rubbed her back and cried too. For Willow. For Rosie. And for Asher.

And for himself. And for everyone in the whole world that has ever loved or lost.

And when his daughter's breathing and tears finally slowed, he felt the warm tingle of fatherhood. He felt the pride of consoling his daughter. The power of love flowing so truly, so wholly, from him into her, and from her into him.

He could not help but laugh at Asher when he excitedly yelled, "Can we live hewe now?"

And he could not help but agree to the idea when he looked into his daughter's longing eyes.

Rex and Willow rocked back and forth there on the floor for maybe minutes or maybe a lifetime until Willow sat up again. And without saying a word, he carried Willow over to the cabinet full of CDs. CDs of Prince and Blondie and Elton John and all of her mother's and father's favorites.

And then Willow and Asher and Rex put on some music and ate Chinese food. They played Go Fish and Candy Land and laughed. They lay on the couch as Rex told them stories about the apartment. The apartment and Manhattan and what their mother, Rosie, was like in it. And right there in the kitchen of 299 East 82nd Street Willow and Asher and Rex were happy. And Rosie was wrong. She would have been too.

When the sun went down, and the room went dark, Rex put a VHS tape into the old television and pressed Play. *Blazing Saddles* appeared on the screen and they all danced and laughed and talked along with the movie in Rosie's honor. In Rosie's memory. In Rosie's wake.

Willow looked her father in the eyes for the second time that evening as they sat there on the couch. And, this time, it was full of so much thankfulness. So much love. So much ease. And then Willow, tangled up in her father and in the happy memory of

Rosie, drifted into sleep with a smile on her lips.

And then Rex smiled too. With all the love in the universe — past, present and future — on his mind.

57

Rex's love crept slowly into the crannies of 299 East 82nd Street until it filled all the rooms. Filled all the rooms and then Willow Thorpe's whole being. And Willow was better with Rex's love inside her.

In no time at all, the scratches on her skin healed and the redness in her eyes subsided. She spent her summer painting a mural of the Virginia coast on her new bedroom wall. She made friends with her classmates at her new school that fall. They even performed the Time Warp for the school talent show. And all the girls teased their hair to make it look like Willow's.

One crisp fall Sunday morning, after a breakfast of homemade chocolate chip pancakes, Rex picked up a bucket of flat rocks for skipping that he had taken with him from Virginia and proposed a picnic in Central Park next to the reservoir.

"Hurry up and get dressed," he urged, and

gave Asher a gentle pat on the head. And then he waited by the door in his baseball hat and jeans. He thought about what it meant to be happy. For all of them to be happy.

Willow's door slowly creaked open and there was his daughter in one of Rosie's old dresses. It was too big on her and dragged along the floor, but Willow looked so beautiful in that floral-printed dress. So at peace. So perfect. She looked so much like Rosie, but Rex could also finally see Willow as herself. Willow outside of those purple leggings and black T-shirt with the horseshoe. Willow as her own little girl. Willow as her own young woman.

"Can we go now?" his daughter asked.

"Sure we can, honey," Rex responded, looking straight into his daughter's eyes. "And you look so beautiful in Mommy's dress."

Rex pressed his hand into Willow's tight curls and rubbed them back and forth gently. And then he drew her into his chest and kissed her decidedly on the forehead. With her curls at her father's chin, and the sound of Asher skipping across the room, Willow smiled with her whole body. Her whole heart. Her whole being.

Everything was good and everything was right.

Epilogue

15 Years Later

Willow Thorpe nervously fiddled with the locket around her neck on another Friday-night date with Aaron Jackson. He was tall with a strong jaw and kind gray eyes, with thick blond hair and soft hands. Willow liked how his T-shirt tightened around his strong shoulders when he reached down for his glass of beer. She liked how Aaron subtly licked his lower lip after taking a sip. But most importantly, she loved how her heart pulsed when his eyes met hers. And how her cheeks tingled when he leaned over the table and brought his lips to her face.

"You said your parents used to come here?" Aaron inquired as he turned his torso toward the stage at Ray's Piano Bar.

Willow inhaled the smell of old whiskey and wooden chairs that were chipping at the corners.

"My Mom said she fell in love with my

Dad here."

She sank into the scene of red lamps and the sense that she was sitting in a seat that perhaps her mother had sat in before. And then Willow smiled, but with a hint of sadness between her brows.

"She thought he had slipped off to get a drink, but the next time she saw him, he was already up onstage with his hands on the keys."

Aaron leaned back in his chair. Willow thought it might have been the weight of the story pressing down on him.

"Sounds like a stud," Aaron said, accompanied by a wink.

And then Willow changed her mind about his pose. It was the comfort of knowing that love had begun here before and could begin here again.

Willow pushed out her chair and made her way toward the stage. Her knees knocked only once before she sat down on the bench, fanned her floral-printed dress out and placed her fingertips gently on the keys.

She closed her eyes, and then pressed her fingers down.

There were three slow notes that moved effortlessly into a tune the whole bar knew.

Aaron and the rest of the patrons tapped

their hands on the tables and shoes on the carpet and belted out the chorus from "Bennie and the Jets."

"Show-off!" Aaron mouthed through a smile. And then he hugged her when she came down from the stage. So tight. So thoroughly.

"How did you learn to do that?" Aaron asked, still buzzing from his proximity to cool.

"A *stud* I know taught me," Willow joked.

As soon as Willow sat down, Aaron reached under the table and placed his hands on her knee. Willow wondered if her father had placed his hands the same way on her mother's knee all those years ago. She wondered if her mother had the same quick heartbeat when he did.

When she turned to face Aaron, Willow wondered if it was love. She wanted it to be love. Big, all-consuming love. Magical, particular, overwhelming love.

Willow thought back to the way her mother described falling in love with her father. The way she described loving her children. How it was "most mad and moonly."

Willow looked into Aaron's eyes and almost found herself yearning for something "most mad and moonly" too.

But then, Willow paused. She had "most mad and moonly" love. She had it for her mother and she had it for her father and she was ready for a different kind of love with Aaron. An uncomplicated, effortless, simpler kind of love. A quiet, tickling, easy kind of love.

Willow kissed Aaron deeply. And it may not have been "most mad and moonly," but it was her favorite kiss she ever had.

ABOUT THE AUTHOR

Brianna Wolfson has honed her voice on the San Francisco storytelling circuit, including *The Moth Gram Slam.* Raised in New York, she currently lives in San Francisco. Her debut novel is largely autobiographical.

The employees of Thorndike Press hope you have enjoyed this Large Print book. All our Thorndike, Wheeler, and Kennebec Large Print titles are designed for easy reading, and all our books are made to last. Other Thorndike Press Large Print books are available at your library, through selected bookstores, or directly from us.

For information about titles, please call:
(800) 223-1244

or visit our website at:
gale.com/thorndike

To share your comments, please write:
Publisher
Thorndike Press
10 Water St., Suite 310
Waterville, ME 04901